Chromosome

Warrior

PSI, Dark Energy, and the Alien Ragnarök

by
Nathan Gregory

Published by
Nathan Gregory Author *dot* Com

Copyright

Table of Contents

Call Me Jill!

"Out of every one hundred fighters, ten shouldn't even be there, eighty are just targets, nine are the real fighters, and we are lucky to have them, for they make the battle. Ah, but the one, one is a warrior, and that one will bring the others back." —
Heraclitus of Ephesus.

It's not my name, though it has been my handle since I lied about my age to join the military.

Yeah, that's right; G.I. Jill.

If I would tell the tale, you'd beg to understand; where was I born, how lousy my childhood had been, what sort of monsters my parents were, that Dickensian sort of crap.

F**k that!

If you must know the truth, I'm an authentic Man in Black, the real deal. That's all you need to know.

Years ago, before The Agency found me, having little money and despite some 'spiritual' gifts but few prospects due to my gender and stature, I decided to enlist in the service. I'm uncertain what I expected, a few adventures and travel the world, I suppose. Better than hooking — not that anything's wrong with that.

Petite, Chinese, and pretty; assets to a hooker, a hindrance to a warrior. I needed to kick someone in the teeth — several someones in fact — until they saw more than my feminine curves.

Schooled in weaponry and marksmanship; I discovered I like weapons.

Rough Landings

I slammed the ground with a resounding thud. I bounced.
Blackness tinged my vision; my ears rang. I think a soft "Oh! F**k!"
escaped my lips. I hadn't expected Portals to be so hard at the
bottom. Well, to be fair, I'd had zero expectations. Although
anything would have been a surprise, this was not the surprise for
which I bargained. I must've fallen a couple of meters. One thing, if
you're braced for it. But off-balance and unprepared, well, they do
say it's the sudden stop at the end.

My Las Vegas wounds throbbed anew with exquisite pain as I
tasted dirt and grass. The ringing abated; I was face-down in a
pasture. I got a whiff of a grassy scent that made me want to
sneeze.

The shock and pain subsided as I struggled to orient myself
when a petite bag of cement landed on my back. Oof! At least I
cushioned Wisceya's baby-bump. I was conscious enough to roll
aside and pull the young fur girl away from the landing spot before
her mother joined us. We pulled Stapleya toward us and hugged
her to our bodies. Teena — our most fragile member — was last,
and she landed hardest. Frail and elderly, a virtual walking
skeleton, I imagined hearing bones crunch.

Wisceya bounded to her feet, unfazed by the rough landing,
and helped me to my feet. Then we both assisted her mother. It
took us a few seconds to orient ourselves before realizing Teena
was not moving.

Wisceya reached Teena first. She began to roll her over. "Wait,"
I said. "She may have internal injuries or broken bones." She was so
frail I feared the worst. I felt her limbs and ribs; her head and

shoulder took the brunt of it. The visible bump on her head and developing 'goose-egg' reflected her harsh impact.

The shoulder didn't feel dislocated, maybe. Or maybe it was, I couldn't tell. It bulged; I'm going with dislocated. The unconscious grunt when we pressed her rib cage suggested broken ribs too. Maybe we should have left Stapleya where she landed to cushion Teena's fall.

Teena had almost died last year, snatched from the tenacious jaws of death by advanced alien medicine. Despite months of recovery, she remains frail and fragile. The Portal transitions are supposed to be simple, like stepping through a doorway. Except, someone removed the floor from this side of the door! Something has gone wrong.

Teena lay unconscious, and Stapleya couldn't rouse her. She needed medical attention; we felt powerless. I said to Wisceya, "Let's turn her over real gentle-like." We did, and I made sure of her breathing. After a few moments, I said to both Fur girls, "Snuggle down either side of her and shelter her. Lend her all the warmth you can."

The chill had begun to permeate my skin. Stapleya and Wisceya hail from a much warmer world and dislike the cold. Even so, their fur imparts a natural advantage. Unconscious and injured, Teena needed all the warmth the Fur girls could lend her. I was starting to shiver.

I took inventory. Short inventory — we had zip, zilch, diddly, scratch, and naught, with a side order of nix. We were bare-assed naked, in a grassy field. Location unknown. Planet uncertain. Grass and a few trees were all I could see. Evening approached, and with the dusk, the temperature was falling.

The world is quiet and growing dark. No sounds of distant vehicles, only the rustle of the breeze in the trees. No hint of light on the horizon other than that which naturally shines from the sky. It's not natural. Unnerving.

It could be Nevia. An agricultural society makes little noise. If this is Nevia, as it is supposed to be, where is the militia that should be guarding the damn Portal? Why did the Portal dump us into mid-air?

Naked, in an empty field, on unknown soil, we were in trouble. I had survival training and skills. Could I manage a fire under these conditions? I have no matches, no flint, no kindling, no knife. Perhaps I could find a sharp rock and dry branches. Assuming I could, did I dare light a fire? Might that draw unwanted attention? Was it safer to face the cold and dark or to risk a fire? Were there predators?

Fire? D'oh!

(*Did you turn off the apartment's hotplate?*)

Where is that damned militia?

Shivering, I stood and scouted around. Then, motioning the girls to stay put and protect Teena, I started for the nearby copse of trees. Barefoot across the field.

I am a warrior, I reminded myself. A warrior can handle barefoot.

(*There once was a barefoot lass, who was warned about stepping on glass.*)

Ouch!

The gentle evening breeze cut like a knife as I walked, and my teeth began to chatter. The question of fire clarified itself; we could not survive without it.

I am a warrior!

Reaching the woods, I scouted for rocks, flint, sticks, broken limbs, anything. Slim pickings, I found an armload of promising branches and a couple of rocks. Maybe I could coax a spark from them.

I am a warrior, damn it!

Violently shivering as I struggled with the problem of how to carry my meager haul, I spotted a faint light. Moving toward our location was a horse-drawn buggy.

Disregarding caution, I ran toward it. Religious fundamentalism and harsh nudity taboos seem unimportant. If they choose to burn me at the stake, at least it will be warm.

I struggled through the brush toward the light. I tripped as I tried to sprint into the dirt road ahead of the buggy. Sprawling face-first into the dirt yet again, I lay stunned for a moment, tasting dirt and trying to recover my wind. I feared the driver would drive around and continue. I managed a plaintive "help" just as he stopped.

A deep male voice intoned with a dark solemnity in an unknown language. His speech sounded like a prayer. Struggling to my feet, I realized he was standing beside the buggy, an immense dark form. His back was towards me, and in one hand, he held clothing, a voluminous black dress.

After a momentary hesitation, I took the dress and slipped it over my head. The coarse fabric chafed my skin, but it blocked the chill.

Once I donned the garment, he faced me and started speaking. Pointless. I kept missing his pitching. I began pantomiming and asking his help for my friends. I couldn't tell if he glockened my spiel or not. After a few futile attempts, he shrugged and appeared to understand. Dismounting the light from the buggy, he picked up a bundle and indicated a willingness to follow.

Pausing to orient myself in the gloaming, uncertain where I'd left my companions, I made my way back to the copse where I'd gathered the firewood. Another moment of orientation, and I headed toward our landing spot. I called out to the girls. To my relief, I heard a soft "Over here." Wisceya's voice carried on the slight breeze. A minor course correction, and we were upon them. The Fur girls' charcoal pelt rendered them all but invisible in the gathering blackness. But Teena's sallow white skin shone in the grass like the pale moon above.

My gigantic black-clad shadow stopped yards away, his back toward us, praying again. I took the garments he held and gave them to the girls. They dressed and covered Teena's still form. I worried over her; she remained unconscious.

Our benefactor, once we were decent, came to us and examined Teena. He muttered something sounding like a prayer, or maybe a curse, and I suspected he knew her. Then, without further words, he scooped her up and carried her to the buggy, leaving us to follow as we chose. As I said, he was a large man, and she was quite frail. Though she is much taller than I, he carried her like a child.

He placed her in the buggy, we climbed in with her, and he started the horse off at a trot. I was beginning to suspect he might be our absent militia as he acted as though unperturbed by events. If so, he was a disappointment as a militia. I expected at least one weapon. Or perhaps the people here routinely carry extra clothing. Preparation, in case they find naked strangers on the roadside. Either way, I am glad he came along.

I can't guess how far we traveled. I'm no equestrian. Thanks to my vantage point, I have learned more about horses in the last few minutes than I ever wanted to know. My concept of horsepower, the four-legged variety, is unreliable. We traveled a long way.

I could not judge the time, dusk had turned into night, and the stars were clear and bright. Unfortunately, the pale moon that greeted our arrival had set, and I could not recognize the constellations.

If not for the sky, I could believe we were in Kentucky, riding with a Mennonite farmer. Somehow Fitz's stories, fur-clad aliens, Teena, and traveling through a Portal myself felt insufficient. This sky left no doubt I was on an alien planet.

A long ride, and then we arrived at a cabin. It was dark, the night air was cold, and I could smell a faint scent of a wood fire. Stepping from the buggy, I worried what night creatures might be mere steps beyond the buggy lantern in the dark shadows.

Our host carried Teena inside and placed her on a bed. He added wood to a small fire and knelt beside her and began praying again. The girls and I, powerless and uncertain what else we might do, sat nearby, and waited.

After a brief while, he arose and went into the other room. He returned moments later with a bowl containing a malodorous liquid. He also carried a porous white stone and a few towels. The liquid was steaming and emitted a mephitic stench; the stone appeared supernaturally hot. He placed the stone against her injury, where it clung as though glued. Then, like a native medicine man, he wrapped her head and shoulder in towels soaked in the foul concoction.

I considered intervening, but we desperately needed his help. The heat might be beneficial. I would've used cold, but we'd already had a hearty dose of cold.

With no other option to offer, I watched and waited, nodding by the fireplace. Fighting sleep while watching over Teena, my mind kept rehashing how I came to an alien world.

Gym-Rats

My thoughts wandered back to that morning at HQ when I first met Teena. Had it really been less than a month? At the time, I knew of Teena from Fitz's book but had not met her; I did not even know she was alive. Fitz's account had left the point uncertain. When we first met, I had no clue she was Teena. She has a habit of changing names and keeping important details to herself.

I perhaps foolishly had attempted to resume my daily workout regimen. My doctor had not yet cleared me for physical activity. He would have objected; he would have me still bedfast. Confident I understood my body better than a mere doctor, I intended to be careful and neglect to tell him. My early morning meditation was disrupted when a stranger appeared beside my bench.

"Are you going to lift that?" I almost jumped at the question. The brusque, faintly accented contralto had perturbed my navel-gazing. The gym offers a retreat to put the brain on hold — a mental haven for physical exercise, meditation, and thought.

I had thought I was alone.

Rousing, I studied my unexpected companion a half-second before responding. "I would have added another couple of dimes. But I decided to go easy; this is my first session in quite a while."

Nodding at the barbell, she said, "That big wheel can be dangerous. Would you like a spot?" Her voice resonated soft and sensual, almost hypnotic. My inner idiot responded, *"What the hell are you going to do? I doubt you can even roll that barbell, much less lift it."*

I chided myself for my words, even though they were unspoken. I try to keep the profanity inside my head. Sometimes it leaks.

She looked like gym rats don't. Exercise? The only machine she should be using is a respirator.

Obviously not a weightlifter judging by her broomstick arms. Not someone you'd encounter in a gym.

Although my mother came from Hong Kong, my father was Irish-American. This woman resembled a much taller and skinnier version of my frail, elderly Irish grandmother. Her gray-streaked black hair in a classic bob and bangs hinted at Asian influence too.

Disturbing!

This frail, elderly woman appeared nearly as Asian as I with her dark bob hairstyle with bangs. I prefer my hair long and straight, though it means restraining it for fieldwork.

Stereotype Chinese styles are not for me. Especially not anymore, not that I ever willingly embraced such a thing. The blunt-cut bob with bangs hairstyle made her look Chinese. That, combined with her pale, sallow skin, evoked unpleasant childhood memories. Taller than the typical Chinese female, though, much taller, a good head taller than I.

"Are you sure?" I asked out loud. My skepticism may have leaked thru my tone. What would she do, call nine-one-one? Biceps she did not have. Well, neither do I so much at the moment. She nodded confidently.

Shrugging, I positioned myself on the bench, at the ready, overconfident in my ability. A couple of reps and a twinge exploded into ragged pain, signaling I had exceeded my limits. I grunted in pain. To my surprise, the fragile-appearing grandmother reached out and grabbed the heavy barbell. She supported much of the weight with a grunt as together we guided it to the rack.

"I'm Dr. Mathes," she claimed by way of introduction as she extended a bony hand, "my friends call me Min." I accepted it, clueless she had given an assumed name. Well, so is 'Teena' for that matter, but I did not know it then. No one told me that Dr. Mathes was Teena's academic alter-ego.

One palm on my pain, the other accepting her hand to lever myself vertical, I said, "I'm Jill. I've been recovering from an injury for months now. I had intended to resume my training regimen, though it appears I must cut it into smaller slices. So, today has been my first session since the injury."

She nodded in understanding as I continued. "I had picked the early hour so I could exercise my body before my brain woke up and figured out what was happening. That, and to avoid embarrassing myself."

She winced. My idiot inner-idiot had tried to escape her box. I pushed her back and drove a couple of nails in the lid.

I smiled and continued. "I'm glad you were here. I misjudged my recovery." I winced and pressed a hand to the pain-wracked scar. I could hear my inner voice chattering; (*The fault, Jill, is not in our scars, but in the evil that men do. The Shadow knows...*) "I must take it slower, I guess," I said aloud while chiding the damned sprite for mangling the Bard.

Everyone has an inner voice, a snarky sprite that pops up at inopportune times. Right? Mine's an idiot.

Few people know I nearly died last year. Assassins of the mysterious *Boskone* attacked our group, leaving me as the lone survivor. I was critically wounded and not meant to survive. Classified mission. Not something I can discuss with a stranger I just met in the gym. Recovery has been long and painful; the enforced inactivity had chafed my ass; I'm fuming to put my ass back in the saddle! I need to find the bastard behind the attack and avenge my dear Estelle.

She said, "We have one thing in common. I, too, almost died. Did, in fact, die."

Softly, she sighed as if speaking to herself alone, "There's more to that story...."

She went on, "Jill, I know who you are. I came here to meet you. I understand the classified nature of your injuries. I'm aware Boskone attacked your group," her voice lowered. She laid her hand on my arm. "And your lover died in that blood-soaked hotel room. I'm so sorry for your loss. I wish I could offer more than words."

She continued in a firmer voice, "I'm one of the architects of this faux *Jade Helm*. We will find vengeance for those lost."

I fought to contain my surprise. I thought only Fitz, Alex, and his innermost circle knew of the attack. Fewer knew my own loss. My private life is, well, private. I never discuss my personal life with colleagues. Almost no one knew Estelle and I were lovers. As for my injuries, even the doctors remained unknowing as to how I sustained these bullet holes. The name *'Boskone'* is seldom spoken, never beyond our tight group.

She said, "Your sacrifice for the mission is recognized, although the job's not complete." Now, what did she imply by that? I thought we nearly destroyed the organization called *Boskone* and were winding down. She continued, "I must run now. May I join you for lunch?"

I nodded, and with that, she stood, smiled, shook my hand, and without another word, exited the gym. She moved in a surprising rush for one so frail-looking. She failed to name where or when we were to meet — just lunch. It's her problem. She can find me. I'm not hard to find at lunchtime.

I stood in open-mouthed silence for a moment, contemplating what had just happened. I wondered about the strange older woman's manner. Memories of another older woman in my life played in my mind.

My poor Estelle....

I grew up in a modest family environment — Fitz would say 'prudish' — where sex was never discussed. Frankly, I found the topic terrifying, easier to pretend it didn't exist. Fear of sex drove my early social life, celibacy through fear.

Virginity became the easy answer. One can be vapid, stupid, and unethical, but as long as you've never experienced sex, you're a 'good' girl. I'm not vapid or stupid, yet I was a 'good' girl, not from a high ethical standard, just out of fear.

Not that I lacked prurient desires of my own. Manifold fears and boundless unknowns lurked. Monsters hid in shadows where I feared to tread.

I grew older, dated, and grudgingly accepted a 'boyfriend' into my circle. I allowed him to beguile me. A mistake, I suppose, I wasn't prepared. I did not 'get it' then; I did not understand why I should bother.

Satisfying the primal urges of a sweaty male did nothing to sate my own primal urges. He came and went too soon. I disliked the way he would disappear afterward, without even a call, until he wanted another go. If that's what sex augured, I decided I didn't need it and told him so in unmistakable language. I may not have been exactly polite. We never spoke again.

Reflecting in later years, I regretted that. I had savaged him unfairly. Our mutual ignorance doomed whatever chance we had together. Any other human endeavor values experience and competence. Virginity's not something to revere, only a correctable perversity of little interest.

Frustrated, I concentrated on my career and training. I decided I just wasn't a sexual person. For a time, I considered myself asexual. I rejected all sexuality and rebuffed anyone who I imagined might desire me. Fear of humiliation no doubt compelled the turn away from sex and its ugly complications. I suppose a few frustrated would-be suitors used unflattering nicknames behind my back. Well-deserved, I'm sure.

Then I met Estelle.

She revealed another path; I finally 'got it' with mondo joy. Though we were different, we fit. Much older than I, experienced and patient, she opened a larger world. Together we explored feelings I hadn't suspected possible.

I moved from almost pathologically asexual to lesbian without entirely realizing it happened. It took a long time to accept that word, 'lesbian.'

I miss her deeply....

Shaking myself out of reverie, I focused again on my intended workout. I had pushed too hard with the weights, though I couldn't let pain and weakness win. I removed weights from the barbell until light enough for a puny girl. Galling to admit it, though until I get back into fighting trim, I am a puny girl. Injuries and weeks of inactivity have taken their toll. I've grown soft and weak. I must start smaller.

Estelle used to scold me for sounding like a man. I would tell her, "Not a man, a Warrior. A Warrior is a greater thing than any mere man. If that makes me sound butch, well, you did bring out the lesbian in me." I don't imagine I'm butch at all, however. I have nice curves and long silky hair. I also have serious biceps; or did before spending weeks in the hospital. I am a trained, deadly fighter, although I'm soft and flabby just now.

But you wait!

I counted out easy reps with the absurdly light barbell until I felt the twinge again. I stopped, no point pressing my luck. I vowed to add a nickel every day until back to my routine load. This will take a while.

Not content to quit just yet, I commandeered a treadmill and walked. I surmised running would be a bit much today. Tomorrow maybe.

Early morning workout complete — mortifying though it had been — I hung my new Tee in the locker. This shirt was my latest pride, thanks to Jessica. She visited a contractor in the Valley yesterday and returned with a souvenir. The crisp black shirt is exquisite. I identified with its bold, iconic logo and stark 'Think Different' slogan.

My collection of tech-company logo tees is growing. Jessica, the quintessential White-Hat Hacker and Cyberpunk, has amassed a polychromatic collection. She inspired my own collecting by gifting from her surplus. As a result, I have shirts from most of the prominent technology companies.

Mine tend toward black, in keeping with my work motif. Though appropriately Stygian, they're not acceptable office wear for a MiB. Anywhere else in the Bay Area, not here. I can strut my collection only on my own time (*HAH! As if...*) or the occasional Casual Friday.

Usually, I wouldn't wear them to the gym either, though, but I couldn't resist sporting my latest acquisition today. Besides, I hadn't expected to work up a glow in this first session.

∿∿∿

I roused with a start; I'd been dreaming. I was not on Earth, in the gym, meeting Teena. Instead, I am on Nevia, worrying whether she will survive the night.

I raised my head and spotted our host. He still knelt beside Teena, still praying over her. It appears he has been doing so for hours. The Fur girls were huddled together in front of the fireplace, sound asleep. They almost look like kittens snuggled together. I roused enough to check on Teena. She was breathing a little easier but still unconscious.

Frustrated, powerless, there was nothing more I could do; I added a log to the fire and settled back in my chair. My dream, or memory track, resumed back in the gym where I left it.

∿∿∿

Drifting off again, Jill resumes the dream narrative of that fateful morning when she met Teena.

The frustration of my first post-injury morning workout left me depressed. I concluded if I went to the gym every day, changed my clothes, and took a shower, in a month or two, I'd be ready for actual exercise.

Showered, coiffed, and attired in professional black, I took the elevator up to my office. I was prepared for another workday. Intelligence reports littered my desk, virtually speaking, and I had work awaiting attention.

Passing the command center, I remembered spotting Jessica. Impossible to miss her, iridescent in a bright orange Tee from an extinct start-up. She can be bolder in her clothing choices than a MiB. Techies walk a unique path, in the MiB, as elsewhere. As I waved to Jessica, I noted yet again Fitz's absence.

It had been several days since I last saw Fitz. I wondered.... what's he up to? My memory track veered backward several months to our first meeting. But, of course, I knew of him before meeting him, too, thanks to his book.

Estelle taught me more than sex. She introduced me to imaginary worlds, fiction, and literature. Erotica too. She would read Anaïs Nin aloud in bed. I learned a lot about love and erotica from Estelle and Anaïs Nin. Estelle not only taught me to embrace my libido, but she also expanded my mind. A scientist by temperament and training, she loved Science Fiction. The trashier and pulpier, the better in her view. I was disdainful of the genre, yet her enthusiasm became infectious.

She had introduced me to Fitz's book. The first few chapters were difficult to read. I found it crass and much too male-fantasy-oriented. Estelle schooled me in the worth of fantasy. I decided if she liked it, I must give it a fair shot. I indulged her, suspecting no other motive than a penchant for trashy fiction.

By the time the hero landed on the planet of the fur-people, I had become hooked. I imagined myself in his fictional world, on a planet dominated by a population of almost cat-like, furry female humans. Fantasies of a libidinous lesbian society fueled my imagination.

When poor Shameya's corpse appeared in our morgue, I remembered Fitz's fictional creations. I had no clue Fitz was already well known to Alex. It was I who suggested calling him in as an unpaid consultant. I'm unsure why. I had no real plan beyond meeting a writer whose work I had come to relish. I'm confident I had no intention of discussing libidinous lesbians with a strange man — not merely because I read his book.

I told Estelle of the corpse; she went off the rails. She insisted she must see the furry remains. I chalked her interest up to scientific curiosity. At her insistence, I arranged a gig for her, also as an unpaid consultant. I had no suspicion of a darker motive than simple curiosity. Her enthusiasm surprised me. I had no clue about conspiracies or mysterious 'Sixth Column' societies. To my surprise, the required reading list of at least one such organization included his work.

Had I imagined Fitz's mysteries would lead to her horrific death.... sigh....

Even after seeing the fur-clad body, I still considered Fitz's tale fantastic fiction. I didn't budge from that view until I met Stapleya and Wisceya. I heard their story and, with difficulty, absorbed that they were, in fact, extraterrestrials.

I found that hurdle somewhat intimidating.

Then we were caught in the conspiracy, and bullets were flying.

Heretics

"A way of life that is odd, or even erratic but interferes with no rights or interests of others is not to be condemned because it is different"
— *Warren E. Berger.*

I awoke to a brightening sky. My dream, hallucination, or whatever it was, paused as I returned to the real world. Well, this world. It feels real. I think.

Our host still knelt praying beside Teena. He had stamina; I grant him that. Dawn came, and he remained in position. The sun rose, and he did not waver.

He stopped a few times to replace the towels and adjust the stone. It was always hot, though how it remained heated was unclear. When he touched it to her skin, it clung like a magnet and appeared scorching hot.

It was perhaps approaching noon when he removed the stone, and it was no longer hot and no longer clung. I touched it, and it felt ice cold. With a final brief prayer, he removed the towels. He then wiped away the stinking liquid and bathed her head and shoulder in clean water. With that, he tucked her into the bed and stood to leave her alone.

His attention no longer on Teena, he turned to us as though seeing us for the first time. He studied my countenance with doubt. After a moment, he granted me a provisional acceptance. His eyes fell on the Nekomata women, and he blanched as though seeing a ghost. I motioned them back, but it was too late. He turned and left the room without a word.

Unsure how to react, I stared at the closed door. Then, as I contemplated my options, I heard Teena moan. She moved, groaned again, and fluttered her eyes a moment before opening them.

She stared ahead with a blank expression.

Then she focused, scanned the room, put a hand to her head, and let out a louder groan.

"Watch that first step," she said. We all three hugged her.

I heard our host in the back room — I could sense him at the door, though he did not open it. Suspecting his reaction one of fear of our alien friends, I motioned them to step outside.

Undoubtedly, he'd never seen their ilk. Though they were covered, the bulky dresses were not burqas. Their clothing did not cover their hirsute faces, did not hide their vaguely cat-like alien features. They are too small to pass for adult women of this world under bulky clothing anyway.

They stepped out into the sunshine, closing the door. As the door closed, our host reentered with obvious trepidation.

He ignored me and spoke to Teena in that strange tongue. She answered in the same language.

They chattered for several moments. Then, she introduced me, with what sounded like flowery language. Though I did not understand a word, I curtsied. He appeared pleased and bowed somewhat. I guess he accepted me now, with Teena's endorsement.

They chattered further. He appeared questioning, disagreeing over something. Shaking his head as though rejecting her words, she kept at him, wearing him down. Finally, shoulders drooping, dejected, he yielded.

She took his hand and spoke, almost whispering. I didn't understand a word, though she appeared almost to say, "trust me, everything will be all right." Then louder, she said, "Come in, ladies, come meet our host."

Stapleya and Wisceya cracked the door and peered inside with an air of timidity. Teena waved them inside. Our host stood head-down, unwilling to look them in the eye. Though more than twice their size, he acted as though terrified of them.

More chatter ensued. Our host straightened with visible effort. He met their eyes and greeted them, though it appeared painful for him. They curtsied in acknowledgment. He smiled.

"My dears, allow me to introduce my friend Yosef," Teena said in English. "Our friend and agent on this world."

I saw that coming.

She went on, "He should have met us when we arrived. He missed us through no fault of his own. The Portal did not appear in the proper place. What should've been simple egress from null space-time became a materialization into midair. We emerged above the ground and miles removed from our expected location.

"This is unexpected. Either the single Portal moved, or the entire planet has shifted its space-time matrix. If the matrix has shifted — the likely possibility — finding our egress will be a challenge."

I asked, "How might that happen?"

Teena shrugged. "My understanding of Portal physics is imperfect; I'm not a physicist, a layman at best — I can only repeat what I've been told. An energy matrix associated with the planet's gravity-well encircles each world. Portals form at the Ley-line junctures when energy streams flow between the matrices of planets. Typically, the matrix is stable and conforms to the planetary surface and the Ley-lines.

"Portal nexus lock into the matrix, bound to a spot on the planetary surface. Energy waxes and wanes. Solar cycles, cyclical pulls of gravity from a moon or other bodies — even the planet's position in its orbit around its star. When the energy reaches a threshold, a stream flows, and a Portal opens. With sufficient energy, it becomes possible to transit the Portal.

"Though rare, we've seen cases where the planetary matrix shifted within the gravity-well. Chaos always follows. The Portal nexus seeks to realign with the surface and stabilize at a new juncture. In extreme cases, the Ley-lines themselves may shift, though usually the Portal merely realigns with a new juncture. Finding a Portal's new location can be problematic."

I asked, "What would have provoked such a shift?" As I did so, Teena sat up and attempted to stand, paled, turned pallid and ashen, pressed a hand to her ribs, and fell back with a grunt.

Through clenched teeth, she said something to Yosef in his tongue. He disappeared into a back room again. Holding still eased the pain, she relaxed a little then responded to my question. She acted rather grumpy. "If we meet a physicist, let's remember to ask her! Our immediate problem is to find our Portal and exit it. Our original layover here was to be two days. We can't miss our window."

As she spoke, Yosef returned with a collection of long fabric strips. They exchanged a few brief words, and he again disappeared into a back room. I could hear his voice; he was once again praying.

Teena asked for my help in removing the heavy dress and wrapping her ribcage with the strips. Ribs immobilized, I then helped her restore the dress. As soon as she was again clothed, she called out to Yosef. He returned, and more chatter ensued. They went back and forth several times; he did not like something she wanted.

"I am asking him to take us to the place where our Portal should be. He doesn't want to do it; he fears I'm too injured. I have tried to get the idea across that a hospital in the next world can provide care that he can't. Difficult, as they have no concept of either a hospital or another world. He understands more of the multiverse than his neighbors but only has the barest inkling. Such concepts are heresy here. This discussion would endanger our lives if overheard."

She spoke to Yosef again, and he left, returning moments later with a plain wooden box. A hasp on the front, secured with a primitive lock. He retrieved a matching key from somewhere in his kitchen.

"Taking supplies, particularly any technology, through the Portals is tricky. Difficult, but doable, at least sometimes. I cached supplies here on earlier visits. We need them now."

She opened the box and pulled out a few items. One looked like nothing other than an ordinary smartphone. The term 'smartphone' jangled in my psyche as though its presence warped the very fabric of space and time. She retrieved the anachronistic items as our host again retreated and resumed his invocations.

Catching my gaze, she quipped, "There's an app for that!" She grinned as she said it. "Yes, it is a smartphone of a sort. It doesn't work on Earth's cellular networks though it does allow us to communicate through an open Portal, and it has a Portal mapping app.

"This is the phone we use to communicate with Yosef. He doesn't like it, but he's trained in its use. He is handsomely paid to use it regularly to pass messages and greet and shelter travelers. There are several Portal nexuses here that are vital links in the war against Boskone. His service is valuable to our cause.

"He acts as our agent and protects his society from exposure to outside forces — our version of the fictional *Prime Directive*. I traveled here and recruited him into our mission long before I recruited Fitz. Nevia has become valuable with the closure of most other Portals. Yosef has been kept busy at times. He's aided dozens of travelers."

I looked at the box. "He acts as though he is terrified of the box, the items in it, and us, above all Stapleya and Wisceya. Why are we so scary for him? It can't be just racism or bigotry."

She laughed sardonically. "Racism comes in many forms, although none more virulent than those accompanying Earth's Utopianism. Intellectuals who pride themselves on embracing the scientific method, their tolerance, and broad-mindedness possess the 'vision of the anointed' and thereby are the most self-righteous and hate-filled bigots in the history of humanity. That's not the case in this society. It's not quite that he's scared of us or the gadgetry. Although there is some fear of the unknown."

As she spoke, she opened a bottle she had removed from the box. I recognized Vicodin. She continued, "He is afraid of his society, his neighbors, and what they might do to him. Any man caught with a woman not his wife, runs afoul of the Ordnung. Thus he is wary of you, even without the complication of explaining your Asian features."

I nodded acknowledgment. Racism stems as much from fear of one's friends and neighbors' reactions as fear of other people. But why am I dangerous to him and not Teena? There must be a missing puzzle piece. Before I could ask, she went on, "No, not racism — simple self-preservation. You might, perhaps, pass for a native if not examined too closely. That is, if you did not speak and betray a lack of the language. I might convince an observer you're my little sister if necessary. Our resemblance isn't close, though they won't be too critical unless suspicions become aroused.

"The girls are so alien their discovery would provoke an extreme reaction rooted in religious fervor. Not only would they be immediately killed – they're demons, you see – but he, and we, would also be killed for harboring them. So you see, we cannot allow their discovery at any cost. If anyone comes, take them and hide in the fields and let me handle it."

She popped the Vicodin and took a drink of water. I seized the moment. "Why is it that he is afraid of me and not you? I know you speak the language, but is it more than that?"

She laughed, clamped her hand to her ribs again, and lay back against the cushions for a moment. She took a few shallow breaths, letting the drug take hold. Then, after a few moments, she said, "Yes, you see, I am his wife."

Lunch with Teena

"Marriage is a fine institution, but I'm not ready for an institution."
— *Mae West.*

Wife! That sort of left-hook is so typical of Teena. It makes hanging out with her, uh, well, interesting. I never know what new surprise she has in store.

Teena is not someone you would imagine as being married. Nor would you expect her to be married to one such as Yosef. The agrarian, religious fundamentalist lifestyle is a poor match for Teena's personality. It seems clear that this was a marriage of expedience.

Despite Teena's intentions and with the benefit of opioids, travel that day was impossible. She could barely move and needed to allow her body time to heal from the fall. We spent three days cloistered under Yosef's roof before attempting to find our Portal. I had too many hours to worry, to conjure regrets and recriminations. Would I ever see Earth again? Was my career as a MiB over. Again and again, I replayed in my mind the events that began that day in the gym — events that led me to Nevia.

ᨑᨑ

During her watchful waiting as Teena convalesces, Jill has ample time to reflect on the events leading up to her meeting Teena.

That morning I first met Teena in the gym was, of course, only the beginning. After leaving the gym, I spent the morning at my desk. The perplexing nature of our conversation weighed on my mind as I tried to work. Unfit for field activity, I salved my discontent by studying the voluminous Intelligence reports I had received. If there's a pattern, I've thus far failed at finding it. Frustrated, it was clear that I lacked essential puzzle pieces.

What had Dr. Mathes meant? She was still Dr. Mathes to me; I wouldn't learn her alternate identity until later. "The job's not done," she had suggested. I had been feeling clueless, powerless, and frustrated, demanding to do something tangible. She had appealed to my need for vengeance.

Shucks, I was the one who had demanded desk work. While languishing in my hospital bed, I bristled at the forced inactivity. Despite my injuries, I had begged Matt and Alex to bring reports and files to study. Although I couldn't do much between the pain and the drugs to combat it, the prospect of lying inert and stupefied was more stressful. I needed something to focus on, and Alex obliged.

Weeks later, my doctor would still have me recuperating in bed rather than working at a desk.

My doctor didn't appreciate how much tougher and stronger I could be than the average petite Asian female. As a teenager, I was strong and quick for my size. Perhaps it was partly due to my compact frame that I became so driven. With intense, disciplined training courtesy of the service, I focused my natural drive. As a result, I became even stronger and quicker.

Muscle-bound jarheads standing a head taller and massing twice my weight were often surprised.

I never met anyone I couldn't take in a fair fight — except I don't fight fair! If I'm ever in a fair fight, it will be because I didn't plan properly. Only one rule applies in a fight — Win!

No one I couldn't take, save this one muscle-bound lunkhead. It was, oddly, love at first sight of a sort, I suppose. Those few whom I allowed close would find that shocking. Especially me.

Whatever toss of the genetic dice gifted my natural talents paid Fitz the bonus jackpot; that guy can bench-press a Buick. Literally! I've seen him do it. He also has other extraordinary skills.

Love? I dunno. Maybe. Yeah, shocked me too.

Then again....

I had expected with my 'spiritual' talents, Boot Camp would pass easily. That was a mistake. I soon learned happiness often consists in getting enough sleep — just that and nothing more. The meat-grinder of recruit training soon passed. My 'spiritual' gifts opened another pathway. I found my way into these esoteric MiB ranks, and in time, this is where I met Fitz. And now Teena.

Anticipating the mysterious lunchtime meeting, I consulted our internal directory. Not much help. Dr. Mathes appeared beside a Dr. Shepherd as a civilian specialist reporting to Alex. I realized why she seemed familiar. I remembered seeing her and Dr. Shepherd in Alex's command center. We had not met, although they had been nearby a few times when I had conferred with Alex. I wondered then why he had not introduced us. Chalked-up as 'need to know,' I suppose.

That set me wondering, so I checked on Fitz. Then Stapleya and Wisceya. On impulse, I reviewed my own listing. We were all assigned to Alex. They are, of course, civilians. We're all unspecified specialists reporting to Alex. The common factor appeared to be that we all knew of Boskone.

It appears I'm no longer a field operative. Reasonable, given my present medical incapacity. I hope it's not permanent; I have some serious ass to kick once I get my strength back.

After weeks of recovery, I found myself on light desk duty. Inefficient use of my talents; beats lying in bed. I must be patient, I suppose. Recovering from multiple gunshot wounds takes time. You don't just go from rebuilding your organs to running a marathon overnight.

I spent my time digging through intelligence, trying to map the enemy's activities. I spent my spare time looking for potential suspicious activities within our ranks. We had uncovered one traitor, stayed vigilant for more.

Even modest desk duty bothered my doctor. He insisted I should be on a delicate regimen of rest and therapy. But unfortunately, he failed to appreciate how driven I am. Searching for my lover's murderer was the best therapy I could imagine. Still, recovery from a near-fatal wounding is a slow process. Though I bristle, I know how lucky I am to have survived.

While my health and strength improved, I wondered about the mysterious Sixth Column organization. I became involved through Estelle, my connection severed with her death. I must reconnect if I'm to engage the enemy.

Today's peculiar lunch date evoked memories of my previous lunch date. With Fitz! Time spent with Fitz a few weeks before, a different sort of lunch date — we forgot to eat.

One day — barely out of my hospital bed — I met Fitz for lunch in the cafeteria. I was unclear on what he had been doing. All I understood at the time was that he had become critical to our mission. I would not appreciate the value of his security and communications skills until much later. Fitz had gone from terrified of Alex to working for him as a top resource. The shift had thoroughly flabbered my gast and left me unsure of how it happened. Given the depth of Fitz's fears of our organization and Alex, I found this shocking.

Unaccountable power is dangerous. Lord Acton taught us that. Any ground pounder knows the lessons from Ancient Greece. Warnings and safeguards permeate the US Constitution. Although I thought I understood those dangers, I never considered us as unaccountable.

Yes, we operate in secret, though we have superiors who hold us accountable. Or so I believed. It was only while with Fitz that I recognized the depths of fear such secret organizations inspire. And the reasons why. Acton warned of that too. "Everything secret degenerates," he wrote.

I discovered this bothered me. I came to understand how secrecy and power make dangerous bedfellows. Yet, I couldn't see an alternative. So, Lord Acton keeps me company in the darkness now.

The Vegas attack took me out of the action. After my sidelining, much transpired, though I only have an incomplete story. Somehow Alex convinced Fitz that he and the girls faced greater danger from Boskone than from the MiB. When I rejoined the living, Fitz was running things. He oversaw an immense organization. His specialized tech skills were supporting a massive peacetime military exercise. Though I only had an inkling of what he did, whatever it was, I knew Alex considered it critical.

I was glad Fitz asked if we might speak alone that day. I wanted to talk to him — and not in the cafeteria where others might overhear. So, we grabbed a pair of trays and ducked into an unoccupied office to eat and talk. We sought privacy for our conversation; I hoped Fitz would speak candidly. I was anxious to learn what had happened since my enforced idling.

I felt relieved no one else saw us. I'm not given to turning weak and feminine, above all not with a man. Yet Fitz and I had become brothers at arms in a manner of speaking. Plus, he was fond of Estelle too.

᭝᭝᭝

Jill worked through the morning. She spent her time studying the latest data, tabulating trends — fitting known operatives into the interactive map she had been building. The morning flew by unnoticed until her wearable dinged to remind her of lunch.

Jostled from my warm, creative fog, I pulled my mind out of the cyberspace realm and realized I was hungry. Not having heard from Dr. Mathes, I assumed she would find me when she wanted to speak. Time to haul ass if I planned to beat the lunch crowd. I locked away my papers and logged out of the workstation. Pushing back my chair, I stood. My wound twinged, not quite painful, just a gentle reminder of the morning's abuses.

I wondered whether I should tell my doctor. That would mean confessing my sins in the gym, sure to earn a stern rebuke. Watchful waiting is the wiser course, I argued. I promised myself that I would run to the doctor on actual pain, these minor twinges not rising to that level.

During the elevator ride, I had gazed at my black-suited reflection in the mirror. For a bare instant, I imagined myself naked. *(to-whit to-who)* My inner knucklehead wolf-whistled the image as it flitted through my mind. I recalled the evening when Estelle and I became Fitz's more-or-less willing captives. He required we disrobe as an alternative to tying us up lest we run away.

Only Fitz would go there....

In my case, it was effective as I was paralytically body shy. But, on the other hand, Estelle, well, she would not let a small question of modesty deter her escape. Despite her prim and proper, almost prissy formal public persona, she was starkly uninhibited.

I well knew she relished any excuse to get naked.

She had her reasons to play the captive with Fitz, and I was content to play along. It feels silly in hindsight, yet I believe I enjoyed it more than I would have admitted at the time. Regardless, I adapted to the enforced exposure — I shocked myself at how easily I accepted it once we were naked. Perhaps an inner exhibitionist lurked behind my ingrained prudishness.

Entering the canteen, I noted once again I timed my arrival with precision. I always strive just to beat the masses, as I'm allergic to long lines.

A tray, a lump of mystery meat, a bowl of soup; not quite gourmet.

As I targeted my usual table near the aft wall across from the pinball machines, I spied Dr. Mathes. From her position, immersed in the head of the massive swarm, she spotted me and waved. Then, she extricated herself from the pack and headed in my direction, skipping the food line. I noted a guard was dogging her heels, rushing to keep pace.

She laid her hand on my shoulder, steering me away from my intended seat. "Let's duck in where we can have some privacy." I nodded as we passed the row of video games and pinball machines. Finally, she turned toward the vacant office Fitz and I had used weeks earlier.

That day, Fitz and I embraced; not as lovers; instead, as dear friends. That was my intention — until a tsunami of emotion washed over us, and a friendly embrace collapsed into grief and emotion.

I'd started crying. I felt almost as though I were standing outside myself — a detached observer, powerless — no control whatever over what the body I inhabited was doing — as though someone else was driving. I was, uncharacteristically, an emotional basket case. I felt disgusted for displaying weakness.

I diverted my brain from the repeating loop through the memory lane of grief. Dr. Mathes pointed to the office, and her guard moved ahead, checked the office for occupants, and stationed himself beside the door. He nodded to us as we entered the private room. She closed the door and latched it.

I surmised she did not wish us disturbed.

She hadn't bothered with getting a tray, but as we entered the room, I spotted a plain paper bag in her hand. I arched an eyebrow, said nothing; if she preferred to brown-bag her lunch, okay by me.

Settling on the couch, I paused a moment. I did not know this woman, her preferences, her rituals. The gentle Confucianism my mother practiced remains my guide. She had stayed her own path even after ostensibly accepting my father's stern Catholicism. Although my bent leans more humanist, I respect the beliefs and traditions of others. She made no movement telegraphic of genuflection. I presumed — like myself — she lacked interest in the religious trappings. After a slight hesitation, I began eating.

A bite or two into my meal, I saw her bag lay unopened. I paused. "Are you eating?" I asked.

She gave a wan smile and pulled something from the bag. A paper plate covered in plastic wrap held an unfamiliar tuber. It was large, black, and ugly, a strange unappetizing-looking thing. Unlike any food item I'd ever seen. She had a pat of butter and a plastic fork. Noting my stare, she spoke. "Vitelotte," she said. She took a couple of dainty bites, then continued. "From an archaic French word that sometimes means 'penis.' High in antioxidants and potassium, a variety of minerals, among other nutrients."

I must have grimaced as she gave a quiet laugh and extended her plate toward me. I forked a dainty sample. She explained, "Fitz's 'root vegetables,' unappetizing yet healing." I put my fork down, uncertain of the strange, ugly food. She continued, "The nutrients in these plants from Fitz's *Planet Oz* are legendary. Perhaps part of the reason the Nekomata lead lives that are so long and healthy despite the harsh lifestyle. The ones grown here on Earth are extraordinary. The ones from *Planet Oz* are almost supernatural. If only there were a practical way to transport them in quantity between worlds....

"Jill, my injuries were more severe than you would believe. I have been grievously injured before, yet this was different. Death is not a binary state, rather a descending scale. I slid off the end of that scale, hit the floor, and bounced. Caught on the bounce by miracle techniques of advanced medicine, I clawed back to life. Thanks to miracles involving peptides, lasers, stem cells, and median nerve stimulation. If the morgue refrigerator had been a couple of degrees warmer...." her voice trailed off. She shuttered, took a breath, and continued.

"I hoped that once we recovered the research from the Asheran computers, we could fix things. Our geneticists might unravel the fertility plague and find solutions. We needed the means to rescue our failing populations, that of the Nekomata topmost. Without intervention, their race will soon become extinct. Even Fitz's prodigious capacity can only do so much. My people will quickly follow, spiraling into infertility despite our technology. The rest of humanity, including Earth's, will soon follow. With billions of lives in the balance, I willingly gave my life for that data!

"Beyond genetics, that mass of data revealed worse troubling information. We discovered our downfall was not solely due to our hubris. Instead, our downfall was a product of an inimical direct intervention. Someone sabotaged our ambitious genetics program and poisoned our AI.

"The fertility crisis was intentional, the plague an engineered contagion. We spread it everywhere we went, unaware. As a result, though you might doubt it from the teeming population, Earth's humanity, too, is at risk. Though the population is robust, Earth's fertility is waning. Without effective intervention, human civilization stands doomed."

The elderly woman paused and took a deep breath as she looked to the ceiling. Then, holding it a moment before letting it out, she released it in an extended sigh.

After a pause, she continued, "A prolonged and painful convalescence can cause one to question the value of life. Likewise, feeling frail and sick reduces the will to live.

"I didn't fear growing old when I was young and strong. But, being old and frail now, that is what's scary.

"Though still weak, ill, frail, and aged, I'm finally beginning to appreciate living again. However, my mission cannot wait while I heal and regain youth and vigor. Our enemy awaits.

"The fertility problem lies in the hands of technicians, engineers, and experts in genetics. The Gharlane problem rests in my hands. Mine, and yours."

I raised an eyebrow, although she plowed ahead before I could interrupt.

"At Ashera, Fitz's Planet 'K,' we had tried many a frontal assault and failed. Repeatedly. We mounted attack after attack, all futile. A surgical strike with a precision-crafted weapon — named Fitz — succeeded where others could not."

I stopped eating; food forgotten, head spinning as I grokked her words. I had read Fitz's silly book several times. Yet even after meeting the Fur girls, wisdom insisted it was a childish bit of male fantasy. Granted, perhaps wrapping a kernel of reality, nevertheless crass male fantasy.

An insane pinball bounded from the mental popper of the mundane. It bounced madly from bumper to pin before settling into an unexpected higher-level phrenic field. Then I understood beyond doubt; fantasy was fact, reality the illusion, albeit a persistent one.

A pause ensued as I gathered my scattered marbles and waited for the mental TILT to stop blinking.

Finally, I asked, "Dr. Mathes, you said your given name was Min, right?" She nodded. "Short for Minerva?" She nodded again, although I didn't wait for her acknowledgment. Instead, I plowed ahead with my stream of consciousness as awareness gelled.

"Minerva was the Roman goddess of wisdom and war. The Greeks called her —"

She interrupted, plunging into my stream, "Athena! Yes, Dear, I am Fitz's Teena."

I stopped talking; mouth stuck open as though the cosmic first cause had hit the 'Pause.'

I sat frozen in my disbelief, incredulous. This frail, skeletal, elderly woman before me was nothing like the Teena I had imagined. Nothing like Fitz's description.

She broke the spell with a wry laugh. "Don't I look the part? Believe me, I know it. Know it? I feel it! In every joint, every bone, and in every muscle."

Recovering, I fumbled for what to say. Finally, I mumbled, "You look so different than he described. Not just frail from your injuries, unlike his description in many ways."

She said, "Dear, a few easily manipulated genes control so much of human appearance. Due to my extensive injuries and death, I required extensive rebuilding. I've reverted to a genotype resembling what I was gifted at birth. Fitz's flame-topped Amazon was custom built for seduction, for seducing him. A few genetic tweaks, and you could have flaming red hair and bronze skin too. Or, if you'd prefer, a sensual pelt like Stapleya and Wisceya. That is easy. Conquering senescence and death; that's more challenging."

"Does Fitz know you're here, that you're alive and well?" Fitz had thought Teena had died but held some hope otherwise.

"Though perhaps wellness yet lies ahead. Yes, Fitz is aware that I live. Petchy and I revealed our presence to him one recent evening over dinner. Stapleya and Wisceya were present too."

Anamnesis

"People will walk in and walk out of your life, but the one whose footstep made a long-lasting impression is the one you should never allow to walk out."
— **Michael Bassey Johnson.**

Teena related the essence of that dinner for my benefit. I imagined the evening from her description. Fitz had been so overjoyed to learn his Goddess still lived that he was not listening. I supplied my own vision, imagining him lost in his own world — preferring to luxuriate in her presence, eyes closed, blissful, unaware. Finally, a double-take as her words took hold.

"Huh?" came the response. "Princess? Quest? What?"

"Fitz, my love," she had explained, "we're not finished, not by quite a bit. This 'Jade Helm' is only a single battle in the war we must fight — even as it affects Earth. The enemy won't stop until we defeat him permanently. I fear our greatest battles lay yet ahead."

Petch added, "We have played our cards close to our vest; we have not told you everything."

I imagined how Fitz roused himself from her embrace. With effort, I'm certain; he pulled himself away from her hypnotic influence. For the first time, he'd genuinely looked at her.

When she first walked in, he'd ignored how she had changed and aged. He took a couple of deep breaths and looked, shocked at the changes he now noted. From the way she told the tale, it bothered her to have him see her as frail and sick.

Though still Teena, without doubt, she was also a completely different person. She had changed almost beyond recognition. She met his gaze and then dropped her eyes, looking at her gnarled and wrinkled hands. There was no masking it, no blaming an undercover academic disguise. She was indeed positively aged, frail.

His voice solemn, Petch continued talking as Fitz reeled. "Worse, we've been slow to realize — to acknowledge — the extent of this conspiracy. It is older, more complex, and more extensive than we imagined."

Growing unease showed on his face. Petch lowered his voice a notch and placed a hand on his shoulder.

"Son, we suspect the forces arrayed against Earth are already known to us. We believe they are the same as those which decimated our home world. We think a hidden alien force is behind this. One so powerful and advanced as to appear almost supernatural."

Fitz raised his eyebrows. "This character we called *Gharlane* and those we had called *Eddore* and *Boskone?*"

Petchy nodded gravely. "Yes, I know you had speculated Boskone was extra-terrestrial in origin. It agreed with my view, something I, too, had believed. What we kept to ourselves was our belief that the enemy originated among our own people." He nodded toward Teena. "We believed extremist factions were at fault. We assumed they established themselves elsewhere following the collapse of our society. Some of us thought they were complicit in the downfall. Until we studied the data which Teena recovered, that is. Now we know our world did not merely die, a victim of our hubris. It was assassinated.

"After careful study, a new vision of our enemy has emerged. We did not know of another civilization capable of Portal travel. So, we assumed the villains were a branch of our people gone rogue and exploiting Earth. We now are confident that idea was mistaken. We now believe they were — are — another utterly unknown civilization. One advanced far beyond the combined science of our worlds.

"Analysis shows they weren't merely present when the AI went rogue. They were the instigators. They caused the destructive turn of our AI. They are the architects of the DNA sabotage that has almost ended our race. It was not a random accident, it was intentional, and the AI did not malfunction; they poisoned it."

Teena chimed in. "Fitz, Humpty-Dumpty didn't fall. He was pushed, and Gharlane, or at least his minions, did the pushing. He is the driver behind all the conspiracies, the architect of the evil that appears to be blossoming here. Unless we stop him, Earth will descend into a level of barbarism uncharted. It will cause the period following the collapse of the Roman Empire to seem like merely the Dim Ages."

Fitz became concerned. Petch had said that Earth also became infected with the fertility plague. That plague had almost wiped out his people and doomed the dinosaur world of the fur-people. So, he had believed with the neutralization of the runaway AI; it would reverse itself. A temporary reduction of fertility on Earth would appear insignificant. But Planet Oz needed babies, multitudes of healthy male babies. So, he had done his part — yet they required far more Y-Chromosomes than one man could muster no matter how prolific.

Wisceya asked, "My home too? Is Gharlane going to push us too?" Teena moved to put her arms around Wisceya and her mother. "Dear ones, no, we see no evidence of Gharlane on your world. As near as we can tell, the plague that affected your people was carried to your world by us — a horrible, careless accident caused by us Asherans — carried to your world by myself, Petch, and all the others of our people who have visited your world. We are working on fixing that, and with Fitz's help, your people should survive. Why Gharlane has ignored your world is a question for which we have no explanation. Sensible speculation eludes us."

Stapleya raised another question. She returned to the original motive for their hazardous travel to Earth and the death of poor Shameya. "What of the monsters? Now that they dare to walk in the daytime, they are killing us. How can we fix that? We need weapons that can kill them."

Petch sounded vexed. "Yes, we will certainly help you." Stapleya looked relieved as he continued. "Though it will not be easy. We're not supposed to interfere in your society, but we have made a royal mess of that. We have stepped on a lot of butterflies. We will try to make amends."

She cocked her eye at him on that. He ignored her. Teena once again spoke up. "We will take these ladies home and once again train and stage a mission. While there, we will figure out what to do with the recalcitrant dinosaurs."

With that, Teena turned back to Fitz, stared solemnly into his eyes. "Fitz, my love, I know I do not look as you remember me. It pains me to have you see me like this, though you already knew I was much older than I appear. I won't tell you my true age, not that it's some deep dark secret, just that I am vain."

"Fitz, I died last year. Believe me, that takes a lot out of a person.

"The wounds I received on 'Planet K' were mortal. When we landed in that lovely Plaza in the city, I was all but exsanguinated from blood loss. By the time we reached the hospital, my heart had stopped. I went straight from ambulance to morgue. We had agents there, and they intervened in time. Our more advanced medicine still offered slim hope. It was close — I almost did not make it.

"The reason I have not been around these months is that I have been convalescing. I have been busy healing, slow and painfully, and far away."

He was about to say something when Petch emitted a soft cough. "Gharlane won't wait. Teena will do what she can, but we must mount our own mission."

ᨁᨁᨁ

Later, the Fur girls headed to their quarters, alone. Fitz had stayed with Teena and Petch, planning their next mission.

"What about butterflies?" Wisceya spoke to her mother in Language as they entered the elevator. They were on their way to the sleeping quarters they shared with Fitz. "Who stepped on them? Why? What do butterflies have to do with Monsters?"

Stapleya shrugged. "I don't believe he meant literal butterflies. I think they refer to a story we have not heard, like Fitz quotes movies. Maybe Jessica can explain the butterflies and why stepping on them is a bad omen. I will ask her tomorrow. Tonight I am tired and miss Matt terribly. They said he wouldn't be back. I like Matt. I know they said he did something bad, but no one explained."

The elevator doors swished open, revealing the hallway outside their shared sleeping quarters.

Wisceya said, "I'm happy to see Teena and Petchy again. I missed them, feared them dead. I knew Petchy and Teena had visited our home since before your mother's grandmother. I knew she was ancient, but to see her looking so aged and frail crushes my heart. It is one thing to live a long time, something else to be old. I am not sure it is better to live long and become aged, frail, and sick, or to die young."

Stapleya continued, "I love the Smoothies. All the People do. Special love for Fitz. It is troubling to learn how much grief they have brought us. Fitz came to give us babies, to save us from the plague Petch and Teena brought. After Fitz came the day-walkers. Cause and effect? Don't know. Now they will save us from the Monsters.

"But what new plague will follow?"

They walked in silence for a few moments. Then Wisceya picked up the conversational thread, "Cannot look back. Move forward only. Can't fix the past. Must kill the beasts. Will Fitz and Petch stop at killing the day-walkers? Or give us the means to kill them all? On this world, I learned to love the night, the sunset, and sunrise. Too dangerous at home. I want to kill them all!"

Stapleya sighed in agreement with her daughter. Finally, they arrived at their room and entered.

Changing the subject, Stapleya said, "We see so little of Fitz. He works days at a time using pills to stay awake, then sleeping like the dead. We used pills some, but our help is not in such demand, not like his. I worry for him, but he promises pills not harm and doctor checks him every day.

"I see the wear on his heart, the worry in his eyes. Little time to ask him questions, little talk. He only work and sleep, much work, little sleep. Time for love is rare, but we cuddle him in his sleep; sometimes, in the night, there is more. Fitz does not know you are with child. I hope we return home before he notices. Males and babies make problems. I hope he comes to our bed tonight."

Wisceya took her mother's arm and stared into her eyes. She said, "We help Jessica, we help with the mission. Jessica says we help, that we follow instructions well.

"Computers are fascinating but too complex. Maybe our children will learn one day. Fitz explained how they are only machines, only do what told, but the art of telling illogical. Fitz understands them. Jessica understands. Some Smoothies do, but not most. It feels good to help, but I want to go home and fight the monsters; they are evil I understand."

"I know, dear," Stapleya reassured her daughter. "Maybe we will go home soon, but I do not think Fitz will come with us."

Stapleya did not know how prophetic her words would be. The next they knew, Fitz was gone. So was Petchy. No one knew where. Teena was absent, mostly. They were supposed to take them home, but the girls are alone now; no one remains who understands their world.

They have friends here, people they work with, Jessica, Alex, and of course Jill. Yet despite that, they are lonely aliens in a very alien land.

Ordnung

"There are two powers in the world; one is the sword and the other is the pen. There is a great competition and rivalry between the two. There is a third power stronger than both, that of the women."
—**Muhammad Ali Jinnah**

That curious dinner marked the moment Fitz last pounded a keyboard in service to the MiB. He abandoned the Air Chair and keyboard to become a superhero on a quest once again. He and Petchy departed the MiB facility soon after, and we have not heard from them since. I deduced I had seen him that last time shortly after the evening described. Coincidentally, in the same room where Teena and I had our introductory lunch.

Lunch with Teena — er, I mean, Dr. Mathes — she insisted we must maintain the alter-ego — had continued much too long. Far longer than a typical lunch. Longer than I was comfortable with. There was so much back-story I needed to understand as she filled me in on events to date — not just the dinner, but so much more. I worried over the time, though she assured me no boss would be cracking the whip over my absence.

She was right, of course. I have tremendous autonomy in my work, more so since I am still on the disabled list. I rarely take breaks during the workday and usually arrive early and leave late. I protested that this was not a sign of industriousness, just a sign I lacked anything better to do with my time. Well, perhaps my personal drive is a factor too, and my determination to avenge my lover's death.

There had been only one other time I had taken such a long lunch, also in that same room. That day, no guard stood at the door protecting our privacy. Though we latched the door, privacy was uncertain. Someone might have intruded on intimate moments considered inappropriate at work. We had not expected things to go in that direction, of course. I was an emotional basket-case and in need of catharsis. I remembered that day and the way I had broken down and sobbed uncontrollably with Fitz.

I realized anyone other than Fitz would have pressed forward. Most would assume permission I had not intended, mixed signals notwithstanding. But, instead, he just mirrored my embrace and comforted me, waiting.

After Teena related the tale of that dinner and the beginnings of the new quest, I put it together. That is when I realized the 'lunch date' Fitz and I had shared in this same room must have followed that evening. He and Petch must have departed immediately afterward. I haven't seen either of them again.

Although I did not recognize it at the time, the giveaway came near the end of our lunch. Fitz said, "I have received some fresh communications from the Four Columns. May I assume you are 'in' for anything that might develop?"

Ignorant of the events he spoke of, my affirmative response to his words provoked another upwelling of emotion. I grabbed him in a mixture of grief, relief, and, yes, lust.

〰〰

Fitz and Petchy, I mean Dr. Shepherd, had once again gone off-world. Their mission: to scout another society where they suspect the evil influence of Boskone. Teena, er, Min, and I had an interim task.

First, we must seek advanced medical treatment. Second, we must take the Fur girls to their home world. And while there, devise a way to deal with the day-walking dinosaurs. Once we mitigate that threat, we will join with Fitz and Petchy. They will then have a strategy for Gharlane. Well, that's the plan.

"We make quite the pair of warriors," Min had said with wry irony. "Our immediate responsibility is to get back into fighting trim."

I nodded in agreement, "But how? Recovery takes time, and you imply some urgency."

"True," she said, "still, there is much we can do. Advanced immunotherapy can prime the immune system for optimal results. Gene therapy can turn on the optimal expression of genetic capability. I have endured two major interventions thus far in my therapy, and I am almost ready for a third. How much I can hope to benefit is uncertain, I am old and worn, but you have greater potential. Therapy, optimal nutrition, and aggressive physical training are available. With good medicine, I promise you will gain major improvements in strength and stamina."

I opened my mouth, reconsidered, paused, reconsidered again. Then on the third try, I put forth a cogent question. "Are you suggesting off-world medical facilities?"

She nodded, "If we are to take on Gharlane, we must stretch our limits and use every possible tool. Earth's medicine is hardly adequate for a full recovery, if that is even possible. Therefore, we must travel to another world to partake of the most sophisticated medicine in existence. Do you trust me? Will you travel with me through a Portal to another world?"

I had some doubts, then. Now, as I anguish over how our trip has gone awry, those doubts have become troubling.

She had explained her people had blockaded Earth's Portals to hamper evil's minions. Consequently, the barricade made it challenging to arrange interplanetary travel from Earth. Portals open according to precise timing, planned such that a militia might greet any travelers. Because coordinating militia schedules across disparate worlds with limited communications is problematic, we must await the availability of an Earth departure window.

I returned to my desk that afternoon, not yet knowing when we were to travel. Min had said to stand ready to embark. She said I need not worry about packing for the trip.

Yeah, I kinda got that — not my favorite aspect of the plan. But, if Teena can do it, I will steel myself and follow suit. Or is that sans suit? Ugh!

The days that followed were routine. I awaited the final word from Min — Dr. Mathes. Waited, while vacillating between anticipation and fear with occasional dips into sheer terror. It is one thing to read a fictionalized account of 'Portals' as a silly plot device. Quite another to stand on the precipice, staring into a genuine inter-world abyss.

Yes, I was a tiny bit scared. Tiny bit? I'll admit it; I was freaking terrified! Who wouldn't be?

At Min's instruction, I told Stapleya and Wisceya of the intention to travel. Needless to say, they're eager. Veterans of their one Portal transition, they appear unconcerned. Their major disappointment is that we're not going to their home, at least not at first. Due to the blockade, we must make two transitions to get from Earth to the world of the medical facility. Only after time in the hospital will we make the third leg of our trip — to Nekomata.

The first leg, to the hospital, will not be the easy 'Rapidly Overlapping Portals' that Fitz described. Instead, we must layover for a couple of days at this quaint little agrarian utopia. She called it Nevia.

I suspect, like Fitz's Planet Oz, the name is a joke or a nickname. People unaware of other worlds do not bother to name their own. Nevertheless, it's as good a handle as Planet Oz is for the Nekomata home world.

Nevia had promised to be a most curious hiatus. But, as she had explained, "We must be careful; the place can be dangerous."

"Why is that?" I had asked. "Are the people violent?"

"Not exactly; the people are pleasant enough. It is just that they live a strict and unforgiving lifestyle. It is much too easy to run afoul of their many taboos. They are a gentle people and will give a pass to strangers over minor infractions. Still, it can be dangerous to depend on their tolerance. Punishments can be horrific."

I looked at her quizzically. "And what, pray tell, does that mean?"

"Pray ... Interesting you should use that expression." Min ignored my arched eyebrow and continued without pausing. "Theirs is a stern society based on a harsh interpretation of fundamentalist religious beliefs. They practice a Spartan dress and lifestyle, shunning all technology. Transportation is via horse-drawn buggies. They have almost no concept of recreation. Play is forbidden, even to small children. Sex is forbidden unless for procreation. Their beds, for married couples, are 'Bundling Beds' – with a barrier to prevent the couple from touching."

Min sighed as though in frustration or pity. "The Ordnung describes the set of rules they live by, both religious and civil practices. These rules keep their members in line with the laws therein. Their communities function as independent entities with no central government.

Each community defines its unique variant of the Ordnung. As a result, they have two versions of Ordnung — one written and one verbal — within each community."

"Sounds like the more fundamentalist societies here on Earth," I said. She plowed ahead with a scant nod in acknowledgment of my input.

"They have a simplistic dress style — in keeping with their harsh religious philosophy. Clothes are handmade of dark fabric. Coats and vests fasten with hooks and eyes. Men's trousers must not have creases or cuffs. Married men may not trim their beards. Women cannot wear jewelry or patterned clothing and may not cut their hair. The length of clothing, like dresses, is also dictated by the Ordnung."

Interrupting, I had asked, "Doesn't that cause trouble for interplanetary travelers? I would imagine such people would take a dim view of naked Portal transitions."

"Yes," she had explained, "They have an exceptionally harsh nudity taboo, with severe punishment for breaking it. So, we must be extraordinarily circumspect."

Oops.

Fane

Yosef's farm home is remote from the settlement with no close neighbors. Their faux marriage is a sham enacted to satisfy the harsh Ordnung rules. An ersatz wife is a much safer deception than an illicit association with a woman who is not his wife. The latter might result in his, and her, execution in a gruesome fashion.

Pretending to marry is a concept beyond imagining under the Ordnung, as no one questions a marriage claim. They have not yet invented government-mandated marriage licensing and all the ugly bureaucratic intrusions that follow. Yosef maintains the pretense during her absences via the fiction of a distant ailing mother-in-law. This deception also explains his frequent travels in support of the off-worlders' needs.

Teena visits often enough to put in a local appearance to maintain the pretext. In addition, she arranges her travels to attend Fane when possible. Nevian social life, such as it is, centers on religion, and Fane is an essential social function where a wife is visible. When other female operatives pass through, they lend support to the illusion too. When seen from a distance, clad in the bulky, anonymous dress, almost anyone could pass as the ersatz wife. Though shorter than Teena, even I could pass for the wife as long as I kept my distance.

In less regimented societies, this would not have worked. But Nevian society discourages socializing and intimacy outside the family. That Teena's people maintain such effort illustrates the importance of this world. Nevia has become a critical transit point, and Yosef's role as facilitator is invaluable.

We used our downtime to study the language. When not rehashing recent events, I'd been working with Stapleya and

Wisceya to learn their language, and now I find myself pushing to learn the rudiments of the Nevian tongue. Unfortunately, my gifts include not a talent for languages. I find the effort tedious, painful, and unproductive.

Teena appears to speak an astounding variety of languages with perfect fluency. Her American English holds a slightly exotic quality, a faint accent that defies placement. Yet no one would doubt for a moment she was an Earth native on that basis or even her American citizenship. At worst, the region of her birth might be subject to debate, and Teena could sell whatever fiction her mission required. When she looks you in the eye and speaks, you believe her. She is silver-tongued.

They say when you can fake sincerity....

Based on what I learned of their society, I held no illusion I could pass for a native here; nor could I master the language. Suspected of being an alien is dangerous here in the same manner as though suspected as a witch in medieval times on Earth. The lack of social intimacy somewhat mitigates the risk, as Nevians are loath to pry into the affairs of others. As long as one maintains the necessary illusions, no one digs too deep.

"Draw the clothing close, cover your head with the scarf and hood, maintain a distance, feigning shyness, and don't speak. You just might squeak by," she had said. Although it might be perilous, Teena suggested I might be able to pass for her younger sister if the need arose. At one point, she suggested that I might instead play the role of the wife while she played the ailing mother-in-law. I believe she was serious, given her current health and condition.

The Nevian style clothing masks her aged and frail condition; thus, she may maintain her role. In any case, I lacked the language to carry forth such a pretext.

The Nekomata women must stay hidden, as no possible disguise or deception will stand scrutiny. The Nevians hold no concept of aliens in our sense. Instead, they associate anything odd or unaccountable with the supernatural. The danger of their being mistaken for a demon was grave.

On the fourth day, Teena appeared improved, and we set out to investigate the Portal. First, we must survey the site of our arrival, measure the extent of the shift. Plotting the present location of the nexus and its stability was paramount. That data was necessary to calculate how much and in what direction the matrix had shifted. Stapleya and Wisceya wanted to join us, though Teena expressed fear of the risk of an encounter. She wanted the three of us to remain at Yosef's home and hide, awaiting their return. The girls did not care to stay there without our host, fearful of possible visitors and discovery. My motive was milder; I just didn't fancy being left out of the action.

It's a difficult decision. There are risks and dangers either way. If left home alone and a visiting neighbor discovered us, Yosef and Teena might return to a smoldering ruin and our charred remains. If the girls joined us and became exposed, we all faced dreadful consequences. After considerable debate, we elected to stay together as a unit, taking our chances. Teena believed she could defuse any tense situation, talk her way out of any trouble.

Yosef must endeavor to avoid encountering anyone, if possible. We must travel a circuitous route to our destination. We must stay away from those who might recognize Yosef and perhaps question his activities. We had our story planned and rehearsed if an encounter with anyone occurred despite our cautions, though avoidance is safer.

Our story was that Yosef and his wife are hosting a visit by the wife's younger sisters. I play the eldest in our little charade, and Stapleya and Wisceya portray the role of children. Their stature, shorter than I, made that presentation reasonable. As such, he provided them heavy veils to wear, masking their faces. That cannot endure close inspection. Instructed to stay in the back of the buggy, they must not meet anyone's gaze. They must not speak under any circumstances. They had picked up a few bits of the language, although useless since any interaction might be fatal. Teena fretted and insisted on rehearsing every possible scenario.

We set out early, long before dawn. I remembered the ride that first night, how long it felt. This trip felt longer. The sun was high when we arrived at where I had first spotted Yosef's dim buggy lantern.

Upon our arrival, debate ensued once again. We wanted to help find the nexus. Cooped in the carriage for hours was frustrating. Unsurprisingly, we harbored no wish to hide in the vehicle while Yosef and Teena — her name here is Sira — traipsed around the field, attempting to locate a wandering energy vortex.

Legion is the name of this woman — can she even recall her birth name? Fitz used the term 'Goddess,' and I wondered.

No one was nearby; we hadn't seen another soul for miles. We demanded release. Finally, we won our way, although we endured a stern lecture. We must stay near the copse of trees and hide among them if anyone comes.

We took blankets and lunch baskets into the trees to set out our meal. We positioned ourselves to restrict visibility from the road. Though cloistered among the trees, we still must watch for travelers. Yosef and Sira headed into the field with the smartphone in hand.

What should have been a simple task, instead turned into a laborious process. It required several hours to map the present location of the Nexus relative to the original point. Teena's injuries slowed progress, hobbling her movements. She was in pain despite the Vicodin. She walked with difficulty, leaning on a long walking stick. She often stopped to rest, holding her side. I worried about her; I offered to do the job in her place, although she declined, insisting she must map the matrix herself.

She'd often dropped odd little comments suggesting a need to protect other societies. I'd inferred there may be a sort of *Prime Directive* she was attempting to honor, however poorly. I couldn't decide whether the task at hand was too skilled to teach, or she held deeper motivations. She was cagey with tech. In any case, I could only stand by, worry, and watch her struggle.

While we waited, occasional passersby traveled the road below us. A few waved and stopped, engaging Yosef in conversation. They expressed concern whether there might be an injury or illness. He assured them everything was excellent, that the family merely paused during a long trip for a picnic. Reassured, they departed without hesitation, without visible suspicion. Despite our fears and cautions, the encounters remained benign; no incidents ensued.

It was late in the afternoon when Teena completed her task and announced she had the required data. Unfortunately, it'd taken far longer than expected. It was too late to proceed to our egress Portal, which was several miles in the opposite direction from Yosef's home. She tried to insist, though Yosef refused due to darkness and her failing strength. It would be necessary to return to his home and begin a new trek tomorrow.

I doubted Teena would be able to again travel the following day. Nevertheless, she stoutly rejected the idea of quitting, determined to proceed at any cost although worn down by the day's exertions. In the end, she yielded, though, agreed despite her objections. She needed medical treatment and rest, not a further adventure. While helping with her clothing and bandages that evening, I noted how precarious she appeared, wasting away under the constant pain and meager appetite. Gaunt, pale paper-thin skin, and protruding bones, the day's activities mapping the matrix had inflicted a wicked impact on her already fragile body.

Teena insisted that once we discovered our egress, advanced medical treatment lay just beyond. She did not wish to linger here under Yosef's care, further endangering him. I worried whether another misstep such as that on our arrival might be in the offing. Another fall might be fatal in her fragile condition. She was not well.

Despite her protestations, Yosef refused to allow her to travel the following day. Fake marriage or no, he appeared to care for her. I felt concerned, too, without any pretense of marriage.

That evening he retrieved the magic stone and accompanying malodorous liquid. He applied it to her abdomen, once again praying through the night and throughout the day. She took a double dose of the opioid and slept through his ministrations. I'm not one to embrace the supernatural, yet his efforts appeared to produce results. By the time the stone turned cold, and the prayers ended, she seemed visibly improved. Whether improvement came from Yosef's prayers, the magic stone, placebo effect, or just time, rest, and Vicodin, I cannot judge.

The following day came Fane, but Yosef intended to miss his devotional, unthinkable as that might be. He intended to stay home and care for Sira, though she insisted she must join him at Fane. She stated that it was crucial that she appear for his sake to maintain their deception. He admitted she was right and consented, although he would not allow her to walk or stand any more than necessary. The girls and I stayed behind with strict instructions against the risk of discovery. The religious service lasted the morning, and on their return, Teena was scarcely ambulatory. As soon as they returned home, she again took to bed with another dose of the opioid.

The following morning, over Yosef's objections, Teena insisted on departing for our exit Portal. We'd already lost several days we could ill afford. She had taken the last of the Vicodin too, which may have been an additional motivation to move on. Besides, she insisted, the medical resources at our destination could do much more for her.

Caesura

Somewhere in a distant galaxy, a massive cruiser of the void stands immobile, powerless against a solitary invader.

Fighting to hold the reins of authority in the sickening light of usurpation, thankful for the moment that only a limited number of his bridge and security crew even knew the Starship had been breached, the captain of the mobile mini-planet Z7M7-Z brooded as he considered his options. Obey or die; he had been told. Resistance is futile. The solitary, gray-skinned intruder had demonstrated the power to counter whatever physical force his crew might bring. Fifty dead crewmen bore mute testimony, terminally smote by a figurative wave of the alien hand.

He wished no more should join them; a frontal assault was off the table, for now. The fate of the remaining forty-nine thousand, seven hundred, fifty-one under his command hung in the balance. However, repelling this invader without additional casualties was improbable.

As the captain watched remotely, the invader sat motionless, his presence filling the large conference room that had formerly been the captain's own briefing room. Watching the emotionless alien presence, he wondered who this creature was and where he had come from. The captain had undoubtedly never heard of the Council of Eddore, or the number two member of that body known as Gharlane. No one of his race had directly encountered the almost supernatural beings. Perhaps if he truly knew them, he might well choose to vaporize his entire ship immediately in hopes of cauterizing the fatal wound already inflicted upon his entire race.

The invader had commandeered the ship's AI and monopolized its computational resources toward ends unknown. For the moment, the invader appeared content to sit motionless, alone, silently communing with the equipment arrayed before him. Perhaps there would yet be some opportunity. But, for now, the captain stayed his hand, watching the invader intently.

᭠᭠᭠

Gharlane was pissed! Cold and unemotional, Gharlane seldom cerebrated in terms scatological and when roused, his choler exceeded base expression.

Nonetheless, Gharlane was pissed! Never had his plans derailed so ignominiously. The sociological meltdown of GL2814-S3 had been proceeding smoothly, and complete demolition of the burgeoning Class 1 Culture had been within grasp, and then, it wasn't.

The unraveling baffled him. The primitive society he was dismantling could not possibly stymie his plans unaided. Either it constituted a fantastic accident, or they had help. However, Gharlane remained confident they had no help, certain there was no one able to help them.

Synchronicity abounds, accidents happen; an inimical alignment of the wheels of chance may occur; keeps the job interesting. But, despite recognizing the occasional happenstance, that program had frayed far too adroitly. This was simply too much to credit to coincidence.

Might an opponent be plotting against him? But who? One of his personal antagonists among the Peers? Backstabbing and sabotage among the inner circle are hardly unknown.

Sector 2814 lay in total waste save for the one inhabited planet. No intelligence on orb GL-S3 of that sector could stand against him. They haven't discovered, much less learned to utilize the natural wormholes and Portals. They had barely contrived the most primitive of intelligent machines.

Decades, if not centuries, away from Class 1 status, they remain confined to one planet. The technological adept of their society does not even control the planet; most natives shamefully forego rudimentary tools of civilization. A Class 0.85 civilization at best, unable to leave its home planet poses, no threat to his plans.

Even this failed intervention is only a minor setback; it will be a long time before he must forcibly intercede — plenty of time to rebuild his failed network and topple that society without resorting to extermination.

Gharlane dislikes wholesale extermination. He prefers to nip trouble early rather than inflict the wholesale destruction necessary, for example, in sector 2837. That civilization, unlike the one before him now, had festered far too long until he was forced to take more direct action, bending their creations into the engines of their destruction.

Primitive societies are much more straightforward. A few "supernatural" manifestations, a burning bush here, a talking snake, and over here a bit of secret-society tinkering. Divert them away from logical thought, and they will quickly devolve into chaotic religiosity. Better to subtly keep them below the threshold of danger, not allow them to become rational and intelligent, let them survive as primitives.

Some of the younger, more liberal Peers had begun to voice disagreement with Council policy, arguing that primitive peoples should develop unmolested. The fools fail to understand that today's Type 1 becomes tomorrow's Type 2 and soon challenge the natural order of the Universe. The idiots would allow unrestrained growth of beings who would cheerfully kill them, destroy the council itself if they became able.

No possible challenger to the Council of Peers may be permitted to arise. It is better to keep primitive peoples primitive, embroiled in fear and superstition than to allow them to rise and face the necessity of annihilation. Besides, they are happier and healthier when they live close to the soil. Keeping them under control and periodically culling the herd with plagues and natural disasters is better by every measure.

Could some bleeding heart be a traitor?

Mulling this thought over, he decided he must investigate the Peers for treason. That would require leaving this Starship so recently commandeered. He did not need to inhabit the vessel to accomplish his mission, although it did provide a convenient and comfortable platform from which to wreak his mayhem. The inhabitants amused him for now, scurrying about as he worked at planting the seeds of their eradication into the AI, a cyber-worm that will spread undetected for years. A few decades and they too shall falter and die as those before, ostensibly a victim of their own technology.

Carefully leaving a shadow in place, lest his unwelcoming host notes his brief absence, he ported to the High Council's Chamber and challenged the Peers with his data. There was almost a fresh opening on the council. After a close call involving a challenge nearly culminating in a duel, he was satisfied no Peer had undermined his work.

Easily resuming control as he returned, he quickly satisfied himself that the crew had not detected his absence and that his interaction with the ship's AI was still underway. Again, he contemplated who might sabotage his work. If not a Peer, there was no other possibility.

Unless.... Could it be? No! Not possible. They were dead! He had seen to that, destroyed by their own creation, the runaway AI that sabotaged their very DNA. None of THAT defunct civilization survived to pose a threat; he was confident. Their home planet is now a lifeless cinder, solely inhabited by the engine of their destruction. Indeed, they must all be dead by now.

Should a few scattered members of their race remain extant, they would now be infertile, aging, lost, and powerless. A defeated people, demoralized and in hiding.

Could some unknown faction yet operate? Is a dying remnant of that decimated world still struggling against his plans? Unlikely as it seemed, he must consider the possibility.

Center

Jill, Teena, and the Nekomata women have found the Portal and made the trip to Field Central, where they are now undergoing medical treatment and healing from their ordeal.

"Are you going to lift that?" I almost giggled at the question, echoes of the day we first met.

"Isn't this where I came in?" I asked, grinning at Teena. It was good to see her up and about. Still gaunt and frail, she appears much more robust than when we arrived. She endured several surgeries reassembling the jigsaw puzzle of her ribcage. Left to Earth's medicine, she would have steel plates and screws embedded in her anatomy. Plus, the horrific scars to match. The result would drive the TSA nuts, destined to set off every metal detector. I shudder to imagine the consequences of Portal travel. Portals do not suffer stainless steel gladly.

These doctors employ radical techniques akin to gluing a broken pot with superglue, except using stem cells. Today marks her first gym appearance. She's barely ambulatory. Though now intact and healing, she's in no condition to spot for anyone with a big wheel. Her doctor and physical therapist appeared about to drag her away lest she might grab that barbell.

Center, a.k.a. Field Central, is considerably different than Nevia. I can't describe with clarity what I expected to find on this side of the Portal. Even so, reality differed from anything I might have imagined. I suppose I envisioned something gargantuan and ultra-modern.

What we found was not my vision of a futuristic medical complex in a globe-spanning metropolis. Instead, we landed in what looked a lot like an Army MASH unit.

Indeed, a Combat Support Hospital is precisely what we found, more-or-less, albeit this one's more modern and capable than anything ever depicted on television. Though rough-hewn and temporary in appearance, the facility was gigantic. There were tents, but there were also modular structures. Some resembled typical mobile homes, and other instances were mundane cargo containers.

Once again, I found myself in a place where I did not speak the language. Pure bad planning on my part; I must break this habit. I spent hours learning bits of the Nevian tongue without a single thought to that of our destination. I never found occasion to test my Nevian, except for a miscellany of interactions with Yosef. Now I wished I'd spent that time anticipating this world.

No problem, though, as there are people here who speak ordinary American English. Quite a lot of them, in fact. I compared it to my visits to Hong Kong. Although thoroughly Chinese, my mother's home island teems with English speakers. No doubt this is thanks to its long history as a British Colony.

The doctors of Center were expecting and prepared for us. Teena texted ahead and let them know we were coming. An ambulance greeted us at the Portal and took us straight to the hospital. Teena went into immediate surgery. She was more critical than I knew. It appears Yosef's magic stone was less helpful than portrayed.

I wanted to hover, to stay with her, but my doctor had his own crazy ideas. I was doing well enough, or so I thought, but he vehemently disagreed. I discovered he had my complete medical workup. He knew about my wounds and the treatments I had received. He knew the backstory, how I got shot and lost my lover in the ambush. It was as though he'd been eagerly awaiting my arrival with no other patients to distract him from my unique case.

The days after our arrival swirled in a confusing blur. A never-ending battery of tests and procedures, therapies, and exercises. The four of us shared a tent, Teena, the Fur girls, and me, although we didn't see Teena much, and she was often unconscious when present; even when awake, she remained tight-lipped.

Her usual answer was to tell me to trust that we were all in good hands. She appeared determined to keep me guessing as much as possible. That damned Prime Directive nonsense I imagined. I determined I was going to have it out with her over this crap soon. If we were going into harm's way, I needed to be fully briefed. 'Need to know' my ass!

I'm a warrior, damn it, not a mushroom. (You don't need to know that, You don't need to know that.)

The Fur girls received medical attention. Wisceya had received routine prenatal exams along with vitamins and such on Earth. Here, she got the five-star treatment. Both were given a clean bill of health.

The baby is progressing on schedule and will be making his appearance all too soon. Teena and the doctors insisted they wanted Wisceya to remain here for the birth. Teena had arranged for it that she might receive the excellent care they provide. However, Wisceya and Stapleya subscribed to a more fatalistic mindset. They trusted the childbirth to proceed in a typical fashion.

Ordinary midwifery would be adequate, in their view. They didn't comprehend the value of advanced medicine as applied to childbirth. Nevertheless, Teena insisted, and Wisceya reluctantly agreed as long as her mother could stay with her. Both were anxious to return to *Planet Oz*.

I received various treatments focused on healing the wounds I received in Vegas. I noted my disfiguring scars disappeared within a matter of days. They said it was something they did to my immune system.

Their stem-cell-based immunotherapy is an improvement over Yosef's magic stone. Still, that bit of legerdemain had seemed incredible, no matter how it worked — or didn't.

The persistent minor pains, the aches from stiff joints, and various minor annoyances soon vanished. I began feeling much better in general and eager to get back to proper physical condition. Once again, I am healthy, my energy growing. Now it is time to regain physical strength. My doctor soon cleared me for strength training, and I was eager to get on with it. I wish to be in fighting trim before I face our foes. Whether day-walking dinosaurs or inimical alien masterminds, I mean to be ready.

I discovered an excellent gym, a busy one, used by staff and patients alike. I shouldn't have felt surprised, I suppose, but I found myself a little disturbed at first by the dress code. Or rather the lack of one. Although nudity was far from universal, it was not uncommon either. It was not the least bit unusual to spot someone jogging away on a treadmill wearing naught save a smile. At first, I found it unsettling to watch body parts bouncing with abandon.

Innate prudishness still dominates my psyche, I fear. Until Center, I had counted the number of nonchalant nude males I've met in my entire life on the thumbs of one hand. Nor more females, for that matter. The nudes of my acquaintance were usually under covers, in darkness. They appeared and disappeared with a hurried furtiveness that prohibited casual review. Even the nude in my mirror exhibits shy and evasive behavior, but the nudes here are nothing if not nonchalant.

I try not to stare, but I must concede a certain fascination. A graceful, athletic, healthy hominid bounding along free and unfettered is mesmerizing. The complex working musculature is fascinating to watch. Surprising how much less flopping around there is than one expects. Regardless of sex. It makes sense, I suppose. Without natural support, our species might not have survived to invent support garments.

The last several months challenged my natural prudishness from various angles. It was one thing to strip to traverse a Portal. I had managed that twice now. It is quite another to mount a treadmill fully nude, in public, with an audience. I had learned to accept the first, somewhat, but I ain't ready for the second. Not yet, at least, and I doubted I ever would be, although the notion frolicked in my daydreams. And nightmares.

Teena watched as I executed a few easy reps, then I racked the weight and resumed the conversation. "Teena, will your keeper allow you off-leash for lunch?" She glanced toward her chaperon and waggled an eyebrow. He shrugged. "General, if you wish, but please no more than an hour, and only a light snack, then I want you back in bed. Your largest immunotherapy infusion yet happens later today. I don't want your blood pressure or glucose levels elevated."

General? Huh! I had suspected Teena carried some rank, but General is pretty rank anywhere. So, I've been dining, scratching, and farting with quasi-royalty!

She turned back to me. "I must do a run-thru of this P-T regimen; then I am free for an hour." She smiled and turned to accompany the doctor.

I'd intended to grab her for a bitch session. I had planned to bend her ears back over her keeping me out of the loop.

I reconsidered.

Between her frailty and her revelation as near to royalty, I opted to reconsider my arguments.

Yeah, I turned chicken.

I had again grabbed the weight to resume my regimen while she talked with her doctor. Then abruptly, I changed my mind. Racking the barbell, I arose and accompanied her. Her doctor led us to a treadmill with digital readouts, and I spotted several sensors attached to her body.

As we crossed the floor, I saw Stapleya and Wisceya and gave them a wave. They were jogging on a pair of side-by-side treadmills. Wisceya was taking it slow, owing to her delicate condition. But her mother was pounding away with vigor. I can't guess Stapleya's age. She may be a multi-grandmother, but she's in exceptional condition.

GMILF? Grand-Mother I'd Like to F*?

Dunno.... Benefits of a harsh stone-age lifestyle, I presume, stay fit or be eaten, perhaps. Which reminds me, I have a date with dinosaurs soon.

Both Fur girls wore their natural pelt. Since learning of the relaxed dress code in Center, they eschewed Earth garb. Can't say I blame them. Not my style, though it works for them.

Teena walked on the treadmill, holding the sidebars at the insistence of her doctor. He cautioned her several times of the dangers of a fall. Then, after watching her readouts a few minutes, he bade her execute a series of gentle bends and stretches. Not exactly Yoga — nothing stressful — just simple moves designed to work her mending body.

After a half-hour of his affable ministrations, he pronounced the session satisfactory. He popped the sensors from her skin and released her for our lunch date. He couldn't resist one last admonition. "Remember a light, high-protein snack, and straight back to your bed. I will be around in an hour to check up on you." With that, he snapped a crisp salute and left. I wondered about the salute. For a military operation, there was little in the way of formal saluting and such. When I was in the service, we saluted everything, sometimes including inanimate objects.

Maybe I exaggerate — a little.

I hope she doesn't expect me to salute her. I gave that crap up. It ain't in my contract.

"Well, is it General now, or may I still call you Teena?"

She dipped her eyes for a moment and grimaced. Then she returned my gaze and answered. "You are not in the service; you are my friend. Besides, that General nonsense doesn't mean squat here. James was just being flippant; he understands how I hate titles. I'm just relieved he didn't use a familial honorific. Great Grandmother sounds worse than General. The only reason I rank around here is that I'm old and have been through hell in this war and somehow survived."

I blinked at the suggestion the doctor was her Great Grandson. Really? He's no child. How many descendants does this woman have, and how old is she anyway? Not sure I want to know; besides, she's probably pulling my leg.

"Okay, but you've used several names. Fitz called you Athena, shortened to Teena; you went by Minerva or Min, or Dr. Mathes on Earth, and Sira on Nevia. Do you have a real name that isn't chosen for the occasion?"

She chortled. "You tell me, Zhang Wei, what name would you prefer?"

(Zinger-roo! She gotcha there! Ya-ya, she gotcha there!)

The world tinged red! I almost staggered as though assaulted. Rage burst from deep inside, catching me off-guard. I must have turned to stone for a few seconds as I wrestled the rage monster struggling to burst free.

I hadn't heard my birth name in decades. How the hell did she come to know it? Blood surged crimson as I coped with the unexpected burst of pain and memory thought long buried.

Recovering, I responded through clenched teeth. "Let's stick with Teena and Jill, shall we? Promise you will never use that name again, ever!"

Taken aback, she was as surprised as I by my sudden upwelling of deep-seated anger. Her shock was genuine and deep. "Oh Jill, I am so sorry, I've hurt you. That was not my intention. I know you changed your name after your parents died. I assumed it was just to pick an Anglicized name to better fit into the service. Was it also to leave your previous life behind after their death?"

I took a deep breath. I needed to calm myself. She had pricked a raw nerve. Not her fault, I told myself. Well, not entirely. Damn busybodies. I breathed, deep, again, deep, and again, forced my anger back into the abyss where I kept it locked away. Allowing that piece of my soul into the daylight never comes to any good.

"Forget it, Teena, though it is something I prefer not to dwell on. I left Zhang Wei behind, as I did everything Chinese when my mother died. A mixed-race child has enough challenges. Not being able to fit in with either society made for a troubled childhood. Hiding both brains and brawn in a world where girls aren't supposed to have either is difficult. Then to be an orphan and one who couldn't conform to the gender roles assigned by society." sigh.... "It was all too much.

"Zhang Wei died, and Jill Smith reincarnated in the recruiter's office. I filed a legal name change, so everything's aboveboard, except for my age. Those records are all sealed since I was a minor, although lying about my age. I've gone by Jill ever since, kind of a play on 'G.I. Joe.'

"After my parents died so horribly, I adopted the service as my family; I became G.I. Jill. I also abandoned my father's Irish surname, although MacGabhann actually means Smith in Gaelic. More accurate, it means 'Son of the Smith' as in the son of the man who forges wrought iron."

"Forgive me, Agent Smith, I only intended to make a flippant joke, not to bring out painful memories or to pry. As for my name choices, yes, I have used a lot of names. Far more than you know. More than you might believe. I have lived a lot of lives, lived in many places, and played a lot of roles. I have been the happiest as Teena, and henceforth Teena I shall be."

"I see," I said, still bristling but trying to play down my anger to recover. Then, lowering my voice and with meticulous, almost mechanical intonation, I continued. "Well, Mr. Anderson, let's leave it at that, shall we?"

Then in a normal voice, I went on, "And please never call me 'Agent Smith' again." She blinked at that and said nothing. I resisted the urge to comment further.

After a dramatic pause, I went on.

"So, what is our next move? You still have a lot of healing to do, and I'm on a path to rebuilding myself as well. We have a mission to pursue. We can't stay here doing physical therapy and bodybuilding forever."

She pecked at her chicken vitelotte in silence as though fearing to speak again. I took the opportunity to decimate my steak. I have been hitting the gym somewhat hard the last few days and needed the calories. Steak, with vitelotte. Ugh. Worth it, though. With a bit of butter and a shot of turmeric and pepper, it is tolerable as a side for a good steak. Now I wonder where I might find a good steak. Kansas, this ain't. How about a nice dinosaur haunch? Bet it tastes like chicken.

The claimed vitelotte health benefits appear real enough. I am lifting almost as much as ever, and my biceps are impressive. Unfortunately, my speed and stamina are still sub-par, although improving. So I'm giving the treadmill a vigorous thrashing now. If I meet a dinosaur, I intend to make the beastie work for his dinner.

I asked for and received a Sabre to work with too. My regimen includes leg lifts, deadlifts, squats, pulls, and pushes. I developed an elaborate workout program. I merged deadly Sabre techniques with a ballet-like allegro/adagio contrasting yen-yang choreography. The Sabre drill mirrors a dance, the moves deadly. I found a practice dummy with painted targets to work out against. As long as my opponent stands as still as that dummy, he has no chance.

It is important to never confuse the rules of a sport with the reality of a mortal fight. People talk a lot about speed, but much less about tactics, control, and the reality of sharp edges. In a mortal fight, one's speed of attack may just determine how quickly one dies. Tactics and control take hard work and constant practice.

It feels good to work the body to exhaustion, eat to inanition, nap and then do it again. If only I had a sparring partner for some gentler, more pleasurable sort of exercise.

I miss you, Estelle. I miss you so much.

Breaking our silence, Teena picked up the conversation. "Our pacing items now become our health condition and Wisceya's birthing. We can't Port to their world until the baby comes.

Meanwhile, I've arranged for weaponry. It is difficult to send non-living matter, metal in particular, through a Portal. The Portals that open near Stapleya's home are fragile, low-energy Portals. A single hairpin can be enough to disrupt the vortex. A far distant Portal is more robust, with a clean, strong, and stable vortex. We will have the tools to deal with dinosaurs, though we must fetch them. They will be waiting for us at a considerable distance from Stapleya's Castle. It will be a dangerous retrieval."

"I see," I said, "We must become healthy and strong and port our friends' home. Once there, mount a cross-country hike to retrieve weapons and kill monsters. Any chance a nice .50 cal might be in the cache?"

She harrumphed. "Even for a strong Portal, cold steel is demanding. I asked the engineers to study the Portal's capacity and do what was possible. Each traversal impacts the vortex. Non-living materials, metals worst of all, are detrimental to the vortex. If you overload a Portal until it dissipates, it can take a long time to return. This is how we disrupt our opponents' Portals, stress the Portal, and cause it to 'pop' and go offline for a while. If we can keep the vortex in a state of flux, the Portal does not re-establish itself.

"Big guns are unlikely, but we need the biggest we can get. They promised us firepower. We just need to survive long enough to find and use it."

I wondered how big a gun one needs to kill a T-Rex.

Teena began joining us in the gym, at first under the watchful eye of her doctor. As she grew stronger and moved into a serious workout regimen, he soon left her to her own devices. After watching my workout, Teena began adapting a few of my moves into her routine. She began putting on muscle, and her feminine curves started to rebound. She ceased resembling a walking skeleton.

My development had plateaued. My gains were becoming smaller and smaller while her development was taking off exponentially. She was gaining muscle mass day by day. I could even see the change in her hair. When we first met, she had gray-streaked black hair. As soon as she began aggressive medical treatment, I started noticing a tinge of copper at the roots. Within days it became unmistakable. Her hair was rapidly growing longer; the round bob was history. We could not pass for half-sisters much longer. She was morphing into a classical, muscular Irish colleen with flaming red hair!

Many associate red hair and Irish. Yet only ten percent display the ginger, although forty-six percent carries the recessive gene. Irish are often dark and sallow with black hair, almond eyes, and a countenance vaguely Asian.

Teena looked younger, though 'colleen' might still be stretching it. Cougar, maybe. She no longer resembled my frail and elderly Irish grandmother.

As she filled out and became more agile, she dropped the shapeless workout sweats. As I noted, exercising nude isn't uncommon on Center, and she looked spectacular at it. I started seeing her as Fitz described in his book. Pulchritudinous, he had said. Okay, I get it.

One day her doctor came by and asked permission to vid her workout to document her recovery. She agreed without hesitation. I was a tad surprised, though I recognized she was not the least bit inhibited. Besides, she explained, they had already documented her condition at every stage. Every stage of her death and resurrection was on file. It's just another medical vid in the doctor's burgeoning case file.

"I couldn't allow that," I stated almost in horror. "I'd imagine the video in the private stash of every guy on the planet."

She laughed at that. Then she leered, lowered her voice half an octave, and huskily declared, "It would be in my stash."

I blushed. She went on, "Seriously, so what? I'm sure plenty of people have my photos. I just hope the ones they bother with are ones taken before I became old and worn out.

"What imagery someone else uses for self-pleasure isn't something I spend time thinking about. Although if I did think of it, I would feel pleased that this tired old carcass might still excite someone."

This did not reassure me. Teena is an insatiable pansexual, utterly without shame. We do not live in the same sexual universe. Every day I spend with her, the more I recognize just how prudish and uptight I am in comparison. She constantly shows me a new world. I did mention the four of us were sharing quarters on Central. I would not wish to mischaracterize our little group. We were close friends alone together. Okay, yeah, we became lovers soon after that day.

My mental wheels spun as I tried to compose a scathing retort. Before I could gain traction, she continued. "Let me assuage your fears to some degree. There are endless supplies of professional, well lighted, erotic videos for anyone who wants them: Live and animated videos catering to every possible erotic taste. Nudity is unremarkable on Center, so no one gets excited over non-sexual nudity. Almost no one.

"Only one who knows us and loves us will bother with a poorly lit clandestine video. Jogging on a treadmill isn't that sexy when it's familiar. Beyond that, anything the doctor records as a part of his practice is confidential to the nth degree. We enforce strict rules about recording people against their will, with harsh punishments.

"This is not Earth, and this is a military operation. Human eyes never see automated security video unless events demand review. Otherwise, we only permit recordings with the express permission of the subjects, even for professional purposes. You noted the formality James used when asking permission. He did so for an important reason. He was asking for a formal contract.

"No one is going to risk a career, or worse, a court-martial, to record an illicit video of a sexy bit of booty. I'm not going to claim it can't happen, but I will state it is far less likely than you imagine. Wisceya's exotic pelt and perky baby bump are unique here. She is far more likely to star in a clandestine stash than either of us."

I hadn't thought of that; I can imagine Wisceya giggling at the idea. She would not be the least perturbed. Hell, she'd probably propose it if she considered the idea. That gal is naturally gregarious.

I resumed my regimen with a long run on the treadmill. On the treadmill, the brain is not engaged. The mind tends to wander, and mine wandered back to our sessions during the last few weeks on Earth.

∧∧∧

During the weeks following that introductory lunch with Teena, we had slipped back into a regular routine. The travel schedule was uncertain; we had a little time to wait. While we waited, I started working out daily. I invited the Fur girls to join me in the gym. I did not expect them to work out with me, just keep me company and be on hand if I pushed too hard again. Scared by my first session, I became wary of hurting myself with no one around to bail me out.

The concept of working out just for the exercise had seemed strange to them. Their natural stone-age life is so physical that they were slow to grasp the cost of a sedentary lifestyle. They had, of course, watched Fitz's training efforts on *Planet Oz*, so the idea was not unknown. But it was something they had a hard time grasping. That is, until they spent weeks on Earth, sitting for long hours in front of a computer. They are, as I've said, fast learners.

The first day they observed while I worked a cautious regimen. I wanted a challenge, but not too much. A couple of times, I felt the too-familiar twinge and backed off.

The second day, Stapleya asked to try the weights. I set her up with a modest load, which she pressed with ease. I then upped the ante a dime, and she handled that too with no strain. She wanted to try more, though I warned her off, cautioning her against overdoing it. "Take it slow," I advised. Tomorrow, if she wanted, we could up it further. For all her vigor, Stapleya is a grandmother many times over. She hardly looks her age, no doubt because of her sensual pelt. I would later learn that she had good genes as well, but that's another story.

Wisceya wanted to try it. Her baby bump was becoming rather prominent, and I felt wary of letting her push herself. She expressed frustration when I started her off at a much lesser weight than her mother's. Was her child Fitz's, I wondered? Likely, I decided, but it was none of my business. She is not bearing the first Fitz'ling among her sisters. I wondered if he suspected. Doubtful, I decided.

Regardless of their other skills, men rarely connect pleasurable copulation with the logical result. Sex is such an inconsequential thing until you find yourself knocked up! Millions of years of evolution planned it that way, I suppose, and that's a good thing for the species, no doubt. Fortunately, it is up to the women to decide how and when to make practical use of the stuff, regardless if we think it's unfair. Thank goodness modern pharmacology gives us distaff warriors more control.

I am not the maternal type.

We continued in this manner for the next few weeks; our workouts became more aggressive. Soon I was hoisting a hefty barbell for a 'puny girl,' and Stapleya and Wisceya were no slouches either. I was still well short of what I had once been able to manage, but I was starting to feel human again. Nevertheless, I will avoid fights with jarheads in the near term. I had not informed my doctor of the workouts. Thanks to my caution and gradual build-up, pain had not returned to force my hand.

The girls and I met every morning for our Earthside workouts. As our conditioning improved, we began extending them. We added more activities and extended the time. Work could wait. I decided getting into condition took precedence, though my desk job was important too.

Weeks passed with no sign of Teena. She had disappeared, and I was unsure what that meant. In the second week, I brought out my sabre, added gentle lunging, and worked my wrist with the basics. That should complement the work of the *latissimus dorsi* of my upper back on the weight bench. Gentle, gentle, work into it easy. We're just humming a little to warm up. Our concert aria will come later.

A sabre serenade requires exceptional skill and energy. It resembles a frenetic ballet, rapid pulsating non-stop dance-like movements. Breath-taking to watch, demanding to perform, it is in many ways a skilled dance. However, do not mistake the dance-like quality for entertainment or mere exercise. Every movement is precise, lightning-quick, and deadly.

A sabre is a romantic tool in skilled hands. I once aspired to such skills, attained reasonable competency. I became pretty good for a casual student. Competent, although I remained a dilettante compared to a true master. Time for a tune-up. Many tools are useful in battle. A screwdriver can be pressed into stabbing service. Knives have their place but mean getting rather too close to danger. A Sabre is safer, effective at arm's length, and exquisite in skilled hands. Guns are much safer still, but noisy and a sabre never runs out of ammunition.

One day midway through the week, Teena appeared at our morning session. The Fur girls, delighted to see her, struggled to restrain their enthusiasm, and maintain decorum.

For about ten seconds.... then they swarmed her.

All three were babbling away in a language unfamiliar to my ears. I realized this was the alien women's native speech. They had become so proficient with English I had almost forgotten how alien they were. I realized I was missing the opportunity to learn their language. I must study their language since I am headed to their home world. Stapleya and Wisceya speak excellent English now. I doubt anyone else on *Planet Oz* does. After the chatter died away, I asked Teena about the planned trip.

"There have been delays," Dr. Mathes answered. Still maintaining the masquerade, she had once again asserted her academic persona. She insists on maintaining the character in private and public. She once admonished us to be wary. She had said, "Surveillance is everywhere these days."

Was there surveillance here in the gym? Hadn't thought of it. Had someone been watching us here? If so, I hoped they enjoyed the show. We had assumed a degree of privacy at the early hour that may not have been wise. My friends had worn only their natural pelt while working out; I had come close to joining. As we were alone, doffing my sweats had been tempting.

I'm glad I opted to stay clothed! I looked around for cameras, didn't see any. That doesn't mean they aren't there. Stapleya and Wisceya had little to risk, whereas I must stay aware of my career.

Unclothed MiB jogging on a treadmill, sweat streaming, hips bouncing, boobs jiggling. All in Hi-Def! Unprofessional. Prim and proper Alex would have a cow. Mortifying! Estelle would have loved it.

She went on. "My ill health and tepid recovery have delayed our plans. I required yet another procedure for which the facility here is ill-equipped. I'm a little stronger now. We will go as soon as I arrange transportation. It may be a few days yet."

To illustrate her improved health, she proceeded to tackle the weight bench. She tossed aside the dowdy academic skirt and sweater, revealing a modest leotard. She did look healthier, more vigorous than she had last time I saw her. I had thought her at death's door a couple of weeks ago, a walking skeleton.

Not that the difference was great. She still appeared quite frail, but her skin was a healthier color, less pale and sallow. Her cheeks were less sunken, her wrinkles less prominent. She seemed to have added a little muscle to her frame, too, although to be fair, I had not seen her in a leotard before. Nevertheless, although she looked less corpse-like, she was thin and frail, yet she talked a good game.

Checking the weight I had been using, she executed a few easy reps before adding a couple of dimes. For her professed frailty, she put me to shame. Which fact says less about her than it does about my own weakened condition. We were both poor specimens. We then mounted side-by-side treadmills and clocked in a decent, if leisurely, run. Not too bad for a pair of invalids. I suppose we both were in better condition than when we first met. Stapleya and Wisceya both gave a terrific accounting of themselves, baby-bump notwithstanding.

After our workout, we repaired to the showers. I was much more comfortable getting naked with my friends in the shower room. Cameras or no, who could criticize nudity in the shower? The others were all less inhibited than I. Earlier I noted a rather fearsome scar on Teena's thigh, and now I spotted another on her side. My Vegas souvenirs appeared minor by comparison. I winced in sympathy.

Weapons

On Center, Jill and Teena have progressed from fragility and healing to training for battles to come.

Center is a wonderful place to heal and recover. As we plateaued in our physical development, our training turned away from raw strength. Although the physical workouts continued, our emphasis morphed toward sharpening weapons skills and agility. Weapons are my forte. I love the utility of a Sabre, I'm fair with archery, and as for guns, let's just say I'm in favor of them. Guns are equalizers. Gun Control means hitting the intended target. Responsible gun ownership means always packing and staying sharp.

I'm not a weak person, although I'm compact. I refuse to be a victim, whether the threat's a predatory animal or a predatory human. Weapons aren't dangerous; predators are. So I'm armed whenever possible, despite others' objections.

I love being a MiB. Having a badge means no one else's opinion matters. My hand cannon's visible for a reason. It is reassuring how polite and peaceable people become when they spot Ol Betsy.

Concealed carry my ass!

If Betsy's visible, you can be confident Ticker is close to my heart. When no gun's visible on my hip, it could be a grave mistake to imagine I'm unarmed. When I can't carry a gun, I carry a knife. When I can't carry either, I still have my training and 'spiritual' gifts. I will turn anything into a weapon. Hope never to learn what havoc I can create with a simple rolled-up newspaper if I must.

I will not go quietly!

Humans are tool-using beings. Until humans attain comic-book "powers of the mind," that's not going to change. Psychokinesis and telepathy are the stuff of fantasy. Until humans develop mental powers that transcend our physical abilities, tools extend our reach. You cannot fight off a mugger or rapist using telepathy. Or car keys between your knuckles.

Weapons are the tools of self-defense. There are no dangerous weapons.

Teena learned the art of the sabre under my tutelage. She impressed me as a relative novice with a blade, and we worked long hours on her technique. Staying balanced, positioned to parry, and thrust with lightning response takes grace and speed. She could not match my speed. No one can — it's a 'spiritual' gift.

As her skill grew, our daily drill began resembling a choreographed Hollywood action film. The difference being that Hollywood action swordplay's not deadly. Although drilling with blunted weapons, we accumulated bruises and worse. I also permitted recording of one of our workouts, though that still sends chills down my spine. I'm told we were glorious, though I can't watch it.

When our training turned to archery, the shoe jumped to the other foot; I had my eyes opened. My archery training, courtesy of Uncle Sam, had been unimaginative. The military taught a conventional regimen, resembling something from a Hollywood swashbuckler. Draw arrow from quiver, nock, and aim, and release to pierce a stationary bullseye.

Boring. I said BORING!

Turns out I'd been doing it wrong. Archery's a lost art on Earth; the 'experts' remain fracking clueless. Teena knew the swing of it. She'd trained under the Fur-People's best Master Archer. Stapleya turned out to be a skilled practitioner with much to teach. Who Knew?

Teena could salvo much faster and with accuracy that I had not imagined possible. Stapleya threw five balls into the air and Teena nailed all five before they topped their arch. Sheer black magic! The first time she demonstrated, my mouth hung open for five minutes. Then, she revealed her technique, and soon I became a thaumaturge too.

Speed lies in grasping many arrows at once to fire in rapid succession. Minimal motion is the key. Her handspan's less compact than mine, and I just can't grasp the numbers of arrows she can. I'm faster and can fire my first volley as quick as she. Quicker. Once I learned her technique, I could fire my volley much quicker than she. Despite that, she fired five to my three, thanks to just having bigger hands. She took points for accuracy too. Though I'd never seen it myself, I came to understand Fitz shamed us both. I had read his book yet discounted his claims. Teena promised there was no exaggeration. Or not much.

Neither of us can match the draw-weight, the sheer power of Fitz and his massive heroes bow *The Lady Seven*. He bested us both in every dimension, draw length, weight, and span. Yet, despite his size and draw, he's also much, much faster. Counterintuitive, isn't it? A bigger man should be slower, so common thought maintains. I'm blazing PDQ; Fitz is more like greased lightning. Teena claimed he could volley ten arrows to her five. I scarcely believed her.

The massive metal-tipped arrows he threw could almost stop a Sherman tank. Possibly even a T-Rex, if lucky enough to hit the walnut-sized brain. His artillery can penetrate the toughest hide, but arrows just cannot wreak enough damage. It takes monstrous damage to bring down a twenty-ton monster. Even Fitz's massive arrows are a pinprick to such beasts. Those monsters are almost invulnerable!

Teena promised guns on *Planet Oz*, so we trained with guns. I believed I didn't need training; I'm already a *distinguished expert* marksman with the badges to prove it. I perhaps only required a refresher to hone my skills following my injuries. I was overly optimistic. Still, any polished skill returns with practice. It took a few sessions before I slid back into the groove. Not with paper targets, either. Just try hitting a bouncing Ping-Pong ball with a pistol sometime. I have my own particular brand of black magic. Fine-honed skills can appear almost supernatural, and ours are finely honed indeed.

Teena's marksmanship became excellent, too, although she worked for it a little harder. Her injuries had been severe; her extended recovery time had atrophied her skills. Several training sessions and she became almost as skilled as I. Closer than anyone I know, anyway. Teena and I were formidable warriors.

Move over Xena and Gabrielle.

It has become an article of faith in certain quarters that guns are evil. If only there were no guns, the refrain goes, there would be no victims.

That's one of the stupidest ideas I have ever heard!

Muggers, rapists, and wild predators don't need guns. Their victims do. Whether threatened by a bear, or just a bear of a man, a gun can save your life.

A ninety-pound woman armed and skilled with her weapon is a fair match for any aggressor. If her aggressor is also armed, well, guns are equalizers. Guns protect the weak.

Compared to the dinosaurs on *Planet Oz*, we're all weak, even Fitz. We need guns. Big guns. How much firepower to kill a T-Rex?

Arrows and sabres won't do it.

Will bullets stop a twenty-ton charging monster? I'm skeptical of anything smaller than an M242 Bushmaster with MK210 HE rounds.

Getting big weapons through the portal is a problem. There are small, lightweight composite weapons, even plastic weapons. Such weapons might be easier to pass through a portal. However, plastic and composite weapons are small caliber and low power. Not very useful against a T-Rex.

I suspect anything we can carry through a portal will be just another pinprick to a T-Rex. I doubt a T-Rex would notice even a .223 Remington.

When we began practicing with firearms, Stapleya and Wisceya became interested. That might be an understatement. They were already familiar with and adept with bow and arrow, swords, and even spears. Their world does not have guns.

A perfect paradise, according to some.

These self-styled elites insist the problems are the weapons themselves — their solution, banning firearms. The Fur people don't have guns, yet they have dinosaurs. They need a few of the firearms those elites so disdain. Dinosaurs belong on the Extinct Species List.

Of course, those elites don't intend to surrender their own guns or their armed guards. They just seek control, to restrict weapons to those of whom they approve.

Call the elites when a T-Rex is on your ass, and they will come and pick up your remains. But, of course, you mustn't have a gun to defend yourself.

Those believing in the myth of Gun Control aren't against guns in principle. They recognize they need guns to disarm an armed citizenry who might otherwise object. They're sanguine with that. It's not that they're anti-gun. They intend to use guns to pilfer the weapons of the people THEY disapprove of having them.

In fact, they are very much pro-gun. They just believe that only they — the reliable, honest, moral, and virtuous — should have them. Thus, only they may own a means of practical self-defense.

When only the elite have guns, by definition, that creates an entire class of unarmed victims. Unarmed prey for any predator, four legs or two, armed or not.

There's no such thing as gun control. There's only the forced centralization of gun ownership into the hands of the elite. History has shown us how that works out. The wholesale slaughter of unarmed and unresistant populations has followed time and again. Elitist politicians are far more dangerous than guns can ever be. Examine the slaughter record of 20th Century Earth, search the word Democide sometime. Yeah, Billions, with a 'B.'

The Fur-people don't have elitist politicians. They don't have guns either and they do have predators. Vicious ones.

The firearms training facility on Center was impressive. The armory stocked an incredible variety of weapons, almost all manufactured on Earth. I found that surprising. I asked; why, with the universe to draw upon, all the weapons at hand came from Earth? Didn't another world make better weapons?

Teena stated that it was no coincidence. After the loss of their home planet to the machines, Teena's people had relocated to Earth. They came to Earth and brought along a great deal of technical knowledge. So much of Earth's technology has off-world roots. I could hear Fitz's beloved late-night talk shows playing in my head. I imagined the conspiracy enthusiasts' stunned faces if I could tell them what I learned. They would understand how aliens had nurtured Earth's technological progress.

Stapleya and Wisceya decided they liked guns. They couldn't spend enough time on the gun range. We started them off with the Colt M1911 .45 Caliber, and it was instant lust.

They wanted to learn every weapon and became proficient with everything in the arsenal. After mastering the M1911, they graduated to the famous *Dirty Harry* "most powerful handgun in the world," the .44 Magnum. Beside a 10.9 mm shell diameter and 1450 ft/s muzzle velocity, the 850 ft/s Colt was unimpressive.

Stapleya showed every sign of orgasm the first time she fired the Magnum BFR (**B**ig **F**rame **R**evolver). It is even more potent with a .50 Caliber 12.7 mm shell and an 1800 ft/s muzzle velocity. Much more than the iconic "Dirty Harry" weapon. Yet even the massive BFR would be little more than a nasty pinprick to a 20-ton T-Rex.

The BFR fires a .50 Cal shell, but it is still a handgun, albeit a large one. The bullet's diameter is 12.7 mm, the same as the original .50 Cal Browning Machine Gun but shorter. The S&W .500 BFR rounds are 41 mm long, total case size 54 mm, whereas BMG rounds are 99 mm long, total length 138 mm. The BMG also loads more powder, 800 grains, vs. 400 for a much bigger kick.

The bigger bullet and greater powder capacity mean the BMG muzzle velocity is over 3000 ft/s. The velocity approaches double that of the handgun; the heavier bullet carries more mass. The BMG is much more potent, but you cannot put such a huge round into a handgun. It needs a long barrel and must mount on something solid. BMG weapons are usually mounted on trucks or even aircraft.

Guns are often considered phallic for a reason, I suppose. But, despite the unwieldy heft and the arm-breaking kick from the recoil, I believe Stapleya fell in love with the BFR. I guess she likes them big. If her people had such tools, they would not live in fear of their predators.

I asked Teena to explain this over lunch one day. I'd long believed that her people treated other human societies as second-class. As though they were somehow bound by a sort-of of non-interference directive. A Prime Directive in the parlance of classic Space Opera. Why wouldn't they supply capable weapons to the Fur-people? Why not let them fight off the dinosaurs?

"A salient point," she conceded, "and partly correct. Our leaders have embraced such ideas. Our ambassadors always tried not to disrupt other cultures. The historical record of cataclysmic consequences of two different cultures colliding is unmistakable. The fate of the culture on the receiving side of 'First Contact' is always dire."

I nodded and added, "The lessons of the Colombian Exchange on Earth are instructive. Certainly, the European impact on the American aboriginals was decimating. However, we often overlook the fact that it cut both ways, though. Europe suffered terribly from the syphilis plague brought home by the Columbus crew. The disease appeared in 1494 Italy and decimated Europe.

"Both cultures suffered from the contact. Tremendous harm resulted from ignorance, unmitigated greed, and the baser exploitative instincts of humanity. Is it possible modern humans haven't learned from this? That even your people cannot competently manage the impact of such contact?"

She grimaced. "Things are a little more complex than you suggest, and the simple answer's that we're working on it. Some people on Earth, and a few others, know of our presence. Our people live in secret on Earth in significant numbers and have for a long time. We have guided Earth's technological advancement with a light touch. We've lived among the Fur People much longer. There are a few other planets like this one. This planet — uninhabited by native hominids — serves as a base for the war, yet many of my people live here. Mine's a scattered, lost, and dying people. Our population's tiny with no real home world now."

"Why not elevate the Fur People with technology and weapons to defend themselves?" I needed to understand. The Nekomata are beautiful people, intelligent and civilized. More civilized than my own countrymen. They're civilized in ways my countrymen cannot imagine. So why must they live a stone-aged lifestyle? It seems barbaric.

Teena sighed. She placed her hands on the table, fingertips together. "We've tried. The problem's complicated by several factors. We intend to elevate them but without destroying their culture in the process. They have a great culture with a rich history, well worth preserving."

I nodded at that. She continued before I could muster something to say. "We've been helping them in minor ways, with medicine and antibiotics, but there are problems owing to the unique physics of their planet. And we've been documenting their culture. Our biggest worry of the moment is to preserve them from extinction and restore fertility. Fitz's energetic gametes have played a crucial role—if they had a hundred of his ilk, they might have a chance. Also, rebounding from near extinction to overpopulation and starvation is a concern too. We hope to grant them control over their fertility."

"Is it as dire as that?" I asked. No wonder she's adamant Wisceya's birthing occurs here in a capable medical facility. She wishes to permit no chances. Every Fitz'ling is precious to the Nekomata. Not only that, but Wisceya's child is her descendant too if I believe Fitz's story. He said Teena was his Great Grandmother.

"Yes," she replied, "If not for Fitz, there would be no children at all in this present generation. Every baby's precious beyond words; we must restore their fertility. We hope that the young ones spread their genes far and wide. Fertility appears such a simple prospect until it's gone. Our scientists are working on the problem. I just hope they can find a solution.

"Reversing one person's infertility in the lab is not enough. We must craft a mechanism that will spread much as did the original plague. Our working theory's that an engineered virus spreads the fertility plague. Most likely carried by insects. The virus replicated in the host and twiddled specific DNA genes in the process. The virus died and disappeared from the host, leaving infertility behind. They need a reversal process that works the same."

I asked, "Why not permit them technology or weapons to deal with the dinosaurs?"

"It's not that simple," she said. "The laws of physics differ in their world. Ordinary gunpowder just fizzles, and electrons spin differently. Much technology either will not work there or works in an odd and diminished fashion. Even basic medicine has unexpected challenges. We're not withholding our technology — it's just almost impossible. Physicists believe that their world's not in our universe at all. Instead, they believe it exists in a sort of parallel universe, a flawed mirror of our own.

"Our chemists have been trying to create an explosive that will enable guns to function there. It has taken years, now success has come. We'll test the prototypes. Testing here presents impossible challenges. The behavior's too different in this world. We must travel to *Planet Oz* and play with guns."

"You're saying that the weapons we're depending on may not fire? And they can't test them here?" She nodded at my question.

"They may not fire, they may fizzle, or they may explode. But we are certain none of these things will happen. We are confident it will work as intended.

"The engineers have done extensive computer modeling and simulation. They are confident they have it nailed. Ours will be the first full-scale live-fire test of the experimental explosive. It's too unstable in this world to test here." With that, she shrugged.

Wonderful! Rampaging dinosaurs and untested weapons. What could possibly go wrong?

Lacuna

While Teena and Jill are training and preparing for battle, we flash back to a few weeks earlier when a previously unknown Portal was discovered somewhere in Northern Mexico.

The three hostiles led a merry chase, but no chase lasts forever. They darted into the tight, dense woods. Cornered, surrounded, and almost out of ammunition, they continued the farce of resisting.

Black-Knights Squad 2 had the enemy in retreat. Direct engagement served no purpose. Outnumbered ten-to-one, they could not escape. Rather than offer targets for their dwindling fire, Sergeant Hacker played a smarter game. He instituted a modified shoot-and-scoot strategy. A strategy designed to coax the enemy to expend their ammunition in vain. He instructed that no fire directly engage the hostiles. Instead, let them waste their rounds firing at shadows. When they no longer took the bait, their ammunition depleted, his men would close in for the capture.

The game of cat and mouse continued. Each feint by the Knights elicited fewer and fewer rounds of return fire. Finally, the return fire ceased. The only noises came from the Black-Knights.

"Easy as it goes," the Sgt said to his men, "the last thing we want to do is to hurt these guys — the last thing, but it is still on my list. Let's take them home as a present to the captain instead, though, if we can."

After several rounds with no return fire, the troops began closing in. When they converged, they found a surprise. Enemy weapons; ammunition exhausted, and their supplies, backpacks, vests, armor, and more. Even the enemy clothing, right down to underwear, was abandoned.

The Sgt boggled at the idea of three enemy combatants stripping starkers—buck-naked and unarmed, and yet somehow eluding his entire squad. He envisioned 'The Invisible Man' unwinding bandages and removing clothes.

Hours later, while briefing the captain, he omitted that imaginary detail.

Or rather, he intended to.

The captain would not have it and pressed the point, demanding to know what had become of the enemy. When the matter of abandoned clothing became apparent, the captain stopped. With sudden brusqueness, he said, "Thank you, Sergeant, you're dismissed." Before Hacker could exit, the captain was already on the phone. As he closed the door, he overheard the captain asking for a Doctor Shepherd.

Homecoming

The magnificent, polished stone table in the center of the Great Room appears carved from a solitary block of marble. Carved in place and polished to a smoothness and glossy sheen that defies belief, jam-packed with every comestible imaginable, a massive centerpiece featuring a gigantic tray of hash cakes. Around the tray, platters, dishes, bowls, goblets, mugs, and plates jumbled in chaotic confusion. The enormous chandelier overhead, the real deal, aflame with candles. Ornate wall-sconces, close-spaced high on the walls burn, with real fire.

Though without electricity, the room is blazingly illuminated. The room would be stifling in any climate. This is not just any climate. Death Valley in summer is merely balmy by comparison. Air flowed as the heat from the candles, sconces and the mass of humanity below rose to exit through the high unglazed windows. Slightly cooler air entered through the narrow vents ringing the outside walls. The constant influx of fresh air maintained the temperature as only marginally hotter than a well-fired sauna. Any clothing would have seemed intolerable. Fortunately, no one was clothed. As the temperature was perfectly ordinary and unremarkable to the natives of this world, no one remarked on it. A couple of off-world guests held their tongues and did their best to cope.

The ginormous room is bright and cheery, packed with family and guests. Musicians reside upon a raised stage in the room's corner; tuneful hilarity resounds with raucous delight. Burlesque entertainers tread the boards with mirth and merrymaking, singing, dancing, juggling, and every imaginative form of amusement. Party songs, impassioned solos, group sing-a-longs, and ballads, a few recognizable as having Earthly origins, most not.

Among the former was campfire classic 'Clementine,' a favorite augmented with unexpected verses never heard on Earth, often bawdy, profane, and anatomically impossible. The folk-ballad parody of a tragic demise has taken on a near-mythical significance, though the why remains unexplained, a nuance of the Nekomata's love for the hero who first sang it.

It's party time at Castle Stapleya. The beloved clan-mother has returned.

Sad songs mourn sister Shameya, lost to the Threshold, her fate scribed in the family book where her life will be remembered. Joyous songs celebrate the triumphant return of Stapleya and Wisceya, dance and celebration for the newborn Fitz'ling, son of Wisceya.

Marching music worthy of Sousa celebrates honored guests from beyond the Threshold, Red and Black Warriors come to vanquish the monsters.

The Red Warrior, taking her third cake from the platter, grinned at the Black Warrior. "Having fun?" The wine slurred her words, just a touch. She leaned in closer, and in a low and husky voice, asked, "Didn't I tell you these people know how to throw a shindig?"

"Indeed," the Black Warrior agreed, taking a giant bite out of her own fourth brownie, along with another sip from her own goblet. "These brownies are wonderful. I would never have imagined being comfortable this way, but distance from Earth imparts a fresh perspective."

"What do you mean by that?" The Red Warrior's voice had taken a silly tone, her manner intoxicated. "Explain yourself!"

"I can't explain myself, I'm afraid," said the Black Warrior. Intoxicated herself and arm-wrestling each word into submission, "because I'm not myself here, you see."

"I don't see," responded the Red Warrior with a yawn.

"I'm afraid I can't put it more clearly," Black replied very politely, "for I can't understand it myself to begin with; it is all so very confusing."

"It isn't," insisted the Red Warrior.

"Well, perhaps you haven't found it so yet," said the Black Warrior; "but when you travel to another world, one where clothes disappear, and everyone wears fur instead, and you have no fur, I should think anyone would feel it a little queer, wouldn't you?"

"Not a bit," rejoined the Red Warrior.

"Well, perhaps your feelings may be different," said the Black Warrior; "all I know is, it all feels very queer to ME. I feel decidedly queer right now. I am queer now."

"You!" said the Red Warrior, with snide contempt. "Who are YOU?"

Taken aback by the sudden turn in the Red Warrior's manner, Black felt a trifle irritated at the Red Warrior's making such short remarks, and she drew herself up and said, very gravely, "I think, you ought to tell me who YOU are, first."

"Why?" asked the Red Warrior.

There was a puzzling question; and as Black could not think of any good reason, and as Red seemed to be in a VERY unpleasant state of mind, she turned away.

"Come back!" the Red Warrior called after her. "I've something important to say!"

This sounded odd, certainly: Black turned and came back again.

"Keep your temper," said the Red Warrior.

"Is that all?" asked Black, swallowing down her anger as well as she could.

"No," said the Red Warrior.

Black thought she might as well wait, as she had nothing else to do; besides, she wanted another brownie. For several minutes Red ate and drank without speaking. At last, she paused, turned to Black, and said, "So you think you're changed, do you?"

"I'm afraid I am," said Black; "I can't remember things as they used to be — and I don't know the words!"

"Can't remember WHAT things?" prodded Red.

"Why are you naked?" asked Black.

"Harrumph! You're naked too! Everyone is naked; you just can't tell under the fur. What words?" Red queried.

"I want to sing Clemmy, but the words seem misplaced." Black began humming softly. Red started tunelessly intoning, "Oh my Darling, Oh My *darling, She is all they claim, Tangerine when she dances by, You're a darling, my queer little lover ..."* Her voice trailed off into a dreamy fog.

∿∿∿

I awoke with a start, mouth dry, and my head spinning. Spinning! Pounding like a timpani solo! I felt as if I were riding a roller-coaster with drummers on either side. I moved and touched fur on my shoulder. Stapleya lay asleep, her head next to mine. Turning in the other direction, I discovered Wisceya occupying the other shoulder. Another tiny fur person lay crosswise my chest, posterior elevated. I tried to place her. Lolita. Or Williya, maybe. Uncertain. No, wait, Lolita is Fitz's pet name for Williya. This was she.

Scanning the room, I spotted at least a hundred tiny furry bodies strewn about. All appeared insensible; at least, I hoped they were just unconscious. I located Teena astride another resident in a compromising pose, both comatose. I couldn't decide what to make of that.

Who in the world am I? Ah, that's the puzzle.

I struggled to regain the memories of last night. Piecemeal, a few memories began to trickle in. Difficult to be certain what's a memory vs. mere intoxicated imagination. I'm quite certain we didn't do THAT!

ON THE DINNER TABLE! OMG! Fur-people standing around, chanting and applauding. I hope I dreamed THAT. Mortifying!

What did I drink? Wow.... Next time, someone please warn me it's loaded. That one's a doozy.

As I was pulling myself awake, I became aware of a different sort of pressure than that on my chest or shoulders. I needed to extricate myself from the jumble of unconscious celebrants. I was near to springing a leak.

Minutes later, I rejoined Stapleya, Wisceya, and Lolita, snuggling into their sensual fur. A quiet nap with dear friends was just the prescription.

∿∿∿

Our arrival on *Planet Oz* had been momentous. It had been almost a year, long enough for Wisceya to conceive and birth a child. A darling baby, spittin' image of his sire. Except with fur. A shame Fitz never knew he fathered the child. I know he has numerous sons here, including many he doesn't know about or only suspects.

I wondered if the child might ever meet his father. It's difficult for us to understand how differently the Nekomata approach fatherhood. Fathers have little role beyond the biological necessity. There are too few males and too many desiring their seed. Relationships between father and child are impractical. Their society had evolved into a matriarchal environment where males are rare and precious. Their seed became a staple for barter much as racehorses at stud are on Earth.

There had been no communications those long months, the return unheralded. The family knew not if or when their wayfaring mother and sister might return. Even so, a sentinel waited by the Portal to greet us when we emerged. She immediately blew a riff from a gigantic horn. I could hear it picked up and echoed through the forest. Although it was not musical; it appeared to be a code or a message, with a reply soon returned. Several blasts echoed in quick succession.

Wireless messaging, Nekomata style. I learned they called these horns *lepatata*, and they are an important communications tool. The large ones can be heard for miles in the forest, and a complex series of sounds carry messages. By the time we arrived at the Castle, a massive celebration was already underway.

My jaw dropped in stunned surprise. I could not comprehend the Castle when I spotted it. Fitz's description had not done it justice; the fortress is immense. I couldn't begin to guess the number of people housed therein. Hundreds, I'm confident, perhaps thousands. It takes plentiful hands to run a stone age.

The Castle itself appeared ancient — Sphinx-like ancient. I was disappointed to notice it lacked a moat. I thought castles always had a moat. Not on Planet Oz, I suppose. I imagined this edifice as the home to this family for centuries, if not millennia. I later learned I was correct. Castle Stapleya is one of the oldest castles on the planet, the origins lost in the mists of time. Uncounted generations had lived within these walls.

Except they are not entirely uncounted. Stapleya showed us her library, in which the enormous family book was prominently featured. So massive it must need several people to lift or move. The tremendous volume occupies a place of honor on a polished marble throne in the center of the room. Within this prodigious volume resides the vital statistics of every family member. Every person to live under the roof of Castle Stapleya, everyone to have ever lived here.

I made a mental note to study this book when I had the chance. However, first I must learn to read Language.

Stapleya gave us a tour of her home. Fitz's descriptions had been woefully inadequate. She showed us the library, the copious paintings, objet d'art adorning the endless walls. Not mere art, many of the wall-hangings were real weapons. Some were magnificent, larger-than-life, artisan-crafted Heroes weapons such as Fitz's giant bow. Others were beautiful and practical weapons intended for practical use on the battlefield. The inherently peaceful Nekomata certainly display a lot of weaponry.

I mis-stepped on a curving stairway, nearly falling flat. *(klutz!)* Stapleya grabbed my arm to steady me. I remarked on the uneven nature of the stairs. I asked, "The masonry is so beautiful and precise otherwise. Why are the stairs so uneven?"

"So you would fall," replied Stapleya, deadpan. I saw Teena was repressing a grin. I cocked an eyebrow at Stapleya, suspicious I was about to be pwned, as Fitz would say. I decided to play along.

"That's considerate. You must have an exceptional stonemason. Rebuilt these stairs just for me? I'm honored."

Stapleya grinned. "Tower steps are built uneven so that those unwelcome and unfamiliar will be off-balance. Family gets used to it, but those unfamiliar, stumble. You are family, of course, but you must be careful until your feet learn the pattern of it. Notice the curve of the stairs, curved so that an invader's sword hand is against the inner wall, giving advantage to the defenders."

(*Not so peaceful after all, are they? Sure, they may seem peaceful now, but they know the art of war.*)

My eye fell on a stunning sabre, a beautiful weapon of outstanding artistry. She occupied a place of honor on the wall near Stapleya's bedroom. Displayed with a matching scabbard, leather harness, and other accessories, she was magnificent. Stapleya's 5G-Grandmother Edda once wielded her. As is the case with Fitz's heroic bow, this weapon is legendary enough to bear a name. Stapleya introduced the sword as the Lady Tyrxing.

I asked to hold the beautiful artifact. I surmise Edda must have been a formidable woman among the diminutive Nekomata. She must have been nearly my size to have wielded such a sword. The noble sword melded into my grip as though crafted just for me. I executed a few dance-like moves with the elegant blade. She sang as though she had been waiting just for my hand to caress her, my arm to enfold her. She longed for a quest, for adventure. It was almost heartbreaking to return her to the lifeless display, as though abandoning her to imprisonment.

The third morning following our arrival, Teena led me to a clearing, a grassy field distant from the Castle. This will be our training field, she explained.

"Training Field?" I asked. "Aren't we done training? We're ready to kill some dinosaurs, aren't we?"

"Yes and no," she said, "further improvements in our strength and speed are possible. And necessary. Second, our super-weapon is not yet ready. We have time to spend before the weapon arrives. Let's invest it by taking advantage of what this planet offers."

"If there is time to spend, I'm all for using it to benefit our strength and skills. However, I don't foresee much improvement. Our development had already plateaued back on Center. All the weightlifting in the world won't improve on that. Over-training can be detrimental."

She smiled kindly at my naiveté. "You read Fitz's book, right? Remember his describing local root vegetables and the concoction he called Grow Juice?"

I nodded. Actually, I had spotted the ugly, black vitelotte among the variety of tubers I had been eating. I had also asked for and sampled Fitz's 'Grow Juice.' Horrible tasting, foul stuff.

Teena took my nod as her cue and continued with hardly a bobble. "The vitelotte and related vegetables are locally grown. Their fertilizer derives from extraordinary materials not available on Earth. Our scientists haven't unraveled that which makes them exceptional. However, I suspect the fertilizer's key. The same plants cultured on Earth and Center aren't nearly as beneficial."

I replied, "I noticed their vitelotte's larger, uglier, and more bitter. The ones I saw on Earth look anemic by comparison."

"Yes, we carried the seeds to Earth and cultivated them there. The Earth transplants don't thrive the way they do here. We believe it relates to factors present in the fertilizer they put on their gardens."

I wrinkled my brow in puzzlement. "I had imagined the science of botany and the benefits of fertilizer as well understood. What's missing?"

"Two factors," she answered. "The first, and I suspect the greater, is one factor Earth once possessed and lost on December 31, 1879."

My puzzlement deepened. "What's that?"

She replied, "On that date, Thomas Edison demonstrated the first practical electric lighting."

That didn't clear the fog.

Before I could interrupt, she continued. "With the advent of the electric light, Earth people began burning less and less wood for heat and light. Ashes from the wood-burning cookstove and other uses dumped into the gardens diminished. As electricity usage grew, less wood ash became fertilizer for the gardens. We note a strong correlation between the rise of various diseases and the decline of wood as fuel.

"Not only wood ashes themselves, the nature of the wood. This superheated, sweltering tropical world is extremely fecund. When cooking, they burn wood that has grown in exceptionally fertile soil."

"Gotcha," I interrupted. "Since wood's rich in the soil's nutrients, the ashes are supremely beneficial as fertilizer. I suppose that makes sense. The body requires sixty minerals along with nutrients such as vitamins and amino acids. Ashes contain minerals present in the wood."

"Correct," she answered. "That and animal dung and composted plant waste they process for similar purposes. So, you see, we need to eat our veggies, drink Grow Juice, and train like hell for the present. These concentrated nutrients will allow us to gain significant improvement over our current fitness."

So, we exercised. Not all exercises were traditional, formal exercises with no purpose other than muscle-building. A stone-age society has endless jobs effective for strength-training workouts. I had often remarked on the rock-hard musculature of the fur-folk, and I soon came to understand. A stone-age lifestyle's hard work!

The first exercise of a more practical bent than lifting weights was swinging a maul. Teena mentioned firewood ashes. A large household, even in this hot, suffocating climate, needs plenty of firewood. Heating water, cooking, cleaning, and other chores need heat, which requires fuel. Without fossil fuels, fuel means wood. Plenty of wood.

The proper tool for splitting wood isn't an axe, a common misconception. The proper tool is a maul. A maul is heavier, larger, and has a broader head. Sharpness isn't a significant factor; you're not cutting wood or chopping it. You're splitting it. There's a difference. A maul ends in a point, although it need not be particularly sharp. Even if sharpened, it will soon dull, and if the edge is too thin, it will chip and break. The challenge is not to break it or damage the edge and to keep it smooth and pointy.

There's an art to swinging a maul, to splitting wood just right. I came to enjoy the satisfying thunk, viscerally! You must put your entire body, every muscle, into it.

Chopping wood's excellent for muscle-building. First, grab a round or partial round of seasoned wood. If the wood's green, leave it a few months. The fur-people had an immense stack of wood just sitting in the sun to that precise purpose. Had, as in past tense. We soon worked through that.

First, place a hunk of seasoned wood on a chopping block. Address the wood such that, when swinging, the maul strikes dead center, in line with the grain. Be careful not to miss; if you must miss, miss on the near side, but mind your toes. Missing on the distant side tends to break the handle across the target. It is much less frustrating to strike dirt and dull the maul than break the handle. Trust me; I broke my share.

Safely swinging a maul takes practice. It can be dangerous until you catch the hang of it. Ensure nothing is nearby to damage, humans and animals in particular. Stand and address the wood, lift the maul high with both arms. Let the maul pull back behind your head only so far as you can do so and still control it. Focus on control over strength and speed. Swing it forward using the strong muscles of the upper back. Bring the shoulders and biceps into the act as it arcs high and descends. Finally, and this is key, let your arms relax just as the maul impacts the wood.

Build up your speed and let the momentum and weight of the maul perform the work, not your brute strength. As the maul strikes the wood, relax your arms to dissipate the shock. You don't wish to carry it up into your shoulders. Powering into the target with tense muscles adds zilch to the impact. Further, it stresses the arms and shoulders; it's tough on joints and tiring. Limp muscles don't transmit the shock and spare the body from strain and abuse.

Do it right, and the wood splits with a near orgasmic crack. Doing it often builds tremendously powerful shoulder and back muscles. I did it until the wood ran out.

Contrary to popular imagery, chopping wood's not the exclusive domain of strong men. It isn't necessary to be a hugely muscle-bound lumberjack to swing a maul with authority. Even a compact lumber-jill can swing a mean maul. It doesn't demand massive muscles, although it allows the application of whatever muscle is available. Plus, it is terrific exercise.

Other tasks of the stone-age household also constitute quality exercise. Carrying water is a surrogate for lifting weights. I also pulled a plow, a hilarious story. Unfortunately, they lack draft animals on this world. Horses, oxen, and such just aren't available. The big and powerful beasts are nocturnal and not amenable to domestication. The best draft animal here walks upright on two legs.

Teena added rope climbing to our regimen. I learned rope climbing in the service, although there, we utilized high-tech gear — a wimpy, watered-down sort of rope-climbing. Teena's Planet Oz regimen used only rope and that with which nature has endowed us. We don't grade based on points scored.

I discovered that scooting up a rope uses a rather unaccustomed set of muscles. Teena claimed that the ability to levitate up a rope, or down, might one day save my life. She darkly hinted that a predator at my heels might inspire alacrity. The only score that matters is binary; survive, or die. I took her advice to heart and discovered rope burns heal quickly with a poultice of vitelotte skins and Grow Juice.

And running. OMG! I hate running. I hated running in the service; I hated it on Center; I hated it with headphones and a vivace tempo. A twenty-minute treadmill jog takes me nowhere and leaves me bored, frustrated, and spent.

Despite the frustration, the treadmill has some positives — no worries of navigation or dodging obstacles, no woodsy predators to give chase. Instead, I can close my eyes and imagine I'm elsewhere as my body sweats its way down the trail to pain and exhaustion.

And Sweat. If you've never been to the fur girls' planet, you don't know sweat! They have four 'S'easons here. *S'izzling*, *S'teaming*, *S'earing*, and *S'corching*.

Running on a forest trail is different, and not in a good way. You are ducking, dodging, twisting, and turning for endless hours — with no music! Plus, the ever-present attention-demanding danger. So, if you see me running, you probably should run too, and pray you don't see whatever I'm running from.

I read Fitz's tale of the runs he described and laughed. While in the service, I often ran ten miles in an hour and considered that near the limits of human endurance. Teena didn't demand an hour's run. She's demanding at least six to eight miles per hour, for five hours or more, carrying a heavy pack. Nor a pleasant slow jog. Forty or fifty miles in a too-short day without stopping? Impossible!

I discounted Fitz's tales as an irresponsible exaggeration. At Center, I achieved fifteen miles on a treadmill workout. I took a half-hour snack and water break at the midpoint and completed the run in just over two hours. I considered it as having attained the best run of my life. I felt pleased, although spent, hungry, dehydrated, and worn. Keeping that up for several hours must be impossible.

There might be something to the Grow Juice theory. After a few days of drinking the juice and eating vitelotte, my performance blossomed. I ran twenty miles in three hours with relative ease, with only two brief pauses for food and water.

In a week, I reached almost thirty miles in a five-hour run. Every day I became faster and stronger. Teena improved as well. She claimed we might yet still improve. I didn't understand how. She demanded impossible, superhuman speed and endurance.

Running on Center is demanding enough. However, running in *Planet Oz's* environment is insane.

The diminutive fur-people make fleet and efficient runners — they make speedy runs between nearby castles carrying little water. We are not following their merchant trading routes. Our routes are planned for the most efficient cross-country travel. We're making much longer runs than their typical trade route and carrying much heavier loads. We must haul extra supplies, food, and water — lots of water.

A running human consumes up to two thousand calories per hour. The precise amount varies depending on pace, burden, and the size and weight of the runner.

A compact warrior, such as I, requires the least, and a person Teena's size, rather more. A bear of a man like Fitz requires immense quantities. The bigger and heavier the runner, the greater the 'fuel' needed. A larger person carries greater reserves, has greater capacity. Everything being equal, I just 'run out of fuel' sooner, though I need less total for a given route.

Water loss is a severe issue as each breath carries away precious water vapor. Plus, in this heat, we lose much more via sweat, ignoring routine urinary losses. Again, depending on the runner, as much as a gallon of water per hour may be necessary to sustain the body. Our mission demanded runs lasting several hours, a daunting challenge.

One morning, I was mulling these issues as I bounded into our exercise clearing to meet Teena. I was stunned, shocked to spot James — her doctor and physical therapist from Center. Surprised, caught off-guard, I self-consciously tried to cover myself, embarrassed at being 'caught' naked for the first time on *Planet Oz*. I'd grown complacent with living unclothed among the fur-people.

Confronting a smoothie male without warning shattered my equanimity. Not only was I unclothed, but his similar state didn't calm my unease in the slightest — quite the opposite. For half a moment, I froze, mouth open, transfixed by his anatomy even as I futilely struggled to cover my own. Fears, antiquated attitudes, and preconceptions persist. I suppose it's just not in my nature to appreciate dangling masculinity.

I repressed a shudder, forced my arms down, and squared my shoulders. Then, recovering, steadying my voice, I managed as much calm as the knot in my stomach permitted. "H-Howdy Doc.

It's wonderful to greet a familiar, uh, face. What brings you to *Planet Oz*?"

He and Teena had been sitting together on a convenient perch, deep in conversation. He stood as I spoke. Then, with a wink, he answered, "I grew bored with the cool breezes on Center. I decided it was time I should visit a pleasant, steaming hothouse. I plan to suggest that we install an over-heated sauna in camp. That way, we can experience the wonderful health benefits without the necessity of an interstellar jaunt. This is wonderful. I can accomplish a year's worth of sweating in a single afternoon. I must come here more often."

With a forced calm I did not feel, I chortled a little at his amiable pleasantry. Chortled! Ha! I giggled like a stoned schoolgirl! At a loss to respond in kind with similarly incongruous banter, I struggled with my eyes. Finally, after a moment's awkwardness, I merely held out my hand and smiled.

As though to assuage my discomfort, he took my hand and extended the handshake into a chaste hug, barely touching — precisely the wrong move for any assuagement. I arced my body lest his maleness might brush my skin. I tried not to seem obvious — I hadn't meant to seem stand-offish; I felt wildly off-balance. Not James' fault, mine. Just the way I'm built. Freud had it all wrong — many emotions flood forth under such circumstances, but envy's not one.

"Teena says you've been progressing well. I come bearing news, both excellent and less than excellent, as well as some unnerving. Since somebody needed to carry the message, I decided to come myself so that I might also conduct a checkup on my star patient."

I hadn't considered it before, but his words jogged my memory. I remembered Teena commenting something suggesting electronics didn't work here. I presume the 'Smartphone' used to communicate through open Portals doesn't function on *Planet Oz*.

Teena, seeming to sense my discomfort at his nearness, drew James back toward herself, placing her body between us. "James tells us that the engineers created a promising weapon for our mission. That's wonderful news. The unfortunate part is that the Portal intended for the delivery is out of commission. Sending the weapon through overloaded the Portal, and it has dissipated. They needed to send the ammunition through another, less stable Portal and, as a result, blew it up too. Our weapon landed thirty miles distant from the ammunition and supplies."

I grew calmer as I digested her words — distance helped too. Then James picked up the narrative. "They knocked out both Portals. We're uncertain when they can be available again. No way to send anything else for now. Also, the possibility of retreating via the Portals is gone."

Almost back to normal but still thinking slowly, I asked, "Why would we retreat via the Portals?" I hadn't considered the idea before.

His face fell at my question. "The Portals in question are rather distant from the nearest refuge. We had hoped the Portal might be useful in case of difficulty. Should time become tight and insufficient daylight remain, the Portal provides an escape option. You could transit to safety on another world and return the next morning. We had also considered it possible to use the Portal to avoid crossing the distance from here to there by foot. Both options are now off the table."

I nodded at that. Yes, it would have been useful to have usable Portals at the site of the weapons cache. Then, we could transit from Castle Stapleya to Center, then from Center to the cache. We would then grab the weapons and run to the nearest castle and avoid several days of danger. Still, we had planned for the worst-case scenario, and the loss of a more accessible option was not a disaster.

"That only means we are continuing our original plan," I said.

He explained, "Yes, but that's the unnerving news. The unexpected Portal failures stranded two of our people. We can only hope that they were able to reach safe haven."

Oh! I sat down as understanding dawned. Of course, someone must carry the materials through the Portals. I hadn't considered that. They would have become stuck, without supplies — or clothes — in a hostile environment. Further, I imagine they were likely not trained runners. So yeah, the odds are somewhat against them.

Teena said, "I sent word to telegraph the castles near both areas. Both to enquire if anyone made it, and to ask they search for our people. So there's a chance, though a slim one."

James continued, "That's why I came here as soon as possible. I hoped that Stapleya's people might telegraph to the remote castles for aid. But without help and luck, they're doomed."

I recalled Fitz's description of the Fur-people's communications system. Without wires or electricity, they had developed an effective means of long-distance communications. Now two lives depend on it.

Sword

Every morning in Africa, a gazelle wakes up, it knows it must outrun the fastest lion or it will be killed. Every morning in Africa, a lion wakes up. It knows it must run faster than the slowest gazelle, or it will starve. It doesn't matter whether you're the lion or a gazelle-when the sun comes up, you'd better be running.
— **Christopher McDougall**

As I said, a running human needs plenty of calories, depending on weight, speed, and burden. Teena needs more than I; she's not as compact and efficient. Nibbling a comestible the fur-people call Journey Cake while running helps offset the deficit. Ten pounds of Journey Cake matches the caloric deficit of a day's run. Seven, nine-inch rounds of the course, grainy cake, another ten pounds to carry. Much too much to consume while running.

Nibbling while running isn't difficult, though digestion draws blood away from the muscles. Scarfing down a pound of dry journey cake while running guarantees distress. Light nibbling of journey cake during a run can add needed calories. Yet, it is challenging to carry or consume enough to meet our needs. It's necessary to maintain a careful balance. Just enough to sustain but not enough to overload the digestion. Journey Cake alone is not the answer.

Considering the body as a machine, it carries a limited amount of fuel. The faster the pace, the greater the fuel consumption. Running a fixed distance at a slower pace is more efficient, just as a car gets improved mileage at a slower speed. We can't afford to slow down for better "mileage." A slow pace is too dangerous. We must sequester ourselves behind solid stone walls before the predators roam.

Sprinting as much as possible is necessary. Six hours at a near sprinting pace requires a tremendous number of calories. Humans can't run such distances. Not without replenishing water and nutrients along the route. Especially water. In the heat of Planet Oz, plentiful water is as vital as oxygen itself.

Cross-country running demands carrying food and water. Unlike our initial runs on a circular training track, we must carry everything. That makes a tremendous difference. A fifty-pound pack adds perhaps as much as an extra three thousand calories deficit to a marathon run. The total approaches fifteen thousand calories for a six-hour run, depending on variables. Journey cake's heavy, although water is heavier.

In stifling *Planet Oz* heat, water is a greater necessity than calories. We need plenty of water, nearly a gallon per hour. Four gallons of water make for a significant burden. Thirty-two pounds before including the pack, journey cake, our weapons, and other miscellanies. Keeping the burden under fifty pounds is challenging. Our mission demands a forty-mile sprint, carrying a fifty-pound backpack. The prospect of encountering predators imposes deadly time constraints.

The water lost to perspiration also carries away salt. Convention says runners need 1500 mg of sodium per hour. Journey cake is salty, although not salty enough.

One afternoon Teena and I took a break from training for some well-earned rest and calories. Observing a group of fur-people tending a nearby field, my mind wandered to my military days as I contemplated the classical studies I endured in the name of education. Finally, I commented, "The Greek poet Hesiod said, *Sow naked, plough naked, and harvest naked, if you wish to bring in all Demeter's fruits in due season.* Demeter, of course, was the goddess of seasons and harvests."

After a momentary pause, I winked at Teena and added, "I never understood why she'd be fond of naked Greek farmers working their fields without proper OSHA-approved safety clothing. Must have been a Greek thing."

Teena snickered. I don't know if she found my lack of appreciation of nude Greek farmers amusing or my less than subtle dig at the benefits of nanny government. She knows I'm not fond of either.

She added, "Still, it was more than poetry. We have artifacts from ancient Greece devoted to Demeter in which men are depicted as plowing without a stitch."

I said, "The Nekomata farmers never heard of Demeter, yet take Hesiod's advice to heart."

Although it's not as if farming is the only activity performed unclothed. "Clothing is all but unknown on Planet Oz," Teena mused, "ignoring incidentals such as belts, harnesses, and packs for carrying supplies and weapons."

She's right. The remarkable heat makes covering the skin intolerable, especially while engaging in physical labor — such as breathing.

Watching the fur-people working in the fields, I noticed they carried drinking bladders. I assumed they contained water, although I later inquired and learned they often contain something stronger, Grow Juice or a variant of it.

Inspiration takes wing....

What an excellent idea; instead of pure water, I suggested carrying Grow Juice. Loaded with nutrients and calories, it augments the journey cake. It's also rather salty and if necessary, adding salt is practical.

After several experiments, an optimal mix emerged, our own custom formulation, Grow Juice with added salt, and mixed with crumbled Journey Cake. I tagged it GoJuice in a flippant comment to Teena, and the name stuck. Like Grow Juice, it adds significant calories and nutrition. The runner's equation demands every calorie and every drop of water. GoJuice and Journey Cake together makes an almost palatable combination. Almost, er....

Our journey must traverse hundreds of miles to the Portal, where our weapons await. Not just a single Portal, we must visit two Portals thirty miles apart. Our path hopscotches from castle to castle, providing for a nightly safe haven. Unfortunately, the castles are not optimally placed, the portals being at the apex of an isosceles triangle.

With the risk of insomniac dinosaurs, we cannot spend much longer than five hours traveling. Anything over six hours approaches suicide. Early morning or late evening risks encountering a predator we cannot outrun or fight.

Circumstances permitted us to run five to six hours max. If not behind solid stone on schedule, our survival chances diminish by the minute.

Of course, one can never be sure where the predators will be. What they lack in numbers they balance with deadliness. At present, there are two day-walking Deinonychus known to prowl. At least one flock of their smaller cousins, the Velociraptor, is also prowling.

The People watch and report any sightings. Sightings get plotted on a gigantic stone map in Stapleya's library. Every time the Criers come round with a new sighting report, we are all on pins and needles. None of the recent sightings are near Castle Stapleya, to everyone's relief.

Teena and I configured packs with water bladders holding gallons of GoJuice. We added rounds of journey cake and made practice runs with the rigs. Our goal was to run forty miles in under five hours to allow a safety margin.

The burden required several adjustments before getting everything packed just right. Despite our efforts, no matter how we tweaked the load, our packs were just too heavy and slowed us down. The real problem is our limited running window each day. If only the day were longer, it would be practical.

Cramming an eight-hour run into five hours just demands too much. Predators roaming early and late enforce limits we dare not encroach. Our safe running time is much shorter than the full daylight hours. We must find another solution.

Stapleya identified the answer. I never fail to find her intelligence and quickness of mind remarkable. I had read of the technique she proposed in Fitz's book, although I had forgotten it.

Even Teena didn't consider it. Stapleya suggested employing support runners as Fitz, Petchy, and Teena had done. Fitz had suggested the concept for their longer runs, and it had worked. Our shorter runs demand a faster pace; whatever reduces our burden improves our odds.

The concept is simple enough. Rather than carry a heavy pack the entire run, we enlist the aid of support teams to carry our packs. The technique would, of course, only apply to the longer runs. If others carry our packs several miles of a forty-mile run, we can sustain a much faster average pace.

The strategy developed for support runners to start with us. At the ten-mile mark, they would hand the packs to us and turn back. The packs can be much lighter as we only need supplies for part of the run.

We'd carry the lighter packs, exhausting the comestibles as we run. A support team with fresh supplies would meet us roughly ten miles from our destination. This way, we'd only carry supplies for a twenty-mile run or less. Although we'd still be running the entire distance, we'd run minus the burden of food and water much of the way. The burden we do carry is much lighter than otherwise, and we would run unburdened for half or more of the trip.

With all our training, refinements, and the support of our friends, it remains challenging. Several of our planned runs will stretch our physical limits. We debated forgoing weapons, although common sense won out. There are other dangers than the day-walking dinosaurs — wild boar, for example. Deer can be deadly when in heat. Even mundane pests such as skunks and raccoons may be present. Unarmed feels unwise.

The fur people's fleet couriers run the well-traveled routes unarmed. Even so, the job of a courier is a dangerous one; losses aren't unknown. We're headed into less-traveled areas and making much longer trips than the routine courier.

᭦᭦᭦

I had grown comfortable with Language, thanks in part to our practice before arrival. The total immersion experience, living in their society, soon perfected my tongue. Although languages are not my strong suit, I felt pleased with my progress. I found I resonated with life on Planet Oz, despite the unbearable heat and the lack of modern necessities.

Modernity felt over-rated.

With word of our weaponry finally delivered, training was now over. It was time to prepare for travel. As we made our final preparations, we hoped to receive a reply to the telegrams. We hoped to learn the fate of the unfortunates stranded by the failure of the gates.

The evening before departure, Castle Stapleya once again partied. They like to party. This time instead of celebrating our arrival, they were celebrating our departure. There were no intoxicating brownies this time; the party was short, bedtime early. We needed to be fresh and ready the following day and could not afford the luxury of a hangover.

There was singing and dancing and, ahem, other activities I won't describe. You would not believe me if I did. At night's end, Stapleya stepped to the center stage and banged the gong for attention. Then, she began speaking, reciting the Legend of Edda, her distant grandmother.

"From dawn to dusk, no paragon had she.
Boundless in beauty, her strength peerless too.
Evil plight hung o'er he who dared to woo.
For he must win three bouts with her lest his seed spill untapped;
The spear to fling; the stone to throw; the spring to leap;
Should he best in every feat, his wooing too shall win,
but he who fails must lose his love and likewise lose his head."

I guess they had more males in her day; else, she would not have been so quick to behead. Of course, their society was female-dominated even then.

That's the opening stanza, as near as I can remember and translate. In any case, the tale goes on and on, telling the legend of the great warrior ancestor. It named her failed and presumably beheaded suitors. It told how one day a strange giant of a man with a poor and scraggly pelt came to call.

Best her he did and begat a child with her before disappearing into the woods. He returned every few months for years, each time besting and wooing her anew and leaving her great with child.

The tale tells not the number of children thus produced. Any number given would be suspect owing to the unmistakable exaggerations. The singular detail I picked up on was the description of this strange male. His description, simplistic though it was, sounded a bit familiar, as if a smoothie had been her suitor.

I resolved I would ask Teena about that detail a bit later. But I forgot about it moments later as Stapleya's speech took a surprise twist that left my mouth agape.

She had a purpose to retelling the legend of Edda, to tell of the magnificent Sabre she carried. And if one believes the legend, with which she beheaded her failed suitors.

The Lady Tyrxing.

"The greatsword has endured the lonely years since her master's passing. None among the generations that followed possessed the strength and skill to wield her. Only now has someone worthy of the magnificent blade come to Castle Stapleya. Someone with a legendary quest worthy of a legendary blade."

Motioning, she drew me to the stage as Wisceya stepped up behind her, carrying two elegant boxes. The first held the Lady. She gently lifted the blade with a thin leather guard and held it before her, edge facing upward.

Stapleya kneeled, ceremoniously intoned words lost as my language circuits tripped out, no doubt short-circuited by the tears streaming down my cheeks. I was overcome by the emotion of the moment, the immensity of the gift, the honor bestowed.

Turning the blade so the edge faced toward herself, she presented it. Bowing, tears streaming, I accepted the blade. Still holding the leather guard, I was careful not to soil the blade with my grimy, sweaty, oily hands.

The second box contained a brand new, exquisite scabbard and belt to match. The belt not only held the scabbard with sword ready to draw but two smaller scabbards. They contained a knife and dagger. A pouch held a karambit, and the belt had loops for arrows, also present with a matching bow—a complete warrior's armamentarium.

Kneeling at my feet, she placed the belt around my waist. She stood and hugged me and ceremonially kissed me on each cheek, stretching to tiptoes to do so. I needed to help her by bending my knees to meet her halfway. I'm no giant, as I believe I have stated, but next to the fur-people, I'm still rather tall.

Parenthesis

"The best scheme… is a stiff uncertain thing."
— **Thomas E. Brown**

Having discovered the Portal in Northern Mexico, Petchy and Fitz made their way to a previously undiscovered human planet. We check in with them a few weeks after landing on Klovia.

"Seems a harebrained scheme to me!" Petchy was pacing around the gym as they debated strategy. Massive dumbbell in one hand, he gesticulated with his other fist as he expostulated. "Crazy idea! Insane! You want killed?"

Fitz grunted but was otherwise unresponsive. He was momentarily preoccupied, prone on the bench as he power-lifted a staggering six-wheeler. Despite the monumental load, he was not exactly struggling. After the initial lift, he began doing easy reps, as though the massive wheel weighed mere ounces.

Fitz is extremely fit, as the reader may have inferred. Several generations of selective breeding had given him advantages. Alien gene tweaking had unleashed his tremendous latent potential. Intense training and optimal nutrition had yielded extraordinary results. The combination rendered astonishing physical abilities on the part of both men.

Petchy does not look the part. He is in good shape for his apparent age and possesses an impressive physique. Still, he appears older, balder, and rounder; a prominent potbelly undercuts his musculature. His biceps are less impressive than those working beneath the six-wheeler. He somewhat resembles the younger man's father.

Fitz on the other hand. …

The pair had appeared weeks ago. They invested time and effort in learning the local language and studying the culture. All the while, they were looking for tell-tale signs of Gharlane's influence. This is a new, uncharted world, accessed from a previously unknown Portal. Petchy and Fitz came to investigate what presence Gharlane's organization has on this world.

And to determine what to do about it.

Petchy soon made the decision to discard subterfuge. These are not stone age peoples like the Nekomata. Their society is — to Petchy's experienced observation skills — under full-frontal assault. They must discard the idea of 'protecting' this civilization from the risks of contact. Instead, they must intervene lest it might follow the downward spiral of his own.

Pressing forward with First Contact was the only logical course. He must recruit these people into the fight for human civilization. They had as much at stake as the rest. Gharlane's tendrils were deep into the society, working their evil magic day by day. The question was not whether to proceed but how best to do so. How could they approach the head of the government and convince her? How could he prove that the fantastic tale they needed to tell was reality?

"Porting into the most secure spot on the planet and saying, 'take me to your leader' is a risky proposition," Petchy said. He waved the dumbbell for emphasis. "Even if not killed outright, we'd not get anywhere. They'd likely confine us with no chance to talk to anyone, much less their Executive. I, for one, am allergic to jails."

Racking the massive six-wheeler, Fitz sat up and looked Petchy in the eye. He stared for several seconds before speaking. "I hear ya! I'm open to better ideas. We must get the attention of someone high enough up the food chain. Someone able to bend the Chief's ear and convince her we are legitimate and serious. Walking up to the front gate won't work. We don't have a lot else to work with. I do have a strange feeling we are on the right track, though. I can't explain it; call it intuition."

"I still don't like it," Petchy growled. It was unlike Fitz to talk of unscientific ideas like intuition. Yet Petchy felt it too. Something was drawing them to take the risk. Something neither had felt before.

"Neither do I," said Fitz, "but the charm is in the very audacity of it."

Petchy nodded. "I must admit it is audacious. Penetrating the shell of flappers surrounding any high executive is challenging. Reaching the Chief Executive of an entire civilization might require more than audacity. Perhaps if we present her an irresistible puzzle..."

Like all other known alien civilizations, these people are entirely human. In all the worlds, Petchy's people have never encountered a sentient non-human species. That is with the possible, although unproven, exception of Gharlane.

All human civilizations are biologically consistent within several decimal places. Divergence from the Earth human norm is insignificant. Minor issues of appearance, such as the Nekomata's fur, are the extent of it. Petch often pondered the mystery of humanity's origins and expansion to disparate worlds.

Might these people then be the source of the human species? Or are they just another tribe descended from an unknown point of origin? Did humanity originate in one place and then propagate via the Portals? Or were we seeded by another, more advanced race?

Fitz and Petchy debated these topics for weeks as they prepared to initiate First Contact, but the immediate question is not human origins. Instead, the question of the moment is more straightforward. How does one go to a strange planet and establish contact — and credibility — with the Chief Executive?

It is not for nothing that one finds the expression 'shooting the messenger' in all human languages.

Deinonychus

"We all have a dinosaur deep within us just trying to get out."
— **Colin Mochrie**

Our first few days traveling were uneventful. Our stopovers were meticulously planned, support runners accompanied, handed us off, and fresh ones met us as planned. A complicated dance arranged by Stapleya via the *Bedrock Telegraph*. No word of our stranded couriers. By now, they must be dead, presumed victims of the predators. Surviving one night was unlikely. Weeks, quite impossible.

Planet Oz is hot and fecund. It rains frequently, virtually every night, often violent and lasting hours throughout the night. Daytime rains are less frequent and milder, but cooling and welcome. Long-distance running is challenging due to the heat. I discovered a new experience, running in the rain on *Planet Oz*.

I've never been a pluviophile, a rain-lover. Rain on Earth often means slogging through mud and muck and is usually cold besides being wet. Then we have lightning and thunder, which impart their own special joys, including tornadoes.

They have civilized rain on Planet Oz, as it usually comes at night while the inhabitants rest. When it does occur during the day, it's not cold, just a sweet, pleasant shower. The well-maintained trails show little mud and muck. Drenching in fresh rain instead of my own sweat felt wonderful and refreshing. A bottle of cherry-scented shower gel would have been the perfect compliment.

On the fifth day, we were running the final leg, approaching the castle nearest the site of our first Portal. We both felt rather stressed as we approached stone-sheltered safety. This had been a long and tiring run, over forty-five miles by the map, our longest and most dangerous thus far. It was dangerous for more reasons than the mere distance.

The declining population of the Nekomata has emptied many castles. Abandoned and dark, their provinces grown uninhabited and wild. We hoped to save three days travel time by cutting through such a region, skirting a dark castle. We could have gone around it, making shorter runs at the expense of more days en route. In hindsight, this time-saving shortcut appears ill-advised.

This region is seldom hunted, the trail ill-maintained. Roadside markers are often absent or hidden by overgrowth. Once, we had to climb over a roadblock created by a fallen tree. The work the fur-people put into maintaining their roads is astonishing. The stark contrast before us clarifies their evident meticulousness elsewhere. Without attention, this trail will soon become impassible as nature reclaims it.

Tomorrow, we make the run to the Portal location. That distance is just over fifteen miles from tonight's safe harbor. There we hope to collect our weaponry and thence continue. The next evening's safe haven resides a similar distance further on. Thus, tomorrow must also be a grueling day. We not only must run some thirty miles, but we must stop halfway — an unavoidable delay; precious time spent searching for our weapons materiel.

We must also search for the remains of the unfortunate who cached it, if any. We can afford but limited time on site. Today's run had been a strenuous forty-five miles. Although less isolated and less total distance, tomorrow's nevertheless is a demanding route.

Another factor is that the Portal nexus of our interest, being so far from a living castle, is unfamiliar. Although near the main trail, it is too distant from any castle safe haven for practical use. Only a capable runner can use it, making the long run to safe harbor. Inconveniently located and infrequently opening, it languishes unused.

This Portal's uncommon feature is that the flux stream is uncommonly robust. Robust enough to transport non-living materials, even cold steel. When not abused by overloading, that is. Once overloaded, when it would next open becomes unpredictable. It may be months before it will again be usable.

Teena and I settled into a comfortable routine. We alternated taking the lead and setting the pace vs. following and watching our six. She had bloomed in the last few weeks. Grow Juice and vitelotte agreed with her, especially when combined with vigorous exercise. No one would mistake her for an ingenue, but she looks younger, stronger, and healthier every day. She began to resemble Fitz's image of his pulchritudinous Amazon. I had come to develop similar feelings for her as well. Nevertheless, I tell myself I am not overwhelmed by her charms as he appeared to be, by his own telling.

I won't claim that she became the love of my life, that I felt about her the way I had my dear Estelle.

Had? Still do! No one will ever fill that void.

Nor had I fallen into a slobbering, pheromone-induced trance, as Fitz described himself. Instead, we found comfort and release in each other's arms. Need there be more?

If so, why?

In any case, age to a lover is a matter of mental attitude; it cares naught about the steady march of catabolism. Fitz's Teena was young and vivacious with a zest for life. The Teena I met had the appearance and manner of one whose long life is all but done. Appearance does matter, if the calendar doesn't, whether we like to acknowledge it or not.

Having some inkling of her actual age blunted our affair, I suppose. That her appearance reinforced that gap was no doubt a factor too. I was hyper-aware of the vast gulf in our ages, unlike Fitz.

I had anguished that Estelle was an older lover. That seems almost humorous now.

One night not long after Stapleya had recited the Tale of Edda, I broached the questions that tale had raised. At first, she would not speak of it, then I asked about the legendary beheading of her lovers.

Teena snorted at that.

"Fairytales!" she had said as she sputtered, laughing at my question. "Human beings are hardwired for stories. The tall tale is an art form, one that occurs in every culture. Anything billed as a 'Legend of...' is a fish story, trust me."

She snickered a few more times before continuing. "Remember, these folks do not have much entertainment. Tall tales entertain and remember those gone before. Even in Edda's day, males were too useful to behead casually. I would never have permitted it anyway. Besides, you have spent time with these people. Can you see them doing such a thing?"

(HUH? Wouldn't have permitted? She was there?)

I cracked a quizzical smile. "I had wondered; it feels so contrary to their nature. How do you know the *legend* was just a tall tale?"

"Because I was there. My son was her lover and the father of all her children. So I have many grandchildren from Edda. She was a fertile mother, just as Stapleya was in her time. Both produced many, many children. The true story of Edda and her life and family is preserved in Stapleya's library, much of it in my own hand."

Teena had met Edda! More than met, she became her mother-in-law. That means Stapleya is her direct descendant too. Is that why she appears so young and virile for a manifold grandmother? Good genes?

Despite my questions, Teena clammed up. She keeps her secrets it appears. I could not estimate how long ago Stapleya's distant, multiple-Great Grandmother had lived. But it was clear it had been several generations. The most I could get out of her was that it occurred when she had first visited the Nekomata.

Estelle had been an infant compared to Teena. What did that make me? Aren't there laws? I know our misalliance in no way implies I am an immature child. Still, you must admit such disparity is remarkable. I began ruminating on why I am only taking much older lovers.

Was this some deep-seated psychosis?

I brooded all that day over the questions that line of thought had opened. We had entered the final stretch; the trail was smoother, and we were pushing ourselves to compensate for lost time. We were behind schedule.

Twice during the run, Mother Nature had wet us down. But she had been parsimonious with her cooling spray, little more than a light misting. We had exhausted our supplies and were pushing curfew. The sun was low, and our support runners, delinquent. No clue why, but their absence raised deep concern.

We hoped to be behind cold stone soon. Our supplies gone; we were running on our reserves, weak, tired, and exhausted. We were pushing curfew, uncertain of the remaining distance to our sanctuary.

Lost in introspection, Teena caught me unawares when she slammed on the brakes. She stopped, and I plowed into her from behind, almost causing us both to fall. Braced in fighting stance, she did not go down, and I somehow managed to keep my feet.

Her bow nocked with a clutch of arrows at the ready; she was zoned, in the flow, hyper-focused on what she had spotted ahead. I looked down the trail to where she was aiming and saw why.

I froze. Panic. Sheer terror!

My inner voice screamed, Oh! Fuck!

Teena whispered, "Back-to-back. There will be another; they always travel in pairs."

A considerable distance ahead in front of us stood a giant chicken. Well, that was my first impression. This 'chicken' was a dozen feet, beak to tail, as tall as Teena and must have weighed at least two hundred pounds.

A deinonychus!

It was standing over and pecking at something in the pathway. Well, not really a chicken, and it doesn't have a beak, a difference

I'm too busy to debate. Yeah, it has fearsome-looking teeth: two points for you, nit-picker.

It had not yet turned its attention on us. If it had, we would already be dead. Our life expectancy measured in seconds as it was — no one saw a deinonychus this close and lived.

Time stopped. For a half-blink, I could not move; my feet riveted to the ground. Staring my imminent death in the face, my body locked solid, unable to move or breathe.

Fight? Flight? Frozen, I could do neither.

Then the adrenaline hit, the fatal demon of fear departed, and I felt my own flow begin.

In a whirl, I dropped my pack, unlimbered my sword, grabbed a handful of arrows, and nocked bow. I whirled to face 180 degrees away, alert for its companion. My movement had caused it to look up, hiss, and turn toward us.

I scanned the forest for another giant chicken and listened for any rustle. Nothing. There should be another. They hunt in pairs. One draws out the prey, while the other sneaks from behind as the unwary victim watches the one in sight. They are smart hunters, for birdbrains.

Well, so are chickens, far smarter and more vicious than most city-dwellers would believe.

Birdbrains. Right.

The Deinonychus started forward rather slowly, as though uncertain whether it intended to attack. My head was corkscrewing from the imminent threat in front to probable danger behind. Dividing my attention front and rear, I was checking both sides on each turn.

As the beast took another step, Teena loosed her first volley, grabbed a fresh hand, and fired again. And again. It kept coming, picking up speed even as Teena's missiles found their mark. It looked like a pincushion, but they barely pierced the skin, a mere pinprick. She had tried for the arteries in its neck and its eyes and had drawn blood.

The eyes are improbable targets at this range, not that you want them closer. A shot square in the eye has a chance of penetrating the peanut brain. Not only are the eyes minuscule targets, but the bobbing head is unpredictable.

Despite the difficulty, Teena scored. One eye blinded, though the tiny organ behind it remained untouched. The beast screamed in pain and anger, then charged. Blinded in one eye and bleeding, it charged in rage and fury.

Deinonychuses are not considered fleet-footed. Don't bet your life on that, though. Attempting to outrun a predator is a poor strategy. Ask any Gazelle. Although faster than humans, deinonychuses are nowhere near as speedy as their smaller cousins. Velociraptors well earn their name. Though much smaller, those *chickens* can sprint over 40 MPH, and they hunt in packs, not pairs.

When stressed, my mind retreats into absurd humor. Such as "Why did the dinosaur cross the road?" Answer: "The Chicken joke hadn't been invented yet." Yeah, like that. Ain't the human psyche something?

I held my stance for a moment, reserving my arrows for our chicken's unseen sister. Teena was reloading for another volley as it came closer and closer. Watching the contest, I realized we're outmatched, negotiating from a position of weakness. Arrows are poor bargaining chips.

Time to open a more intimate dialog.

I'm not easy, but I can be had with the right approach, a candlelit dinner, some soft music. Unfortunately, this gal is not making the kind of overtures that endear me. Therefore, I must respectfully decline the invitation to dinner. I shall send the Lady Tyrxing with my regrets.

I launched my volley, drew my Lady, and shouted to Teena, "Watch our six," as I guided the Lady Tyrxing into battle.

Teena whirled to watch our behind for the missing monster, her last volley at the ready. The wounded nightmare was still coming, albeit slowed by the arrows it had absorbed. Weakened and bleeding, it came on, angrier than ever. Seeming mortally wounded, it must die soon, though not before killing us. These beasts do not quit.

Our only hope lay in two prospects; that my Lady could end this beast, and its truant sister remained absent.

If sis was hiding and about to join the fight, we had zero chance. One of these monsters is more than enough.

The beast charged with a blood-curdling screech. I answered with an adrenaline-fueled battle cry of my own; the blood-curdling vehemence startled even me. I charged with my Lady in full lunge, a suicidal move against a skilled swordsman. Deinonychus, though, lack swordsmanship skills. And swords; although they have their own weapons and methods.

My audacity and my scream of rage appeared to unnerve the beast. It hesitated an instant and turned its head so the remaining functional eye looked square at me. This was its fatal mistake, as it gave Teena an opening for her last volley.

Teena's fire took the beast full in the face as we closed, ending its remaining eye. But, despite two missiles to the eye socket, the pygmy-sized brain still functioned.

Damn it!

Guided by sound, scent, and inertia, the beast charged. Not yet admitting defeat, blinded and wounded, it came on, fury undiminished.

I probably should have turned tail and run. But adrenaline was driving, and I was in the zone. I couldn't have turned away if I tried.

The Lady Tyrxing sang a magnificent aria as we closed, her song the center of my hyper-focus. I felt time slow, and my sense of action and awareness merged. As the beast neared, I was wholly in the flow. It felt as though a supernatural force took control, guided my moves.

I ducked, rolled, and lunged with all my might, dropped and rolled aside. The final lunge was near orgasmic. Long evenings polishing the razor's edge paid their dividends. The beast fell, beheaded in a single blow, although not before a monstrous claw gashed my side!

Motherfucker! My inner voice screamed. Aloud, I grunted something indecipherable as I fought to stifle the inner voice. Profanity ill-serves women, I tell myself.

It was a dying blow, weak and ineffectual; else, I would not be telling the tale. Nonetheless, I shall require something more than a band-aid.

As I regained my feet, Teena leaped to my side, still in warrior flow, her last arrow nocked.

She's kidding, right?

Between us, we had put over twenty arrows into that beast. Other than blinding it, the projectiles had an almost insignificant effect. What did she hope to stop with a single shaft? An aggressive rabbit?

With a bloody hand, I passed her my few remaining missiles. I could not use sword and bow simultaneously, and my Lady was the better negotiator.

Despite my wound, I remained upright for the moment, sword in hand. I held the other hand against my wet side, perhaps to keep my organs from falling out. Perhaps stem the bleeding.

We held that position for several heartbeats, scanning, listening. Beginning to feel weak, I turned my attention to my wound, noting with relief that my injury was less than I feared, although on a stone-age planet without antibiotics, it was quite severe enough. At least the blood was seeping and not gushing, so there were no severed arteries.

My feeling of weakness likely was from the adrenaline crash and fatigue, not blood loss. Though my side was a red-splattered mess, the actual volume of blood was trivial. I am amazed we are alive. A human against a Deinonychus has the slimmest of chances.

But then, I AM a warrior!

We're not safe yet; there should be another. Teena was retrieving arrows from the corpse, sorting and dividing them between us. I restocked my belt loops and prepared for another round.

Wounded and weakened, it was unlikely we would survive another round. We intended to, and doubtless would, fight to the death.

Minutes dragged on. Blood trickled down my thigh. The sun moved inexorably toward the horizon. Even if this were the sole day-walker, her nocturnal cousins would quickly join us. We had to get behind cold stone, and soon.

Deciding we were not under imminent attack, Teena retired her weapons and turned to my injury.

"Not exactly a scratch," she mused as she examined my wound, "but not too horrific either. Peritoneum creased, no penetration. No internal organs punctured. I'm glad Stapleya provided a good first aid kit."

Teena cleaned my wound with a burst of sterile water under pressure. I'd best not elaborate. A battlefield procedure I learned about in basic but had never seen used in practice. Surprised by her technique, I presumed she had practiced. I wondered when, in her long life, that had been a valuable skill.

Aiming comes more natural to males. Yes, I know, gross, but it is sterile. Counterintuitive, but effective.

I gritted my teeth against the pain as she stitched up the gash. She then applied a poultice made from the dregs of our GoJuice. I won't elaborate that either. The dressing eased the screaming pain a little. Finally, she wrapped a tight bandage cut from our water bladders around my waist. Teena obviously has significant experience with battlefield medicine.

She asked, "How's that feel? Do you think you can travel now?"

I winced. "I think I can travel; I just hope these stitches hold." We could use a roll of duct tape about now.

With that, we started at a slow trot. We needed to run pell-mell; the sun is getting low. I gritted my teeth to ignore the pain. We passed the spot the Deinonychus had been pecking at when we first saw it. It was a bloody battleground. We found what became of our greeting party.

And the beast's sister.

Good for them that they had managed to kill one of the devils, although it cost them their lives. Four humans and two Deinonychus died here today; two humans survived. A good outcome in the annals of human-dinosaur intercourse.

Teena grabbed more arrows from the corpse as we passed. They had given a good account of themselves. They had killed the beast, although it died far too slowly after wounding.

We picked up the pace as well as I was able. As I realized my intestines were not in danger of falling out, I pushed myself, ignoring the pain. Dusk was heavy when the Castle came into view. Thankfully, it had not been far. I was getting wobbly from fatigue, adrenaline, dehydration, and possible blood loss. We were already outside way past evening curfew.

As we approached the Castle, a watcher in a window high above the entrance spied us. She blasted a riff from a lepatata just like the ones used at Castle Stapleya. We approached the big front door, already secured against the night beasts.

We banged the door and shouted. Despite our noise, there was no response. They were not about to open for us. Hard to blame them; entire castles have died that way. Opening for unfortunates trapped outside past curfew risks the whole castle. Once closed for the night, the big front door is not opened for any reason.

Protocol calls for sacrificing anyone trapped outside. A harsh protocol from my perspective. Though cruel, better to lose those outside rather than expose the entire castle to risk. Our surviving the night requires an alternate solution.

As we stood by the door agonizing over the conundrum, a T-Rex thundered in the distance.

The big boys were awake!

Predators would be upon us in moments. We were near panic when the bugler sounded again. I looked up as a rope dropped from another, lower window.

Our running had, predictably, loosened my stitches. My battlefield bandages were a bloody mess. The exertion of climbing a rope did not portend betterment.

Considering the alternative, I accepted the challenge. I dropped weapons, belt, pack, everything. We would retrieve them later if we survived. The pain and further aggravation of my injury mattered not. It was nothing to the prospect of meeting that obnoxious loud-mouthed fellow bellowing in the distance. Or as more likely a flock of Velociraptors, though just as fatal.

Teena grabbed the rope and held it while boosting me up. Even with her help, not an easy climb. They say pain is what lets us know we are alive. Each pull left me more alive than the last. I screamed thru gritted teeth. I could feel stitches tearing, the wound opening. Gushing now, blood was making a slippery mess of the rope. I felt faint and suspected adrenaline and dehydration might not be the cause this time.

About half-way to the window, I faltered. Teena saw my weakening and shot up the rope. She levered herself underneath me as I sagged, piggybacking my weight on her shoulders. Then, pushing upward with surprising strength, she boosted my faltering carcass toward safety. Hands grabbed my arms as I neared the high window and pulled us both into the upper chamber. As we landed on the cool stone floor inside, I swooned a dead faint.

Illuminated by a sharp pain-prick, I came wide-awake moments later. Someone was restitching my wound. Weak and light-headed, the pain made me retch.

"Tell me a joke," I quipped between clenched teeth, "if you're going to have me in stitches." No one laughed.

Teena grunted at my gallows humor as she passed me a drinking bladder and commanded me to drink. I did and soon ceased to worry about the surgery. The taste was familiar; something more than Grow Juice was in that particular bladder.

Hours later, I awoke to the sounds of rain. It was dark, the middle of the night. My wound, cleaned and bandaged, my body bathed, and I slept in a fresh, clean bed. Teena lay beside me, also fresh and clean after our ordeal. Noticing my slight movement, She reached out and took my hand. "It's okay, we made it," she whispered, "sleep and heal."

Our hosts were heartbroken to learn of the loss of their friends. That two of the day walkers had also died gave slight solace. Observers had only documented two day-walking Deinonychus, though we suspected more. It's a big world, and distances between castles are enormous. That we had helped kill such monsters was a victory. The bad news is that the known day walkers were last seen over 100 miles away. It's likely these were not them.

The fact is, we don't know how many there might be. So far, there have been no day-walking T-Rex spotted nearby. The only known day-walker of that species was last seen months ago and hundreds of miles away. So as far as anyone knew, the one we heard, along with any of her relatives, are nocturnal. But don't bet your life on that hypothesis. Arrows and a sword are less useful than a roll of toilet paper against a T-Rex.

The following morning Teena retrieved our equipment as soon as the door opened. Our packs were the obvious casualty. Night creatures had torn them to shreds, no doubt drawn by the scent of GoJuice and Journey Cake.

Our weapons weathered the nighttime dangers with scant detriment. The arrows and knives scattered, some arrows trampled, scratched, and damaged, a bowstring broken. The damage was minor, arrows and bowstrings easy to replace. The packs, too, we could replace.

The Lady Tyrxing lay where I dropped her, still in her thick scabbard, unharmed. The casing itself sustained significant scuffing but was otherwise undamaged. I embraced her, cleaned and polished her blade, and oiled her leather belt and scabbard. She had earned some TLC.

Almost Dead

"Almost dead yesterday, maybe dead tomorrow,
but alive, gloriously alive, today."
— Robert Jordan, Lord of Chaos

We rested the next three days as I recuperated. Teena had wanted to run ahead to the nexus with only fur-people as companions. I vetoed that idea with vehemence; two well-trained, capable warriors almost died! Not to diminish the Nekomata, but four of their best had fallen. They are competent fighters but lack our size and strength, as well as our skills and training.

And my sword.

I refused to permit Teena to tackle the dangers without the Lady Tyrxing and my skilled arm to guide her. We'd experienced firsthand the impotence of bow and arrow against dinosaur hide.

"I lost one lover to violent death, damned if I will permit another," I yelled. "That's a stupid idea." I had lashed out seemingly in anger, although it was more in fear. She bristled in frustration, claiming I was over-reacting. She retorted that I was refusing to listen to her idea. I went nuclear on that. "If you want me to listen to your ideas, get some better fucking ideas!"

That got to her; she was the closest to being angry I've ever seen. "I've never heard you F-bomb before," she said. Her astonishment appeared genuine.

"Keep saying stupid things, and you'll hear a lot more!" I fired back sharply, not using my 'inside voice.' I usually keep it inside my head; I feel profanity ill serves women. That doesn't mean I don't know the dialect. Sometimes nothing else will do. Patton summed it up best. Profanity serves a purpose, but it must be eloquent profanity. I was feeling quite eloquent right then.

I continued pushing her buttons, offending her sensibilities. I eloquently reminded her of how I'd saved her life and claimed she owed me the courtesy of staying until I was back on my feet. She said we had worked together to defeat the beast and save both our lives. I rejoined that not only was I opposed to losing a lover, but her loss would strand me on an alien planet.

I think that last scored a hit.

Truth told; I do not fear living among the Nekomata. They're lovely, friendly people. Although I lacked Portal navigation skills, I knew others would come searching. I was in no danger of stranding, and we both knew it. She became quiet but perforce admitted I was right.

We spent the next three days in bed, but even Lotus-eating can pall. It was not the blissful interlude you might imagine. Teena is an enticing and playful bedmate, but I failed to uphold my share. Due to the pain and our quarrels, I was irritable. When I became too cranky, I drank the enchanted Grow Juice and let the world drift away. I'm still unsure what that mixture was, but it's potent stuff. I hoped it was not addicting; I don't need withdrawal pangs on top of injuries.

Our relationship had been growing closer. Exactly what we were to one another escaped definition. In one of our more intimate moments, I asked, "Teena, my love, forgive me if this is too personal. I know you're much older than I, much older even than Estelle was. You spoke of knowing Edda and that your son married her. Forgive me, I must ask; just how old are you?"

She was silent a long time. I feared I had made a terrible mistake; I could sense her pain. I could see the dark clouds in her eyes, almost expected her to cry. She did not, yet I could see she was blinking back tears.

Hesitatingly, she began. "Sweet child, I have been expecting you to ask. This is painful to talk of; I have been thinking how to answer, about how to discuss it with you since before that day we met. I intended never to allow you to become so close, to avoid the intimacy that would lead to this moment. But I am weak and needy and lonely. So again and again, despite my better judgment, I take inappropriate lovers."

She kissed me, not as a lover but as a parent might kiss a child. She sniffed a couple of times, still on the verge of tears.

"Indeed, I knew Edda. I was already much, much older than your Estelle when I met her. My youngest son was much older than she, a detail we hid from her."

She snuggled against me as though she had said all she was going to say. Unwilling to amplify her pain, I said nothing more. We held each other in silence.

After an eternity, she sniffed and began anew. "I am old enough to have been born on and lived a lifetime on Ashera before my home world died. Fitz had called it 'Planet K' in his book, from something Petchy said. I am the elder matriarch of Ashera. With few exceptions, all the survivors are my children or their descendants. Everyone you met at Center is my descendant.

"So you see, I am ancient beyond words."

I had thought she was semi-royalty because James called her *General*. I gulped and took a breath before I answered. "I was beginning to suspect something similar. But how is it you have managed to live so long?"

She sighed—another long pause. "You know that the runaway AI that killed my planet was part of a massive genome research project. Before it went off the rails, we succeeded. We unlocked the genetics behind aging, senescence, illness, and death."

"So," I asked, "you were running that project? Or one of the researchers?"

"No, dear, I was one of the test subjects. I was a student, in debt and struggling to complete my matriculation. I volunteered to let them experiment on my genome for the basest of reasons, money.

"It is ironic that I have outlived them all, the researchers, the other subjects, and am still going. Cosmic irony, a joke on a grand scale.

"The genetic research became lost when the AI took control. I am the sole example of the breakthrough. My genome is the result of that research, but we needed the original work to uncover the path to success. The mission with Fitz was as much about recovering that data as it was killing the AI. We needed it to replicate the original work, as well as unravel the infertility plague. We succeeded, although at a horrific cost. Thousands died, myself nearly included.

"It was questionable for a while, but I am vibrant and alive now. If not for my strange fate, my entire culture would long be extinct. My people survive because of a freak accident. The genetic project worked, and I was off world when the final catastrophe struck."

She paused for a moment as though recounting the tale was painful. I suppose it was. I held her hand and said nothing, waiting for her to continue.

"Our colonies survived for more than a century, but in time they too fell victim to the plague. I escaped — pure dumb luck — and managed to keep my fertility for many lifetimes. As a result, I've birthed hundreds of babies and have many thousands of grandchildren. Generations of great-grandchildren I've never met.

"Much of the living population of my people has sprung from these tired loins. Two other test subjects outlived our race and bore many descendants, but they are all but gone. My line was the longest-lived, the most fertile but the plague has caught us too.

"We bred among ourselves for a long time, though many of us mated with Earth humans too." She shrugged. "Our people assimilated, living on Earth, it was difficult not to. The same goes for this world. Their descendants do not suspect they carry other-worldly genes. Unaware that they have grandparents who were not native-born. Our declining fertility means only a precious few remain fertile. Those who are fertile are often as challenged as the Nekomata."

I remembered Estelle and her preoccupation with Rh blood factors. She had thought of them as possible indicators of Alien genes. I wondered, were Teena and her people responsible for Rh-negative blood? Does nearly seven percent of Earth's population trace back to Teena's people? To Teena herself?

I pondered this as she continued. "My fertility dissipated centuries ago. We were once 25 billion souls, now but a few thousand. Unless we succeed in reversing this, there will soon be none. Even our long lives will end. Eventually, accident or catastrophe will end the last of my children."

Another long silence, then she resumed in a soft, fragile voice. "Jill dear, I can't tell you how old I am because I don't even know. I have lived in so many different societies, lived so many different lives. So many close friends and family have grown old and died. I had to reset my age and fake my identity so many times. Staying in one place too long without growing old invites scrutiny. I am challenged to guess within a hundred years. I won't speculate or give you a number. You know more of my life story than any other living soul outside of Center. Please, I beg you, don't tell anyone else, especially not Fitz."

With that, she turned over, her back to me, and I spooned her. After a while, I realized she was sobbing soft and low. I had forced her to revisit the death of her entire civilization. Possibly worse, I had forced her to confront the pain and reality of her long life and the trauma of seeing so many loved ones grow old and die. We are not built to endure so much loss.

I usually call little spoon, but not this time. Instead, I stroked her neck gently and tried to soothe her soul.

She cried a long time and finally, we slept.

By the fourth day, I was almost back to normal. My stitches removed; I had a horrific scar. Grow Juice is astonishing. Not only does it carry exceptional nutritional value, but it also speeds healing too. A poultice of the smashed skins and leaves is a potent topical healing agent. The Doctor says if I keep a plaster on the scar, it will soon disappear.

We had quarreled several times over Teena's desire to tackle the run to the nexus without me. I reminded her that returning here required retracing steps. That meant even more lost time. Our plans called for moving forward, not backtracking.

Teena was fumious to travel. Due to her pressure to continue, I felt determined to resume after only three days recuperation. I still feared she might leave me.

We talked with the Castle Doctor. She agreed that while I might still have some tenderness, I'm fit enough. My wound, though ghastly, was not so severe. Although, a smidgen deeper, and I would be singing a different tune. With three days of Grow Juice therapy, I should have recouped the blood loss too.

The doctor would have preferred I rest another day. I would have too but for Teena's urgency. Nevertheless, she admitted I should be able to handle the run. That is, provided I avoided tackling another dinosaur. She proposed a compromise, allowing me to take it easy the first day out.

Instead of running the entire 30-some miles our route required, she proposed I ride the first leg. Riding would give my wound additional hours to heal. In addition, the shortened run will allow my body the opportunity to ease back into the rigors of distance running.

Not everyone who travels between castles is an able runner, and some cargo is too heavy for a runner to carry. So, when necessary, the fur-people use lightweight two-wheeled buggies similar to rickshaws. There are no horses, mules, or even oxen for draft duty. Instead, teams of fleet-footed young girls pull the rick-buggies.

There's a reason, I learned, that horses and other animals are not on Planet Oz. Most people are unaware, but humans are the most efficient runners of all animals. That sounds shocking and counterintuitive, but true. The primary reason is that we humans have the most efficient ability to sweat of all the animals. We do so and cool our bodies better than any other creature. Our sweating ability is a big part of how we can thrive in the extreme heat of Planet Oz and why there are so few mammals, especially large ones. Most other mammals cannot cope.

A cheetah can vastly outrun a human for a while. As they run, their body temperature rises until it hits about 107 degrees. At that point, the cheetah collapses. Some researchers, I learned, tested that with instrumentation and a treadmill. Felines, especially big ones, cannot cool themselves well enough; they don't sweat except through the paws. Yeah, cats have sweat glands in their feet, and when overheated, they can leave wet footprints. The pads are too limited in cross-section for efficient cooling, thus explaining why cats are not on Planet Oz. Dogs cool themselves by panting, also an inefficient mechanism.

Ostriches are the only creature that can outrun a human over extreme marathon distances in most circumstances, but they don't sweat and run with their beak open to take in cooling air. Although they have massive lungs and a long neck to help dissipate the heat, in an extreme climate, they still cannot cool themselves sufficiently. Nonetheless, they are formidable competitors.

Horses can out-sprint a human. They also sweat profusely, but their ability to dissipate heat is inefficient compared to a human. A horse has six times the mass of a human but only 2.5 times the skin surface. The horse has the advantage in colder climates. As the temperature rises, a horse becomes unable to keep going. Horses would be all but useless on Planet Oz.

A fit human can outrun any animal over marathon distances in a very hot climate, if we have sufficient water. Period! Including dinosaurs. Any animal, no matter how fleet. Many animals can sprint faster for short distances. Humans can keep going and going – like that damned pink bunny – long after any other creature collapses.

The Fur girls have an advantage over us. They, too, sweat profusely, but the wicking effect of their short fur helps cool their body. Counterintuitive, I know, but their fur is a cooling adaptation to the climate. Their sweat stays in place and evaporates instead of dripping away. Nekomata runners become sweat-soaked and stink to high-heaven in their exertions, but their efficient cooling makes them capable of extreme marathoning in a catastrophically hot climate.

Castles that are near can send cargo, trade, and even passengers via rick-buggy. Teams of runners take turns pulling the cart, spelling each other as they tire under the burden. Busy routes often have 'trains' of rick-buggies with their cargoes of trade goods.

Fitz mentioned rick-buggies, their cargo, and trade between castles in his tale. He had undersold the extent of the inter-castle commerce. This traffic explains the tremendous effort spent maintaining the clean and smooth forest routes. The shortened safe travel window due to the shift in dinosaur habits harms this commerce.

They are not to carry me the entire trip, but only the first leg. After that, I will run a while, soon to be met by a rick-buggy team from the other end. The process is much as we had employed support runners, except slower. Although they can carry heavier loads, rick-buggy teams are slower than a less-burdened runner.

I'm much more burdensome than their usual passenger. So they supplied a team of no less than ten runners to meet the challenge. Two to pull at any given moment, with pushing from behind on the upgrades. They would trade-off every mile or two in order not to overtire any individual.

I must still run several miles, though much less than otherwise.

Plans complete, we asked they notify the Castle at the other end of our day's journey that we are on our way. We would expect their rick-buggy runners to meet us on the final leg of the day's run.

Teena and I gathered our supplies, and as soon as the morning curfew sounded, we started for the Nexus. We made excellent time despite the buggies. We could have run it faster, but not by much.

I chaffed at the arrangement; I did not want to ride, pulled by my friends. Yet, when I began to run for real, I appreciated that our friends had been so solicitous of my well-being.

Medically, I was intact. Even so, I found I was weaker, and running was more painful than expected. That claw had put a nasty hiccup in my hustle. Easing into the first day's run had been an excellent idea. My wound twinged as I ran, but by the end of the day's abbreviated run, much of the pain had dissipated. I believe I could have made the entire run but glad I didn't have to.

Our escort should have turned back sooner. But they insisted on accompanying us further than planned. We were quite near the nexus when we stopped them and insisted our friends hand over our packs and turn back.

It was time I stopped acting like an invalid.

They still had plenty of time for the return journey, but we did not wish them to take unnecessary chances. Those Deinonychus had been about much too early for comfort.

We also worried lest they delay their return too long and raise new alarms for their safety. With the recent loss, any unexpected delay would be worrisome to their family.

Our friends had another motive. They had wanted to escort us all the way. They wanted to discover the precise location of this unfamiliar nexus.

Since learning of the worlds beyond, the Nekomata have become curious about the Portals. They were paying rapt attention to any factoid about the Portals and inter-world travel.

Fearful of another unfortunate tragedy as with poor Shameya, Teena discouraged them. Safely navigating the etheric void requires skills and training they lack. Well, I lack them too. Nevertheless, one day they will join the Interplanetary human family.

I hope we Earthers do too.

We had only just bid our friends adieu when the stone marker denoting the nexus hove into view. All mapped Portals carry an identifying marker. The majority are subtle. The markers are unidentifiable unless you know exactly what you are looking for. Yet, some are more elaborate than others.

This nexus had a stone structure to identify the spot. However, we found an elaborate pile of rocks formed into a stone pyramid, not just a simple stone marker. What would be the purpose?

I asked Teena, "Who built this? What is it for? How come there is a pyramid here?"

She shrugged. "There isn't, according to my knowledge. There was a long, low wall bracketing the Portal, but this is different. We don't have time to unravel the mystery now. Look for our weapon, and let's hit the road again. We'll investigate another day."

Examining the area, I surmised someone had dismantled the stone wall. They had used the stones to build a rough pyramid. But why? We started looking for some sign, any clue where our weapons materiel might be. I began to suspect it lay beneath the pile of stones. Nothing was visible elsewhere. I began examining the rocks, looking for those last disturbed. After some examination, I picked a spot and began moving rocks. I had been shoving rocks aside for perhaps three or four minutes when I let out a startled grunt.

"Here, Teena, here's something. It's a body!" I began removing rocks and tossing them aside with haste. A moment later, Teena was helping, and in seconds we had uncovered the still form.

"That's no corpse!" Teena exclaimed. At her words, the body opened his eyes and groaned. He was alive.

Dehydrated, emaciated, and frail, he had survived ten unbelievable nights in dinosaur country.

We helped him to his feet and provided water and Journey Cake from our packs. He improved immediately.

"Thanks," he said, "I knew you would come. That damn Portal blinked out when I arrived. Stranded and alone, I was certain I couldn't survive. It was painful work, but I managed." He waved at the makeshift pyramid. "How do you like my castle?" Extending a hand, he said, "I'm Obadiah; friends call me Obie."

A rustle from the trail startled us. We unlimbered weapons as we whirled to meet the threat. Instead of a predator, it was our rick-buggy team. Contrary to our admonitions, they had stayed behind us, following us. They were intent to learn the location of the Nexus. Teena, though perturbed they had disobeyed her wishes, felt relieved they had. We had a use for their buggy.

We introduced them. Obie didn't speak Language, so we interpreted for him. The Fur girls' eyes widened in amazement at his feat of survival. He had dug out the ground and built a rough stone pyramid. He carved a space underneath, a tiny coffin-sized cavity where he could spend the night. He had come out in the daytime to hunt and find water, berries, and such, but he spent much of his time hiding in fear.

I wanted to know, "How come they left you alone? Didn't they scent you and know you were there?"

He shrugged. "I sequestered animal droppings among the rocks. I hadn't expected it to work, but I guess the stench was sufficient to mask my own scent. The only beasts I heard nearby were Velociraptors, I presumed."

Teena nodded, "Yes, a T-Rex would have smashed those rocks aside with one blow. Even a Deinonychus would have dug you out. A flock of Velociraptors would have encamped around your pyramid, awaiting your exit. Had they scented you, they would have never left."

"You were lucky!" I interjected. "You survived because they didn't scent you, didn't investigate. Luck does not begin to describe it. You should be dead!"

We debated our next move. Finally, we decided to send him back to the castle with our escort. Obie, weakened by his ordeal and not a trained runner in any case, needed the buggy. Otherwise, he would find it impossible to cover the distance in the available time. They had plenty of supplies, and with ten runners and a buggy they could carry him to safety. The Fur girls, excited by the prospect of a male, were eager to take him home. They were babbling in Language at, and about him.

Teena listened to their commentary for a few moments and smiled at their enthusiasm. Moments later her expression turned to one of mild concern. She spoke to them with stern words. "Listen to my words, daughters. This young man should not grant babies." Their faces looked shocked. She continued, "Fitz and others who came here to provide their seed in trade carried fur in their souls. They also carried sons in their loins. Their sons would breed true, with a proper pelt. His are not the same. He will grant babies mixing Smoothie and People. Also, he is as likely to grant daughters as sons. Be aware before letting him sire."

I whispered to Teena in English, "Did I just witness the invention of racism on this world?"

She reacted with surprise at my suggestion. Then she laughed. "Nah, these people do not think in such terms. They have almost no concept of race. Racial enmity does not arise in a culture until it begins to decay. Viewing the world through the distorting prism of race is a hallmark of a diseased civilization."

She shrugged. "They will still take him to their home, and bed. They will just be more careful about letting him impregnate a fertile womb. Before coming here, Fitz underwent genetic tweaking to increase his sperm count 500-fold, as well as to favor sons with a proper pelt. Obie does not have such tweaking."

I shrugged. "Accidents happen," I said.

She nodded. "If they weren't aware of the concerns, you know how challenged their fertility is. I doubt he is fertile either, though I don't know for certain. So few of my people are. Even with unconstrained access to the castle's beds, the odds of insemination remain low. And these people love their children. Even a hybrid smoothie female – should the genetic dice roll that way – would receive as much love as any other.

Fitz had his genes tweaked to ensure a perfect pelt, as well as to ensure sons were his legacy. The genes for their pelt are dominant. Even without the tweaks Fitz received, any hybrids would likely display a near-normal pelt. The chance of a badly flawed pelt are slim and, even if extant, would cause little harm. In the worst case, such a child would still be loved."

I paused, wondering. "Perhaps the clan-mother may consider all this and decide otherwise. The need for babies is paramount." "But," I asked, "Is it possible, even knowing, she might still present him with her nubile daughters?"

"Maybe," Teena admitted, "if so, at least she's informed. Besides, if necessary Center's medicine can intervene and tweak the genes. The genes for their pelt are well understood."

I leered knowingly at Teena. "Looks like he's gonna get some."

"I'd hesitate to put it so crudely, but yeah, not just some; rather a lot."

I smiled. "I wonder if he suspects what's in store?"

Teena laughed. "I doubt he will complain."

I remembered Fitz's comedic treatment of his first night in Castle Stapleya. I understood the fears and anguish he'd experienced because he didn't understand their society. Not everyone is as open sexually as the libidinous Nekomata, a failing Fitz and I shared. Despite weeks on our quest, time on Central and here, I am still bothered by their free-wheeling ways.

I am working on that.

Obie is not Fitz, and his culture is much more relaxed about such things. Further, his people know the Nekomata culture. He would not be surprised by unfamiliar cues and mismatched expectations. After a moment's thought, I agreed, he will be fine.

Before departing, Obie produced a rather large leather pouch, the cargo over which he, and we, had risked our lives. I opened it to find there were two weapons, not just the one promised. One was a monstrous, heavy abomination, too immense for mere mortals. I had never seen anything like it.

At least four times the weight of the smaller gun, this thing is monstrous. I later learned it was a Riesen-Pistole WTS BMG Single-shot, bolt action handgun.

WTF BMG is more like it!

Calling this thing a hand-anything is a reach. The idea of firing it terrified me. The second was a much smaller Magnum BFR! Unbelievable! The gigantic BFR was tiny beside this monster-killer.

Each was loaded; otherwise, there was no additional ammo. We knew we must travel to another Portal site in hopes of finding munitions. I had expected one naked firearm. Discovering two, and that they held ammunition was a pleasant surprise. No wonder they broke the Portal. We were not anticipating such a weapon, and given the sacrifice in getting them to us, I wondered if the engineers on Central had made a wise choice.

Damn engineers and their technological hubris!

I examined the ammunition. The single shell held by the BMG was odd-looking, with a red tip. On closer inspection, I realized that this was not just a big, heavy bullet. It appears to be the category of shell identified as HEIAP, explosive, armor-piercing shells. I knew such ammunition exists for .50 Cal weapons. The original BMG, the truck-mounted 1910 Browning Machine Gun, fires such rounds. Anti-tank weaponry from WWII used exploding shells. Explosive cannonballs date to the Civil War.

Those weapons are NOT handguns!

This thing is technically a handgun; portable artillery is more descriptive. Certainly not something one would fire one-handed. This monster is better suited to Fitz. I am uncertain I could even discharge it while standing and using two hands without the recoil knocking me down. I wanted to brace it against a tree, rock, or something, not my shoulder. This thing fires full-sized BMG rounds, albeit awkwardly, and requiring a reload after each shot.

Even without the untrusted, experimental nature of the explosives, exploding shells seem unwise. Firing them from a handgun – especially including this one – feels impractical, dangerous even. I find explosive handgun rounds unsettling on a good day. With the added factor of experimental, possibly unstable explosive formulations, the prospect becomes terrifying. If it works, it might positively stop a raging T-Rex though. It certainly should blow a big enough hole in one to slow it down.

With a shrug, I tucked the BMG into my pack for later study. Unloaded! Not taking any chances. Teena did the same with the BFR. We must run.

Time was against us, and we still had a long road ahead. We said goodbye to Obie and our escorts. As they turned back toward their Castle, we headed onward toward our evening's safe haven.

Klovia

The morning started with a bang. Not literally, nothing exploded. Nothing that is, except the morning quietude, shattered by raucous alarms. Alarms that disrupted the daily breakfast briefing. Alerts triggered by the unaccounted presence of intruders inside the security barrier. It is not possible to enter the secured area, yet they were there. That was the 'bang' that disrupted morning in the Executive Mansion.

Before they could disband the briefing and hustle the Chief Executive into the bunker, the all-clear sounded. Uncertain, the aides paused and milled about. The Chief of Staff pressed her ear and listened a few moments, then nodded at the rest. The briefing resumed amid speculation as to just what had happened.

An hour later, the Chief Executive asked the Chief of Staff about the incident. "You'll never believe it," she said, "two men appeared inside the secure area on the front lawn. They were naked and unarmed and taken into custody without incident."

"What?" the leader responded. "You're suggesting that two intruders, without tools or weapons — or clothes — walked into the most secure lawn in the galaxy."

The aide grimaced. "We see no evidence that they walked into the area. They were just there. No camera recorded their entry."

What some might mistake for shock or surprise, others recognize as the leader's intuition — a brief moment in time when the leader went elsewhere.

Motion halted. Posture erect. Paused. Head tilted, eyes closed, visualizing the scene. Or praying. Someone once derisively tagged these frozen moments "the still point of a turning world." The less favorable proclaimed such moments the result of a mental disorder, a few dare to go so far as to attribute such moments to a stroke or physical illness. Having one's every moment scrutinized permits few eccentricities. Unfortunately, the Chief Executives' mystic eccentricities invite scrutiny, debate, and, frequently, derision.

Some thought she used psychic powers to guide her governance. But, despite the critics, it was one of the reasons she held her office election after election.

Then came the decisive response. "That's just not possible. Tell Security Chief Breen I want a detailed report and analysis as soon as possible. Schedule a personal briefing."

"Madam," the aide asked, "is that proper use of your time? Shouldn't you just trust your people to handle it?"

"Maybe I should, but I'm not going to," she said. Then softly, she whispered, "Trust the gut. Always trust the gut." Then, louder, she told her aide, "Make it so."

Potiphar Breen's face contorted, purple with repressed rage as he struggled to maintain equanimity. Fighting the urge to laugh in his face, the Lieutenant told himself this was not funny. Maybe so, but he found it hilarious, despite Breen's vitriol. Breen castigated the Lieutenant for no more than being the bearer of unsettling, if comical news. Breen lacked a sense of humor and took anything humorous as a personal insult.

The incident was unremarkable, save for two factors; the intruders were in a place where no human being could possibly be; they were as naked as newborn babies. Other than that, nothing remarkable happened.

Intruders often attempt to access the Executive Mansion in some manner. There's no shortage of those believing they have vital information for the Executive.

Of course, they always insist they must deliver it in person. In today's climate of rising unrest, there are those who might wish to harm the Executive.

What Breen wanted to know — expounded with loutish and raunchy language unsuited to his station — was how they had managed that trick. The 'why' of their nudity piqued not his curiosity. Perhaps he didn't believe it.

Nudity was not something Breen often contemplated, never in connection with Presidential security. No, his only interest was the how of it, how they entered — the why was of minor concern, if any.

With the intruders in custody — and in prison jumpsuits — the security team began investigating. Breen would have been happier, the Lieutenant thought, had he shot them on sight.

The fear of threat subsided. Once it was apparent that there were no further intrusions, the Lieutenant reviewed the surveillance. The intruders materialized from thin air in the middle of the video frame. Something must be wrong with the recording.

That just can't be possible. The recording's altered; faked — no other explanation fit.

The Lieutenant checked other recordings that surveyed the area from different angles. They all showed the same, but obviously, they were tampered with. They had to be.

Calling the head Security Technician, he gave instructions on how to analyze the recordings. Also, he insisted they be compared with backup copies from the secure data mirror repository.

Fuming as he waited, Second Lieutenant Rice considered his next steps carefully. He had no wish to again incur Breen's wrath. One excoriation by the foul-mouthed and ill-tempered Security Chief was sufficient.

He considered the problem while observing the live detention cell feed. The intruders had little to say, and what they did say bespoke an unfamiliar tongue. He watched and listened for clues to their origin or purpose. Instead, they sat in silence as though waiting for the next shoe to drop.

Deciding they should wait a while, Lt. Rice instructed they not be offered food or water for now. Let them grow a little hungry. A few hours without food may render them more malleable, more cooperative.

He ordered recordings of their few words sent to linguists. He wanted to know the language they were speaking. He would not permit them to hide behind a language barrier. Little did he suspect just how foreign was their tongue.

〰〰

Hours later, the Security Technician reported back to the Lieutenant. Her analysis was thorough and impeccable. One does not work this close to the highest office in the known universe by being sloppy or careless. She required every datum triple-checked and cross-verified.

The videos proved undoctored — both the local copies and the archive backups verified as exact and unaltered. The cryptographic hash was unaltered, timestamps in sync, no frames dropped or skipped. All three cameras told the selfsame tale. Further, peripheral cameras outside the immediate area showed no evidence of intrusion or tampering. The intruders had not crossed the field of view of any other camera.

What the cameras reported had occurred, no matter how impossible that seemed. The Security Technician produced several stills, enlarged and cropped to maximize the details. They revealed a shimmering, as though caused by the refraction of light by rising heat. The distortion appeared extremely faint, not quite visible to the naked eye. It would have gone unnoticed by anyone. It was invisible without digital enhancement and enlargement. Still, it was there.

The shimmer hovered unnoticed, all but invisible in the clear air. After several minutes it brightened. Two naked men stepped from the shimmer as though stepping from behind a waterfall. The shimmer then returned to its previous state of near invisibility.

The Technician visited the lawn and took high-resolution living photos. First, she photographed the phenomenon from various perspectives. Then, she ordered cameras with wide-range ultraviolet sensors trained on the shimmer from different angles. She intended to track the field with every tool available.

With cameras recording, she reached out and touched her hand to the shimmer. Nothing happened. She became aware of a faint sensation as the tiny hairs on her skin entered the field. She had come to think of it as an energy field, though what form of energy, she had no clue. No sensors detected anything abnormal in the electromagnetic spectrum.

She moved her fingers back and forth, in and out of the field. Her hand penetrated the shimmer with no visible effect—that faint sensation bordered on imperceptible. When the sleeve of her TechSuit touched the shimmer, the feeling stopped. She sensed an intangible pop as it dissipated. Squint as she might, she could detect no further presence of the field. It had vanished.

The Technician called for extra personnel and tasked them with reviewing past security files. She wanted to know if this phenomenon was present before today.

That review process was still underway, would be for days. Already they had discovered two occasions when the faint shimmer appeared. It had flickered for a while and dissipated. Once, it manifested during a packed state function with no one the wiser.

As she watched the recording, she wondered what would happen if a guest wandered into it. The thought had barely breached her reverie when the video replayed that precise scenario. Then, finally, a matronly woman dressed in high fashion obliged her. Cocktail in hand, she blithely walked into the shimmer.

The shimmer crinkled and vanished the instant the woman's stemmed glass touched it. She appeared to react subconsciously, jerking minutely, as though having brushed a silken cobweb strand. Gone without a trace; disrupted, the shimmer did not soon return. The woman continued, oblivious. The shimmer dissipated on contact as though the glass had broken it.

Although unable to explain the phenomenon, she believed the intruders had used it as a conduit. She wondered how and what lay on the other end.

∿

The Lieutenant played the recording of the intruders' capture for the tenth time. They had done nothing after appearing. They just stood and waited to be noticed and arrested. They offered no threat, no resistance—silent save for one cryptic expression which had until now gone unnoticed. The Lieutenant had to crank up the volume to hear the words. The younger spoke sotto voce, almost as though talking to himself, "Take us to your leader!"

The elder gave him a cursory odd look but said nothing. At least it did not appear there would be a language barrier.

Besides the video record, there were graphs of data from motion sensors ringing the Lawn. Overlaid against the video timestamps, the motion sensor data matched.

Flummoxed by irrefutable proof of the events, unable to debunk the impossible, Second Lieutenant Rice faced his duty. He gathered the materials, straightened, and steeled himself for the coming confrontation.

He must present the analysis to Security Chief Breen. He did not relish the duty. He only hoped he didn't have to disturb the man from a nap to do so. 'Potty' Breen is not a tolerant man.

Chief Executive Kassa paused outside the detention area. She disliked the idea of a prison in the basement of the Executive Mansion and had long ago ordered it abolished, the space reclaimed for storage or other uses. However, this day saw the reversal of that order for the only time since she assumed her office in Service of The Empire.

No less distressed by the idea, she accepted the necessity for the moment. Her intuition told her this would be a short-lived reversal. She doubted the prisoners would be there long.

She stood several minutes watching the screen, observing the strange men. They did nothing remarkable. Did they suspect she was watching them? Uncertain, she decided. They sat there, saying nothing, doing nothing. The pair acted as though they were prepared to continue doing so forever if they must.

Linguists were unable to identify the strange language the pair had used among themselves. However, Potty assured her they had made at least one statement in *Standard Language of The Empire*.

She assumed they spoke SLoTE; everyone did, didn't they? Although Potty may be crass and obnoxious, he was also wolf-cunning and bulldog loyal. Less to her personally, more to his sense of mission and duty. Although still, she counted him as a friend. She trusted his judgment.

She acknowledged a few remote provinces maintain archaic languages despite the prohibition. The Empire no longer rules with an iron hand. Though not permitted, the old tongues persist among the disenfranchised and radicals.

The Emperor had decreed a single tongue, just one of his radical reforms. His ultimate transformation came when he stepped down and dissolved the office of Emperor. His reign transformed the Empire into a Republic in every way save the name and cemented his place in the pantheon as the last Emperor.

The Empire continued without an Emperor, the Empire existing in name only. Since the Reformation, one heard only SLoTE in education and commerce.

Our bodies have five senses, she mused — touch, smell, taste, hearing, and sight. Our souls also have five senses, intuition, peace, foresight, trust, and empathy. The senses of the soul are more subtle but no less valid.

Closing her eyes, she strove to draw a fresh intuition. Inspiration came not. Intuition is not forced, it comes, or it comes not, but it may not be summoned. She must confront them, or not. The decision was hers alone.

Absent fresh intuition, shoulders squared, hand on the door, she took a deep breath. Exhale, and again, then she stepped into the room.

The guard followed on her heels. Tilting her head toward him, she said, "That will be all." He startled almost as though slapped. She amplified, "Thank you. You may leave us."

A carefully composed, blank expression replaced his momentary shock. Then, with a nod, the guard abandoned his post, stepping out into the hallway and closing the door.

Chief Executive Kassa did not consider that he might hover just outside. She did not care that he would watch the proceedings on the screen. She was under no illusion they were alone. The Chief Executive was never alone, even in the most private, personal activities.

She well knew her every motion, her every facial expression came under review. Her every moment was recorded and monitored, subject to scrutiny. It came with the job. She trusted those doing the monitoring were her friends, protectors, and supporters. Thinking otherwise was the pathway to madness.

Absolute monitoring is a condition of any job in Service Of The Empire. All public employees, no matter how low their station, must accept the surveillance. Unconditional, mandatory scrutiny is a condition of public employment, no matter how lowly the station.

Every action, no matter how private or intimate, is on display to the Citizenry. The "Vision of the Empire" holds all recordings of public employees. VoTE makes them universally available. Any citizen may access VoTE to review any moment of any public employee's life for any reason. Anyone may question any act, whether public and official, or personal and private.

It could be a lonely life. Who would partake of intimacy under such public scrutiny? The price of Service, she never considered it.

The prisoners stood and faced her when she entered. Otherwise, they remained expressionless and said nothing. Fearless for her safety, one might suggest the bars between her and the prisoners as the reason.

One would be wrong.

Her intuition told her that the younger could bend the bars if he wished. When looking at him, she believed it.

She sensed much more than mere muscle. She sensed psychic force of unimaginable strength. She felt it ripple through her soul. Similar energy emanated from the elder too.

The reason she felt safe lay in her intuition. These were friends. She had no doubt, though she knew nothing of them.

She seated herself in the lone chair. Then, with a slight bow, the prisoners resumed their seat on the bed. They appeared to be waiting for her.

"You're not from around here, are you?" she studied their faces as she spoke. The younger one sat impassively. The elder smiled.

"No, Madam, we are not." His SLoTE was perfect, without accent. Terse and succinct, he did not elaborate.

"Your unconventional arrival created a stir. I presume that was the point."

His eyes twinkled; he cocked his eyebrow. "If we had instead appeared at the front gate and politely asked to chat, would we be speaking now?"

"I suppose not," she agreed.

"But for our dramatic entrance, you might think me insane when I tell my tale."

Smiling, she responded, "Insanity is relative. It depends on who has who locked in what cage."

Petchy laughed long and loud, till tears streamed down his cheeks. The younger man grinned and shook his head. She smiled, accepting her intuition as accurate. These strange men were friends.

Drying his eyes on his sleeve, laughter subsided. He lowered his voice for dramatic effect. "A storm is nigh upon us. Anyone can hold the helm when the sea is calm. Leadership is about weathering the storm. We need to talk to the leader, not just the one holding the helm.

"I am Doctor Shepherd. This is Fitz," he said, indicating the younger. "We come seeking alliance. Not to put too fine a point on the argument, but civilization is in danger. Yours and ours. We need each other."

Petchy knew that by briefing the Chief Executive, he was informing the entire civilization. He may as well brief Gharlane himself, a calculated risk.

He asked for Service of The Empire Privilege, in hopes of limiting the risk. SoTE Privilege is frowned upon by the citizens and restricted by law. Abusing Privilege promises swift Executive Recall.

The Citizens of The Empire are unforgiving of politicians who would hold private meetings. Public servants are not permitted secrets.

Privilege has its limits. Meetings held under Privilege are not restricted from review by members with security clearance. Privilege is not private.

Nor are the citizens forever excluded. The law mandates Privilege release within a definite time frame, defaulting to one day. Only a unanimous vote of the Security Council may extend Privilege. Only once had the Council voted to extend the Privilege, and that barely for a second day.

The meeting that followed garnered massive attention. Soon, on all inhabited worlds, the citizenry was reviewing the Privilege recordings.

The Council had taken the unprecedented leap of extending Privilege a whole week. The Citizenry arose in protest, and whispers of Executive Recall began circulating. Fearing revolution at the ballot box, the Council rescinded Privilege. They released the recordings early before the week had elapsed. Nevertheless, it was the most prolonged period of SoTE Privilege in recorded history.

Upon their release, the disaffected cried foul. Dissenting voices proclaimed skullduggery afoot. Claims that the delay meant the recordings were untrustworthy echoed across the cybersphere. Critics decried the records as frauds.

Public hearings in which Security Council members testified to veracity accomplished little. The critics refused appeasement. Investigations sought to expose the trickery, and although all failed, critics chattered.

The cries of trickery were not unfounded. Once Petchy pitched his case, the most obstinate Council members faltered. They agreed to violate their public oath.

The recordings thus released were honest in most respects save two omissions. First, there was an initial hour-long meeting edited to remove a few inconvenient details. Second, during this briefing, the council members became scared out of their minds, became willing to risk career suicide to keep these secrets. There soon followed a period during sleep-time, wherein Kassa herself ducked surveillance. During this time, she traveled off-world with Petchy and Fitz.

Potiphar Breen insisted on coming along, which meant doctoring his VoTE recordings as well.

Although he shouldn't attract scrutiny, Breen's proximity to the Chief Executive invites examination. Of course, another in his position would draw far more attention. But, given his penchant for loutish mannerisms and uncivilized speech, few bother to view his recordings.

Those who do so seldom repeat the mistake.

Gunpowder

"My ancestors started a very dangerous gunpowder business in 1802, and my great-grandfather and his father were both killed in gunpowder explosions."
— **Pete du Pont.**

While Petchy and Fitz were busy cracking the puzzle of Klovian society, Jill and Teena have been busy gathering the weapons and ammunition and are preparing to test them on Nekomata. We rejoin them during the test of the Riesen-Pistole BMG.

"Well, well, this is a fine mess, huh?" Teena surveyed the divot in the side of the tree with impenitent ire. She bit her lip while poking her fingers into the still smoldering cavity.

I watched her in stunned silence, my ears still ringing. The putrescent reek of the explosive hung in the air like a fetid, purple cloud. Worse, with the open breech weapon, effluence had coated everything nearby. I struggled not to retch at the stench.

We'd dodged a disaster on this one. Teena had been confident in the work of her engineers. She'd wanted to take the weapon straight into battle. She owes G.I. Jill an apology, though contrition is not in the offing just now.

We'd argued over the test. Teena had wanted to build a hunter's blind high in a tree and stake bait nearby. Then, once set, just wait for that early rising T-Rex to come to the breakfast smorgasbord. "Why waste a precious round on testing?" she had argued, "Kill the damn monstrosity and have done with it!"

I had quoted my first rule of engineering; Never trust an Engineer! Engineers solve problems. If there are no problems handily available, they will create their own.

"What, are you crazy?" she had asked. She held a somewhat higher opinion of Engineers than I.

I spoke softly, not rising to her provocation. "That is a possibility I have not ruled out. But let me break it down Barney style for you. That explosive is untested on this world. All the computer models in the universe are just toys. Until calibrated against real data, they are worthless. You can't trust a computer model until it is proven to make reliable predictions."

"This is a controlled experiment," I insisted, "and I'm damned sure going to be in control of it. That confounded weapon's dangerous!" Only I didn't say confounded; I was getting emotional again.

One of her great-grandchildren had given his life, it appears, to bring us those shells. However, we didn't find his remains, just a pouch of ammunition sitting in the open near the Portal location. No other sign of human visitation. Loath to waste one on a 'worthless' test, Teena chaffed to test against a live target. She wanted vengeance.

We'd had a dozen .50 Cal HEIAP rounds, plus the one that had arrived in the chamber of the BMG itself. Unlucky Thirteen! Now, a dozen HEIAP rounds remained, and no WTF BMG! Useless!

Exploding shells, experimental explosives, and experimental propellants! It's not an experiment if you know it is going to work. But, despite the Engineer's assurances, this is definitely an experiment. My hard-nosed obstinance appears justified, given our test results.

It appears the experimental explosive explodes rather too explosively. The BMG had performed a spectacular RUD on the first firing. Nevertheless, it works, excess enthusiasm notwithstanding.

I'd insisted, over Teena's objections, on letting the unfortunate tree hold the weapon. Teena has the benefit of lifetimes of experience, yet I grok weapons better than she. My intuition was vindicated.

Imagine the poor drub who had held that beast while firing it. Could even Center's physicians reassemble such an unfortunate? Doubtful, I'd wager.

Nevertheless, we still had the Magnum BFR and two dozen rounds plus the five in the BFR cylinder. Heavy tungsten slugs — heavier and harder than lead — not exploding HEIAP rounds. Consequently, I trust them somewhat. Although Teena was now converted to my own hyper-cautionary outlook.

Our original test rig is now unusable, demolished in the explosion. Rather than attempt to salvage it and inflict further damage on the poor tree, I selected another. Far away from the stink of the first one, I might add. That explosive smells awful! There were plenty of trees to pick from. I assembled a bracket to hold the BFR from the scraps and a few sticks and attached my cord for remote firing.

I aligned the BFR with the target, stepped behind another adjacent tree, and tugged the cord. The ear-splitting report resounded, though not as loud as the HEIAP shell detonation. The unbelievable stench made my eyes water and my stomach retch anew. I don't know what is in that explosive, but it is as smelly as it is potent.

The block of wood I had set as a target became a pile of toothpicks, the BFR still smoking. The shell-casing jammed the cylinder. The **Big Frackin Revolver** held together for the test. It appears obvious the specialty propellant unleashed far more explosive energy than the BFR designers anticipated.

I examined the gun, the test rig that held it, and the tree. All survived their ordeal without obvious damage.

The wooden target hadn't. These shells aren't explosive, yet one could hardly tell it. The violence rendered to the target appeared little less than an explosive shell.

The BFR, in theory, lacks the stopping power of the BMG with HEIAP rounds. However, it should be quite capable of killing a Deinonychus. If we'd had the BFR that day....

What effect it might have on a T-Rex, I'm uncertain. I decided I had given the BFR short shrift when I panned it as little more than a pinprick to a ten-ton monster. Given the heavy tungsten projectile and the overzealous propellant, I must reconsider.

Studying the wooden target, I concluded a precise shot might drop even the most enormous monster. It all depends on precision, with perhaps a bit of luck. A clean headshot or one straight to the heart ought to execute any enraged beast.

Despite the test results, I fear another RUD, a *Rapid Unscheduled Disassembly* for the acronym challenged. How often will the weapon fire such shells before it disassembles itself as the BMG had done?

〰〰〰

Relieved at possessing a working weapon, Teena's ire softened. The conundrum now becomes how best to wield it. Any way you dice it, the shooter must risk facing a horrific predator.

Teena had proposed a hunter's treestand high in a towering tree, too lofty for the predators — the idea being to set bait and camp high in the tree awaiting clientèle.

The downside is that you can't control what sort of pest will come for the bait, or when. Such a high encampment promises intense discomfort with the added spice of real danger. There are other nighttime predators too, although I'm certain none could be as dangerous as T-Rex, Deinonychus, and Velociraptors.

Pterodactyls aren't nocturnal, although they're just as carnivorous and predatory. They prefer eating rodents, rabbits, and fish and don't bother humans. I'm not sanguine that humans high in a tree would receive the same courtesy. They might consider such as home delivery, a theory I'm not eager to test.

(*"Ptero" means winged, and "dactyl" refers to a foot of poetry. They are not flying reptiles but wing-footed poets like Mercury, teller of stories and messenger of the gods. That is how science and fantasy mingle, paradactylically speaking.*)

And then the snakes. Ugh! Arboreal hunting's not on my bucket list. Besides, if motivated, a T-Rex can knock down any tree a hunter might deem a suitable perch. If you surmise I'm not enthralled with the idea, you're getting warm.

Teena and I debated the possibilities and permutations. The debate had begun long before retrieving the weapons. Our strategizing began in earnest during the return trip. We needed to consult with Stapleya and Wisceya. We four are the only people on the planet with the requisite marksmanship skills.

There will soon be a cadre of trained shootists, no doubt. Stapleya will send her best soldiers to Center for proper training. In time, plentiful ammunition and weapons will find their way to the fur-people. The engineers will eventually tame the volatile explosive. We're still in the early experimental phase of this project. The Nekomata will be killing dinosaurs for decades.

Still, we'd hope to dispatch a few of the worst offenders sooner rather than later. I just hope the BFR doesn't explode before exhausting our meager supply of ammunition.

We plotted and planned all during the return trip to Castle Stapleya. I kept the BFR loaded and handy against encountering another predator. The road remained clear; we made excellent time.

∧∧∧

Six days passed without further encounters of the beastie kind. Curfew approached as Castle Stapleya neared. We met four support runners led by Wisceya, bearing fresh packs of GoJuice and water about ten miles out. Their timing was perfection, as our supplies had expired less than a mile earlier. We could have run the final leg without fresh supplies at the cost of becoming spent and dehydrated. Better to have plentiful supplies.

The climate on 'Planet Oz' is brutal and unforgiving. Perspiration is an under-appreciated physiological process. Death by dehydration is a real prospect. Few on Earth have a clue, trust me.

Of course, word of our adventures had preceded us, and the girls wanted to see my still horrific scar. They marveled at my luck in surviving such a close encounter and chatted at us on the final leg. They brought us current on the news and gossip during the weeks we were away. They told us someone was waiting for our arrival but shook their heads when asked about the visitor. "It's a surprise," said Wisceya. She refused to say more and appeared to be in a hurry, so we focused on the miles ahead.

After we had been running a while, one of the girls pulled out a small lepatata and blasted away. We were much too far out for such a small lepatata to be heard at the Castle. I could hear a distant, much larger lepatata repeat the message. These people had a fine-tuned system of message relays.

One mile or so from the Castle, on each major road, sits a stone watch-house or pharos, as the locals call them. They remind me of tollhouses one sometimes sees on Earth, minus the barricades. They are not here to block or tax travelers. These structures serve to greet, or announce, travelers and count traffic. A gigantic stationary lepatata mounted on the roof serves for heralding.

As we approached the pharos, the horn heralded our arrival, much like that first day. Abandoning her instrument, the bugler then fell in behind us, carrying a small pack of her own. Sturdy as the stone structure appeared, spending the night therein is risky. Velociraptor safe, probable, Deinonychus proof, doubtful. T-Rex? Don't ask. She had been waiting to announce our arrival and worried because we were so late. We were pushing the Deadline.

Capitalization of that word Deadline is appropriate, I later learned. We quickened our pace.

A pair of day-walking Deinonychus are in the area, we're told. Spotted twice in the last three days, the locals are in stark terror of an encounter. I can sympathize. Good thing I didn't know; I might have wintered at the previous abode.

I patted the BFR in my belt.

We spotted Castle Stapleya's mighty front door and a furry crowd inside, holding it open. They wanted to close that door. We sensed their air of compelling urgency. They motioned us to hurry, so we gave it our best sprint the last several hundred yards. We approached the immense front door on a dead run, darting inside without slowing down. The gigantic door slammed shut with a tremendous thud. Night bars slammed home as they secured the door, making it fast against the night.

We listened for sounds from outside. Minutes passed sans ominous exterior noises, and we began to relax. Some minutes later, a lepatata high in the Castle sounded. Deinonychus spotted nearby! We had been minutes or less from a deadly encounter.

I almost swooned when I realized how fine we had cut it. Curfew comes earlier every week, or so it appears. As the wave of nausea and fear passed, I patted the BFR. Then with a start, I recognized opportunity's song. I bounded for the observation perch high in the castle.

Owing to flying predators, among other dangers, Nekomata castles do not have garden roofs. Further, the roof serves for catching rainwater, with rooftop cisterns for storage. This stone-age culture understands basic plumbing and sanitation. They catch the rainfall and channel it into the cisterns. An elaborate system of gravity-fed plumbing does the rest. I wondered if that was Teena's influence. Had she, or her people, seeded them with plumbing know-how? Had the stone-age fur-people created the elaborate system on their own? Or had the Asherans given them inspiration? Maybe not, as these castles appear much older than even Teena, and the plumbing looks designed in.

I wonder who had built them....

Although rooftop observation is problematical, more suitable high windows are just below the roof. Watchers encamp therein to track the big predators in morning and evening. As I interpreted the bugler's riff, a Deinonychus was visible from the east window. I wondered if it were close enough for a handgun to be meaningful. I decided to find out.

The east observation window is higher and safer than any hunter's blind. If only the Deinonychus will come close enough to the castle.

I burst into the bedroom, which doubles as the east observatory. One of the fur-people sat at the window focused on the forest. I didn't remember her name, but that did not matter. We were sisters in the hunt.

I came up to her and whispered: "Where is it?" She pointed. I looked out into the gathering gloom. I didn't see it. We watched together. "There," she said, pointing. The beast was much too far away for a handgun, even with my natural skills.

We watched it for several minutes. Teena, Stapleya, and several others crowded in behind us. Perhaps five minutes more elapsed, the beast came no closer.

About that time, Lolita came in with a big platter of food. She had intended to feed us since we showed no signs of abandoning the hunt for a proper meal. I saw the meat and hatched another idea.

Grabbing a couple of steaming ham-hocks, I tossed them out the window. "Hey!" shouted Lolita, then she stopped herself as she realized what I intended.

The Deinonychus we had been watching sniffed the air. Turning and sniffing, it let out a bellow, a call to its mate. The second Deinonychus answered nearby, closer yet unseen. The pair began moving toward the bait I had dropped.

I grabbed more of the meat and threw it into the kill zone. As they approached, I turned and looked at my friends. "Firing this indoors is bad. It is going to be loud in here, loud enough to damage hearing. Give me that piece of parchment and go in the other room."

Lolita handed me a small piece of parchment that had been on the food tray, a quizzical expression on her face. I tore it, chewed it, and stuffed my ears. Makeshift earplugs, how had we overlooked earplugs? We had focused on the weapons themselves and overlooked the most fundamental of accessories. Idiots! All of us, but particularly me, a firearms expert! Some expert.

I ordered them out of the room and closed the door.

As I completed preparations, the predators entered my kill zone. Propping myself against the stone wall, I braced against the recoil. Body and hand firm, I drew down on the vicious predators below. Could I get them both? Doubtful.

I knew the report would be insane. My makeshift earplugs were all but worthless. My ears rang for days afterward.

Note to self; Get these folks some proper ear protection.

My first shot was a perfect headshot, and the beast dropped. That felt good! Before I could fire again, the mate bolted. My second shot hit it in the side, I think, though it kept going. My third shot may have missed, although I told myself I had grazed it. By then, it was lost, out of range. Further fire would have been pointless.

I speculated the wounded beast might soon die. Nighttime predators would remove all traces by morning, but the fur-people would search anyway. Predators appeared, sniffing at the carcass, quarreling over first dibs.

Stapleya, Lolita, Teena, and the rest came back into the room. We took turns at the window, watching the ghastly scene below. At first, there had been only small creatures, rats, and such. Then, a giant snake appeared and grabbed a rat as it was eating the Deinonychus. A noise from the brush and they all scattered. Moments later, a flock of Velociraptors descended on the scene. Soon there was nothing left but a few bones. The bones, too, were gone by morning.

Nightlife on Nekomata, not exactly a tea party.

I massaged my arm and shoulder as we watched nature, *'red in tooth and claw'* at work below. The BFR has one hell of a kick. My ears were still ringing, my head spinning, and I was nauseous from the stench of the explosive propellant. I sat there, trying not to puke while luxuriating in the afterglow. It felt awesome having dispatched one more hell-beast. Perhaps two. There will be celebration at dinner tonight.

Although I must freshen beforehand, my reek might cause my friends to lose their appetites. I had just completed a 35-mile run with all that entails—running on an insanely hot and fetid world, all the while consuming vast quantities of pungent GoJuice. That is natural enough and benignly unbearable. Then we add the stench from firing the Big Fracker. The malodorous explosive ejecta infused my hair and body with a corpselike rotting stench. The smell would make a maggot retch. This fragrant lotus blossom needs a bath!

Presently I sensed a presence, I tensed. Perhaps I sensed pheromones or some subtle sound. Then a clear, familiar sound pricked my ears. A soft, deep and masculine cough belied a presence other than fur-people. I remembered Wisceya had hinted at a visitor to Castle Stapleya. Old insecurities aroused as I turned to face the visitor. The fur-people parted, opening space between myself and the new arrival.

Alex stood before me. My boss. The head *Man in Black*.
Is here!
And I am out of uniform!
O! M! G!

Mentor

The Universe lives by the quantum flow. An endless sea of energy, matter, and sentience coalesce from the etheric void. Matter's form means little; sentience derives not from matter.

A brain is a receiver for the quantum flow. Flesh matters not. The winner of any contest is the strongest mind, the strongest conductor of the quantum flow.

The question then becomes, can you summon power from the Universe at will? Only the strength of will, quality and purity of mind matters.

Mentor is a multi-conscious intelligence. A melding of individual entities into a single far-flung consciousness.

A super-sentience, born of the quantum flow. All minds touch Mentor. Mentor touches every mind.

Mentor is the ultimate galaxy-scale Swarm Intelligence. The living intelligence of the Galaxy itself.

Mentor is integrating the latest sighting of Gharlane into a vision of the cosmic all. Gharlane is not of this universe, but an inimical invader.

Mentor seeks to find and kill the invader. He has been molding a precision-crafted weapon to that end for centuries. The weapon nears readiness.

Potiphar Breen sits motionless in his office chair. His head tilts and drool slimes his chin. The hour is late, and the staff have gone home. He is quite alone. There is, of course, a possibility someone is watching. The **V**iew **of T**he **E**mpire records his every move, his every utterance. Every snort and gurgle, every wheeze and whistle. Every Tourette's-like syllable, every breaking of wind. Every disgusting noise he emits, awake or sleeping. High-resolution cameras record the drool on his chin as he sputters and gurgles.

Potty knows this.

Breen knows he is not watched now, although it would make no difference if he were. Perhaps a citizen may review the recording. It is unlikely anyone will bother. Most look away.

That's the point.

Appearances suggest Breen has fallen asleep in his chair failing to notice the hour. Sleeping in his office is not rare. His naps are frequent and often inappropriate. The histrionic sound effects and stomach-wrenching visuals are the constant subjects of derision.

Profane and derogatory commentary adorns his public social, as those few who do take notice express their disgust. Somehow, despite near-universal revulsion, he holds his office against all comers. He wins every election by a comfortable margin, a fact that drives his critics to vociferous indignation.

Potty takes naps.

Appearances are deceptive—Breen is not asleep. He does not sleep. The fractals adorning his office attest to wakefulness.

Breen is quite busy.

Kinetic art on an otherwise inactive screen. The display spins and gyrates, a psionic mirror of intense activity behind closed eyes.

If VoTE watchers note the frenetic display, they might suspect strangeness afoot. Breen does not have VoTE watchers.

Public figures' fans follow their every moment. Breen has approximately zero fans. When someone watches, Potty knows.

Watchers soon discover someone more interesting, someone less revolting to watch.

The Security Chief possesses his own 'Mystic Eccentricities.' Unlike the Chief Executive, his psychic experiences occur unnoticed.

She pauses in dramatic fashion and gazes toward the infinite with the look of eagles.

Potty takes naps.

She consults her intuition.

Potty takes naps.

She would laugh at the idea of a connection. She does not imagine herself as a puppet of an alien intelligence, nor does she wonder at the ease with which she wins every election.

Potty takes naps.

When she needs things done that a Chief Executive may not do, she consults her intuition.

She trusts intuition, not lying eyes and ears. She does not know the Breen others see. She sees him with different senses than those of her followers.

Had his VoTE audience — minuscule to nonexistent though it appears to be — deduced his actions, he would face charges of treason.

Had anyone believed it! Few believe in things psychic; fewer believe Potty Breen intelligent enough for treason.

Both camps are misguided.

That's precisely the point.

Riding an insubstantial energy vortex to another world is an improbable mode of travel. One may as well attempt to ride the swirling winds of a great-plains twister.

The Chief Executive exudes undaunted confidence. Public service and mandatory surveillance long ago dispelled her sense of modesty. Kassa was accustomed to public scrutiny in even the most intimate moments.

That no one watched made it all the more surreal. Skyclad, she approached the Portal with a smooth gracefulness, unfazed by her state or that of those she was to travel with; she trusts her intuition.

Materializing on an alien world shook her equanimity and left her feeling unsteady. The transition itself gave her a slight nausea. As she collected herself, she pondered that for the first time in years, she was not under observation. As far as the **V**iew **of T**he **E**mpire watching public saw, she was asleep in bed. There will not be a video for release. She was genuinely private.

The deception troubled her, though she was no stranger to subterfuge. She supports surveillance. Public employees keeping secrets is dangerous. It leads to malfeasance and corruption. If not for surveillance, public service would spawn a class of elite, above-the-law power brokers selling favors to the highest bidder. She supports the mandate while breaking it.

At various times throughout her career, she had used deception to evade surveillance. She has employed a body double before. She does so not from malicious intent but in pursuit of her official duties. When she practices subterfuge, it is an honest and responsible artifice. Her deceptions stem from the highest of intentions. She trusts her intuition.

Breen accosted the big alien. "May we talk, sir?" With a nod, Fitz stepped into the unoccupied office with the Security Chief.

They stayed inside for half an hour. Then, as though nothing transpired, Fitz continued to his intended meeting. Whatever his discussion with Breen, it was forgotten.

He crossed the encampment to the temporary structure. Inside, Petchy was briefing Kassa on Gharlane.

Petchy asked, "Where have you been?" Fitz stared at him blankly. "What do you mean?"

Petchy said, "I expected you a half-hour ago. Did you get lost?"

Fitz shrugged. "I came straight here. Ask the Security Chief, I passed him in the hall outside the mess tent, and we spoke briefly."

"What did Breen want?"

"Nothing. A brief exchange of pleasantries. I think Breen merely wanted to remind me that he was here to protect the Chief Executive. Nothing important."

Petchy pushed again. "But what did he ask?"

Fitz looked puzzled. Confused. He found the question painful. Expressions wrestled on his face; then, he shrugged. "Nothing, I told you. He wanted to remind me he was here."

Kassa watched the exchange with interest. She placed her hand on each man's arm and commented, "Potty has that effect on people sometimes. Ignore it. I trust him."

Somewhat mollified, Petchy dropped the matter, though he remained suspicious. Breen is an odd one. He never appears to really DO anything, yet he seems to be everywhere. His fingers are in every pie. Petchy worried that there was more to Breen than meets the eye. He knew not how right he was.

Cruiser of the Void

"I've seen things you people wouldn't believe. Attack ships on fire off the shoulder of Orion. I watched C-beams glitter in the dark near the Tannhauser gate. All those moments will be lost in time... like tears in rain..."
— **Death soliloquy of Roy Batty, Logan's Run**

The massive ship stands quiescent near space-dock, isolated and alone. Petchy and Fitz had convinced the Chief Executive of the threat. When the Captain reported the incursion, Chief Executive Kassa had ordered an immediate quarantine. The Z7M7-Z sits parked a safe distance from the deep space station, isolating the ship and her people. Thanks to the Chief Executive's swift action, the threat is contained. She granted Petchy and Fitz permission to lead an investigatory team. Portal transport not an option, a shuttle carried Fitz and Petchy plus a team of specialists. Space travel was a novel experience for both. Despite having visited many planets, neither had been in space. Space travel — Fitz loved it!

Technology develops non-linearly in that it does not progress uniformly across human civilizations. Technological progress does not march in lockstep. The Klovians are ahead of the Asherans in some areas of technology, particularly space-travel. Petchy's people had developed space travel but made little use of it owing to the ease of Portal travel. With the decimation of Ashera, they no longer possessed the necessary infrastructure. The Klovians had not discovered Portals, thus pursued space-travel technology. The Asherans mastered quantum mechanics instead. Their understanding of quantum science is key to mastery of the Portals.

Ensconced in the Captain's briefing room, Petchy stared in silence. The clip replayed for perhaps the tenth time. Or was it more like the one hundred and tenth? The entity that had taken control of the Z7M7-Z has to be Gharlane. No other explanation sufficed. The raw power on display sent terror deep into his soul. Petch had long believed their foe was powerful. Not just powerful, this was supernatural.

As the Captain and his crew stood powerless, they had collected volumes of data on the incursion. Video, audio, sensor scans including the complete electromagnetic spectrum. Now quarantined, the impact of the incursion is the subject of intense analysis.

It is unlikely the entity would have allowed the recordings if there was anything to learn. Nothing revealed useful data beyond the obvious surface events.

That is nothing, that is, except one sensor, one instrument. A general-purpose environmental monitoring instrument had given Petchy pause. Part of the ship's ordinary instrumentation, the instrument records ambient environmental data. It tracks everything it is possible to measure, a virtual smorgasbord of data. A continuous recording of environmental parameters — humidity, temperature, CO_2 levels, radiation EM to ionizing, everything worth monitoring.

The interesting factors were none of these. Nothing ordinary was in any sense useful. The data that caught Petchy's attention was the most uninteresting possible. It originated in one odd sensor. Dubbed the Psionic Egg, the sensor detects mental energy, or so some claim. Not everyone agrees. Some claim it monitors the space-time continuum itself.

Some say it taps into the etheric flow of the cosmos.

Still others claim it is reflecting random motions of atoms, nothing more. Disparaged as a pseudoscientific gimmick, it's called by unflattering names of varying disrespect. Often called disdainful names ranging from 'Mood Detector' to 'Galactic Lens,' it receives little respect.

The Egg is a scientific curiosity owing to no one knowing quite what it detects or how it works. Known for decades, it is a popular toy among scientists and technologists. It became a popular toy by defying the laws of physics. And yet, it finds practical use.

The heart of the Egg is a tiny quantum tunneling device useful in a variety of technological ways. Some devices based on it take the form of executive desk toys and jewelry. Eggs make their way into all types of instruments, including common mobiles. Egg-driven fractals often adorn idle displays.

Data from the Egg is nothing more than a stream of random numbers in which the randomness varies. Randomness in a number stream, the lack of predictability, is a property called entropy. The more difficult to predict, the higher the entropy, a much sought-after commodity. High-quality random numbers, having a high degree of entropy, are useful technological properties. Despite the irreverence afforded the Egg, it fills a useful niche. Countless applications where high-quality random numbers are desirable, make use of the egg.

Factors not well understood affect the degree of entropy. Over longer timespans, the entropy is excellent. Over shorter periods nearby mental activity, plus factors unknown, distort the output.

The Egg's data often seeds displays of meaningless although mesmerizing fractals. Fascinating, as the plotted images appear to reflect the thoughts of nearby humans. The mental effort of a player deciding which game piece to move or which card to discard affects the display.

The effect had proven a factor in contests of mental skill. Although not quite mind reading, the patterns appeared to yield an advantage to some.

Psionic Egg driven displays were long ago banned wherever serious gamers play. Not because they enable cheating. That hypothesis remains unproven. The mere appearance of possible influence is enough. The mere idea that a display might yield a window into another's mentality was enough.

The general-purpose instrument of Petchy's attention contains a Psionic Egg. It is used as a convenient source of entropy, as is the usual case. Yet the instrument also records the data stream itself, the same as any other data. This is what caught Petchy's attention. The recording mirrored the activity of the intruder.

The Egg had gone ballistic as the entity interacted with the ship's AI. The activity stayed at unprecedented levels throughout the entity's presence, save one brief period.

The activity dropped to the background level for a period. Then just as inexplicably returned to the previous off-the-chart activity level. Petchy had been reviewing the entity's activities during this period of silence. The interaction with the AI had continued unabated, during the period. The entity had continued sitting, motionless to all appearances. Petchy examined the data and decided that the entity had departed, visual indications aside.

Even though no visible Portal was evident, Petchy soon determined otherwise. Data from the visible and electromagnetic spectrum confirmed the presence of a Portal. Not just once, a Portal had appeared a total of four times during the incursion. It popped into existence and vanished a brief instant later. The interval of existence had been quite brief, unnoticed before Petchy investigated.

The Portal appeared when the invader first appeared and repeated when he departed. The same sign repeated at the beginning and end of the Egg's quiet period. Each time, the Portal existed for much less than a second.

Petchy surmised that the invader exerted on-demand control over Portal formation. The hypothesis unsettled him — his understanding of Portal science denied any such possibility.

Meanwhile, Fitz was pursuing his own mission. The quintessential computer jockey, Fitz was in his element, or should have been. Accustomed to being the expert others called upon, he was nursing an inferiority complex. In this environment, he was the neophyte, a position he found ignominious. His ego was taking a bruising as he fought to engage the project.

Fitz knows computers.

He knows every variant of Unix, whether Linux, BSD or MacOS. He knows specialty variants such as the security-focused editions of Tails and Kali. He knows them inside and out, every major version, the features that make each unique and useful. He knows encrypted file systems and encrypted communications. He knows Elliptical Curves and Asymmetric Encryption algorithms. He knows machine language and assembly language programming.

Fitz even knows Windows.

Klovian computers do not use Windows or Linux. The ship does not use computers. Not the cumbersome machines Fitz calls computers. Processors, CPUs, Storage, all notably absent. Or well hidden.

Fitz never heard of swarm intelligence.

Consider the lowly honeybee. Each individual bee possesses limited brains. Yet when ten thousand bees swarm, they form a coordinated intelligence without a coordinator. The same swarming behavior occurs in ants, termites, fish, and birds. The group's ability to make optimal decisions exceeds that of the individuals involved manyfold.

Computers may operate in clusters, but a cluster is not a swarm. A cluster of computers may cooperate on a task. A render farm will divide and share a complex job across a massive cluster. A render farm does not spontaneously develop new complex behaviors. A swarm exhibits self-organizing collective behavior exceeding the individual's programming.

Groups of humans cooperate on a task, yet they do not swarm. Nature did not provide the natural tools for swarming. A jury is an example of humans cooperating on a task. A jury often mirrors the decision-making of a single dominant individual. A leader who dominates the jury makes the actual decision, and the group agrees.

The other eleven jurors endorse the individual's decision, sharing the responsibility. How often do we hear of 'yes men' who exist to endorse the leader's decision? This has the effect of diffusing the responsibility. It does not improve the decision-making ability of the group. Shared responsibility shields the decision-maker from the effects of bad decisions. It does not lead to better decisions, as the 'yes men' contribute little or nothing to the decision.

The decision-making ability of a jury is no better than the single dominant individual. In human society, leaders make decisions. A jury is a cluster of people, not a swarm. The same dynamic applies to most human endeavors. Human ventures tend to succeed or fail based on the charisma of a dominant leader.

Swarms do not have a leader. Each member of a swarm has limited intelligence and influence. Each member applies its limited intelligence cued by the behavior of its neighbors. Without a single guiding intelligence, complex behavior emerges that far exceeds the individual capability.

Fitz, though familiar with cluster computing, lacked understanding of swarm computing. His extensive knowledge of computing doesn't even qualify him as an apprentice aboard the Z7M7-Z.

His virgin-apprenticeship status chaffed, the challenge burned. Working beside the Klovian experts, he was pawing through the system, studying the architecture. He was primed for new principles and concepts.

Occasionally something odd happened. When facing a challenge, Fitz found himself "zoning out." He would lose track of time for minutes or in some cases hours at a time. An observer might think him asleep. He was not aware of falling asleep. He would insist he was working hard.

Slow progress made him question the value of his contribution. Natural perseverance led him to continue. He found himself lapsing into a meditative state. Meditation was helpful in his attempts to unravel the mysteries of Klovian technology.

He began to progress. Each time he refocused his attention, his understanding had grown. Each hurdle surmounted empowered him for the next.

Looking over his host's shoulders, he fumbled his way toward understanding. He asked questions of his companions; he talked to the AI itself. Conversing with the AI itself was a surprisingly productive approach. He fought to remain calm and focused against the tsunami of information.

He took naps.

Knowledge is additive. Each new fact hangs from the tenterhooks of existing knowledge. Each greater concept hangs from the protruding nubs of lesser concepts. The gap between concepts understood and ideas newly learned began to narrow. Menial tasks opened pathways to extending the metaphorical tenterhooks of his knowledge.

He was learning as his Klovian friends worked to uncover damage the invader had inflicted on the AI. The damage was subtle and would have gone unnoticed but for Petchy and Fitz's warnings. It remained unclear what the purpose might have been. Subtle changes in the AI structure were present and would have profound effects. Worse, it was designed to propagate from the ship to any other system it encountered.

They reinforced the quarantine.

It took time, but Fitz reached what he considered the 'bits is bits' enlightenment phase. He finally grokked the concept underlying the Klovian AI computers. There is nothing he would call 'ship's computer' in a traditional sense. There is no cluster of computers. There is no such thing as a server room or a computer in that sense.

That was a difficult mental hurdle, Fitz expected racks of computer hardware. Instead, the ship itself is *alive* with computing elements. He grasped how many millions of individual elements comprised the ship's intelligence swarm. He began to understand the difference between a swarm and a cluster, a mob and a jury. He understood how bees swarm.

Despite profound differences, he found the basic principles consistent with his experience. He began to hang new concepts on the solid framework of computer science he knew so well. Fitz began to gain confidence and develop expertise.

He almost appeared to tap into a cosmic reservoir of knowledge.

Alex

Meanwhile back on Nekomata, Jill is digesting the revelation that her staid, uptight, button-down boss Alex is an Asheran.

I realize now I should have been suspicious. Petch and Teena strolled into the heart of a super-secret government organization. Invited right in, based on their manufactured identity as noted academicians? No vetting, no deep background checks? The MiB just accepted them and followed their every suggestion?

Hindsight; What a concept!

Teena and Petch had sold it well; I never for a second questioned it.

Now who's the fool?

I believe Petchy played it a little too close to his own vest. If I accept what I'm told, Alex did not know Fitz was Petch's protege. No more than Fitz knew that Alex, the head of the MiB organization himself, well knew Petchy. All his anguished speculations over fifth and sixth columns and alien influences. And futile attempts to reach Petchy's people. Sigh....

When he wheeled Fitz out of the hospital in chains, Alex had been unaware of Fitz's mission. Fitz played dumb, and Alex didn't catch on until months later.

A classic case of the left hand's cluelessness of the right hand's occupation. It appears the first real awareness Alex gleaned of the operation came when he finally, belatedly read Fitz's book.

Alex put two and two together and arrived at six for a time. Although by the time that poor Shameya's corpse appeared in our morgue, he was on the right track. Of course, he knew where she was from but couldn't reveal he knew it. Not and maintain his secret identity. By then, he had connected Fitz's story to Petchy and Teena. He knew or thought he knew the story, although he could not reach Petchy for confirmation. Alex decided to recruit Fitz, though he could not divulge the larger reality.

Petchy appeared, read Alex into the program, and Fitz joined the MiB. Even after finding Petchy and Teena in MiB HQ, Fitz never suspected Alex was in on the joke. Fitz did not trust Alex and might not have believed it anyway.

I guess I'm not the only sucker for tall tales.

"Agent S-Smith," he spoke with hesitation, stuttering. I never saw Alex flustered before.

Teena winced in sympathy at his awkward use of my professional handle. We had discussed how I hate 'Agent Smith.' It hit me, prima facie, she is his superior; Hell, she might be his great great grandmother.

We had stared at each other for seconds, our mutual discomfort palpable. Neither of us should find deshabille remarkable now, yet here we were. Our relationship had always been professional, with proper MiB attire. Always formal; commanding officer to agent.

This is deuced awkward!

Declining his honorific in response, fighting to control my hands, I gulped and said, "Hello Alex."

The spell dissolved. A slight wince and his wonted cocky smile beamed forth. The Alex I have worked with for much of a decade returned.

We were once again professional MiB — albeit minus the traditional black.

"Jill, Dr. Mathes, much has happened in your absence. Dr. Shepherd believes he has found a way to approach Gharlane. We need to Port right away."

Teena said, "Drop the vernacular please, we're not on the clock here. No one here cares about secret identities."

Alex nodded acknowledgment. "You're right. Habit. But we still need to go right away."

Teena said, "We can't just run out the door and Port. The Portal is miles away, and even if it were open now, which it's not, we'd never survive."

Alex shrugged. "I had hoped you two would arrive early enough to travel today, though I suppose not. Tomorrow, first light. We've places to be, people to see."

Teena said, "We need a bath after the day we've had. Jill and I had hoped to put the giant soaker in the master bedroom to good use. Stapleya, Wisceya, Jill, and I are doing so. Plenty of room for you to join if you like, as I'm sure you know. You can brief us while we all relax."

Terror flickered across Alex's face. Was sharing a tub with four women a scary prospect? Or was it just sharing a tub with me that unnerved him?

I admitted a momentary disquietude myself. I'm in no more hurry to share a naked soak with Alex than he with me. Unpleasant visions played in my mind as deep-buried anxieties pushed to the surface. I pushed back, told myself that though a male, he's a gentleman. I resolved to place Stapleya between us anyway.

In all honesty, I don't fear Alex or anyone. I'm not Fitz, but I am a warrior. I know how to handle a threat. My general trepidation for males aside, I trust Alex. I'm not some nervous virgin. Old wounds.... Sigh....

Teena picked up on Alex's fear and took it in a direction I'd not considered. Did my personal apprehensions lead my thoughts astray?

Am I so narcissistic?

"Alex," she said, "you can say anything in front of Stapleya that you would say to me. Or Wisceya. They're family and quite aware of Gharlane. They understand the threat he presents. They worked in Headquarters with us for months, and on Center, too. They understand the score and may well have valuable input." His discomfort was obvious, though he acquiesced.

I felt embarrassed for thinking it was about me. *Get a grip, Jill;* the damned sprite chided; *not everything is about you.*

Minutes later, we cocooned ourselves in the giant tub. Gentle horseplay ensued between Teena and Wisceya. As I watched them, I realized with a slight double-take how Teena had changed. Having spent the last few weeks in her constant company, her transformation had snuck up on me. Indeed, vitelotte, GoJuice, Journey Cake, and unrelenting, inhuman exercise had done wonders.

Teena appeared almost an ingenue beside Stapleya and me. An unknowing observer would place the four of us close in years, Teena and Wisceya vying for youngest.

I take that back, partly.

Her mammary endowment belies the youth her face proclaims. She appears as Fitz had first described her. Pulchritudinous in her buxom curvaceousness and unkempt flaming mane. Raw, unfettered, almost supernatural sexuality.

I wondered, how could that be?

She'd been so different when we met a few months earlier, so aged and decrepit. Her metamorphosis is startling. She had been so near death then; it is difficult to believe she's the same person. Yet even she was skeptical of full recovery. Her appearance was modified, not her natural image, she'd explained. Her enhanced attributes created via genetic manipulation and engineered for seduction. They'd fine-tuned her pheromones to lobotomize the males they waft past. They had weaponized her body.

Her accentuated natural attributes endowed tremendous powers of persuasion and manipulation — Asheran genetic technologies. I need to learn more about these things.

Teena must have lived centuries, maybe a millennium; she implied that even she was unsure. Stapleya must be quite along in years, yet she appears little, if any, older than her youngest daughter. How old is Alex? I must ask.

Alex watched the horseplay in silence, a subtle smile haunting his face. Whatever fear had attempted to surface earlier is now absent. He was careful not to brush against me in the water. I hoped he didn't, tried not to dwell on it. I'm coming around, but I'm just not the hedonist Teena and the Nekomata are.

After a few minutes of horseplay, he put his arms around the Nekomata women, and they snuggled against him. I think Wisceya was fishing for a little brother for her son. I saw Alex push her hands away a couple of times; she was indeed distracting. That gal is naturally handsy.

Teena moved closer to me and put her arm around my shoulder as Alex cleared his throat and began to explain.

"A few weeks ago, Petchy received a report of an unmapped Portal. Investigation led to an undiscovered world, one where Gharlane is active."

He must have thought my expression quizzical, as he nodded in my direction. "Yes," he continued, "Fitz and Petchy went to investigate. They have spent the last several weeks on Klovia, an Earth-like, human-populated world. That's where we must go.

"Similar to Earth, although with more advanced technology. They're close to Ashera in general technology yet have never discovered Portals. Instead, they developed spaceflight."

Wisceya had stopped playing tickle-the-pickle underwater. She was now paying rapt attention, sex-play forgotten. She asked, "What is spaceflight?"

I took her hand, "I will explain later, dear. You saw airplanes on Earth. Imagine a plane that flies between planets, much slower than stepping through Portals. Much more difficult too."

Then to Alex, "I assume you mean something more expansive than Low Earth Orbit."

He nodded, "Yes. They don't have FTL travel. Their solar system is a complex one with several habitable planets. They've perfected an EM drive based on microwaves. It renders any destination in the solar system reachable within days. They have a fleet of ships flying between worlds.

"More importantly, they've recently commissioned a new class of ship. They built a massive ship in a hollowed-out asteroid, their first true starship. It carries a huge crew designed to travel to the nearest stars at high, though sub-light speeds. The trips would take decades, maybe centuries. The EM drive makes it possible."

Wisceya whispered in my ear, "What is FTL?" I patted her hand as her mother gave me a wan grin and then shushed her child, whispering, "Later." Despite motherhood, Wisceya is little more than a child herself.

Again, our attention was on Alex. "The first such ship was on its maiden voyage, midway into a three-month shakedown cruise. They were near the edges of their Ort Cloud when Gharlane — or an entity we believe was he — materialized on the ship. One lone being took total control of the entire ship. He killed several of their crew and molested their ship's AI system."

I wondered; how does one molest an AI? I voiced the thought aloud to no one in particular.

Teena tackled my query. "Perhaps molest is not quite the word. We tend to anthropomorphize our machines. It's a computer, not a child. I suspect in this case Alex is suggesting corrupting the programming or inserting malware." She nodded at Alex.

"Yes," he said, picking up her cue, "something like that. That's in line with what we believe happened to the AI Fitz, Teena, and Petchy tackled on Ashera. Although we don't know yet, not definitely, we believe Gharlane did something similar there. In any case, the malfeasance spread throughout all our computers. It propagated across our entire network. We practiced universal connectivity, every computer, everywhere, able to communicate with any other. So the contagion spread like wildfire, corrupting data and ultimately destroying our entire civilization."

I mulled this over for a moment. "Why did it spread so? Didn't the network have security controls? The idea of building a system fundamentally for every human interaction that is incapable of defending itself is insane. I mean, really insane. Of course, this is Fitz's field of expertise, but I know he takes pride in keeping systems secure. Didn't Asherans do as much?"

Stapleya chimed in. "Fitz said no villain could break his encryption. I did not know what he meant, but Fitz and Jessica explained the concept of encryption. It makes me sad to see a world where evil people make such things necessary."

Alex nodded to her and dropped his gaze to the water. He closed his eyes as though gathering his thoughts. After a moment, he raised his eyes, focusing on the far wall near the ceiling. When he spoke, his voice was soft, unlike his usual commanding demeanor.

"Years ago," he began, "I read a story, in National Geographic, I presume, about an African tribe, I don't remember their name. They lived in primitive huts made of animal skins over a frame built of sticks — dirt floors. A skin served as the doorway. When a man left his hut or was sleeping, he placed a stick on the ground in front of the door, blocking the threshold. That stick served as his lock. It was a secure lock because none of his tribemates would cross a doorway blocked by a threshold stick. It was a civilized rule for a civil society."

The four of us stared at him. I stole a glance at Teena, assuming she had heard the story before. But I guess not; he had her rapt attention. He had the Fur girls enthralled too. He had us wondering what a primitive tribesman had to do with computers. Alex is a good storyteller.

"We treated our computer security like that tribesman's door stick. A simple password was secure because no one would enter a system protected by a password. Civilized rules for a civil society. A talisman serving to keep honest people honest."

I could tell explaining this was stressful for Alex. Harsh memories from a terrible time, a time when their whole society died. I know Teena felt stressed when she confessed her life story.

"Common locks are a talisman no different than that tribesman's threshold stick. Ordinary padlocks and door locks are easy to pick, easy to open. Including quite expensive ones. Little deterrent to those willing to discard the societal contract. A talisman for a civilized society. How often have you seen an elaborate lock on a glass door? Who needs a key when the glass is breakable? Locks do not keep bad people out. They remind decent, honorable folks of the boundaries. They define the demarcations. They are no different in principle than the tribesman's threshold stick."

A soft knock interrupted Alex's storytelling. Several Fur girls entered the bath bearing overloaded trays of food and drink. Drink included a native beer often served with evening meal. The celebration echoed the halls, but our soak and meaningful conversation had taken precedence. We had missed the food. Our friends brought trays to us, earning our profound gratitude. Being an intimate of the queen bee has its perks. Low trays set next to the tub, we ate our dinner, lounging in luxurious style.

Teena picked up the narrative. "Our society was once open and relaxed. We had few who would dare violate a civilized code of conduct. People were trusting to a fault. We were rather like some utopian vision of 1950s middle America; only ours was real. If you dropped your wallet on a street corner with money and your ID in it, you would find it returned. Odds were that someone would go to great trouble to find you and return it, and your money would be intact. Though unlikely, if one of questionable character kept the money, they would still return the wallet and ID."

Teena continued, "Our network, our version of the Internet, connected everything. There was almost nothing resembling encryption and little security. Indeed, nothing as robust as the complex asymmetrical encryption processes Fitz brags about. Foolish, in hindsight, I know. We had the mathematicians, the basic theoretical knowledge. We didn't have robust encryption because we didn't think we needed it. We knew the process in theory yet didn't bother. Security was too inconvenient.

"Gharlane's malware tore through our world like wildfire, gutting everything."

Alex resumed his role of storyteller. "Klovia is similar now in various ways. There are some differences, though. For one thing, they have not followed our folly of universal unsecured connectivity.

"Connecting everything to one massive insecure network enables such attacks. Disparate systems only connect when they have a good reason. When Gharlane messed with the ship's AI, it could not communicate. Therefore, it could not spread the contagion. Thanks to Petchy and Fitz, they quarantined the ship before any opportunity to do so arose.

"Another factor is that Gharlane's tactics included methods we encountered on Earth. Focused societal decay. This was the first sign Petchy noticed, even before learning of the ship's encounter. The ship's AI became corrupted by the introduction of malformed data. Gharlane inserted false constructs designed to undermine the system's logical reasoning.

"Bad data is not only effective against Artificial Intelligences. It works against human intelligence too. I don't mean to suggest the computer malware can infest a human brain. Even so, a sort of malware can similarly undermine the human intellectual machinery—seductive ideas that appeal to human nature's baser instincts. Ideas, memes that infiltrate at a visceral level, bypassing logic and intellect. Greed, selfishness, and Utopianism.

"Life is unfair. The universe is unfair. The laws of physics are unjust.

"A reasonable person accepts that fact and deals with it head-on. Instead, an infected mind rails against reality and embraces nonsensical ideas. They push for a type of 'fairness' that does not, indeed, cannot exist in the real world. They demand outcomes, not opportunity. They see themselves as the elite, entitled to enforce their vision of Utopia on the world — even if it means destroying the world to save it. Once it attains a critical mass, this Utopian sickness spreads with alarming rapidity."

Alex paused to grab another sandwich. Teena jumped in. "Earth was the first place we recognized this. We were unprepared. That a free people could be so turned against their own society as to want to tear it down? The idea seemed preposterous! It's one thing to recognize corrupt ideas as influential and dangerous. Quite another to see evil at work on such a scale.

"We're still struggling to find a workable method to fight it. Not certain it is possible. Once a person believes something, no matter how ridiculous, changing their mind is difficult. Evil, selfish memes spread with an ease that is startling. I'm guessing from Alex's comments, Klovia's experiencing something similar."

Alex nodded. "Petchy had seen what was happening on Earth. He has a whole team working to find a way to address the problem. On Klovia he recognized similar signs. Klovia is not as far along the path as Earth, yet similar destructive memes are at work. That this is the work of Gharlane remains unproven, though it appears a likely hypothesis."

As he spoke, the sandwich Alex had been holding disintegrated into a spectacular snackcident. Its contents dumped on him and in the water. A soft "shit!" escaped his lips as he chased the escaping food. Teena passed Alex a towel and helped scoop the bits from the water. He winced at the mess and muttered, "Thanks, Mom."

(*WHAT? Thanks, MOM??? AYFKM? She's his mother?*)

The voice of my inner sprite reverberated inside my head. I froze, mouth open. Stapleya was wide-eyed; Wisceya seemed puzzled. For a moment, neither Alex nor Teena realized what he had said. I suppose it was the relaxed environment, fatigue, and the sudden minor crisis. The alcohol undoubtedly contributed to lowered inhibitions.

Teena started to speak, saw my face, and then the Nekomata. Realization dawned. She fixed Alex with a pointed stare. "Nice move there, son," she said.

Her expression hovered somewhere between laughter and anger. At her words, Alex blanched as realization dawned.

She went on, "I should expect the head of a secretive organization might be better at keeping secrets. A good thing we're among friends. I hope they can keep secrets better than you." She turned to me. "Yes, Alex is my youngest son. I suppose I should leave it at that and not say more...."

Youngest son? Did she mean....

Stapleya interrupted. Her tone one I never heard her use before. A tone of command. She is, after all, the head of this Castle. She always ruled with serenity and tranquility. I sensed she had been building to this for some time. The unveiling of this secret must have triggered a slew of deep-seated resentments.

There was spank in her voice!

She said, "Teena, we love you like family. You said we were family. You've come here all my life, and you've been almost like a grandmother to me. I know you've kept secrets from us. Now I find you can't even claim your own son to us? This is one step too far. While visiting Earth, we learned the concept you called your *Prime Directive*. We understand the intent is to protect us. I appreciate the good intentions you harbor.

"But damn it! You keep secrets beyond reason. You keep secrets that should make our lives much better. I have been on three other planets now; I see how others live and how primitive our lives are." Her voice rose with a touch of shrillness. Wisceya shrank back, trying to go unnoticed.

Stapleya, on a roll now, stood up in the tub and towered over the seated Teena and Alex, her voice at parade-ground volume.

"How dare you withhold technology and science from us! We're dying here, not just due to a lack of fertility, but predators we cannot defend against. How many years did it take to allow us a gun? How many have died for lack of suitable weaponry?

"You spoke of Klovia and their not needing the *Prime Directive*. Yes, I understand the fear of overwhelming our culture. But damn it, Teena, that should be our decision to make now, not yours. This must stop!"

Alex tried to put his arm around Stapleya and tried to soothe her. But, riled and agitated, she wasn't buying just then. I glanced at Teena and saw she was crying. Then I looked again and realized she was smiling through her tears.

Teena spoke up, "You are absolutely right, Stapleya. I am so pleased to see you stand and claim what should be yours. You are due. We have kept secrets, though, in our defense, I will plead necessity. It is also a fact that physics does not work quite the same here. Electronics are useless; simple explosives are difficult. We would have shared more if we could.

"Some past leaders have known the full truth. Edda knew everything and even traveled off-world to Center for weapons training. That's why the legend referred to her as an outstanding warrior. Not for battles she fought, rather the rigorous discipline she mastered. She brought many reforms and improvements to your world, did she not?"

Stapleya asked, "You knew Edda? I understand you're an immortal, ancient even though you do not look it now. Edda lived a long time ago; I only learned of her from the legend and the book. Nothing in the book mentions technology secrets. How is it you have lived so long?"

Teena nodded, "Yes, that is true. We chose not to write secrets into the Castle book where someone might read that shouldn't. I'm not an immortal. Though I have lived a long life, I will die one day the same as anyone. Edda was my daughter-in-law. No 'almost' to it. I am, in fact, your grandmother, with a few 'Greats' in front of the title."

She reached over and took Alex's hand. "Please allow me to correct that oversight now. Alex is my baby, my youngest son, of whom I am proud. And yes, he married Edda and was her husband and the father of her children."

She paused and let her words sink in. Then, in slow motion, Stapleya and Wisceya's gaze swiveled toward Alex. Well, so did mine.

He squirmed, and his face turned red. Then, squaring his shoulders, he gave a nervous laugh.

Looking to Teena for confirmation, or perhaps permission, he hesitated a moment before beginning.

"So many years have passed, lifetimes. Remembering now is almost as though it happened to someone else, as if a story I once read long ago. But, yes, I was Edda's husband, the one who claimed her in that silly legend, though it wasn't that way. I loved her deeply for many years. The most difficult aspect of healing after losing a soulmate is to recover the part of yourself that departed with them. I almost failed."

He sighed again, paused before continuing. "We spent many a peaceful evening's soak together right here in this very tub. The prospect of joining you ladies in this same tub was disturbing in a way I find hard to explain. I didn't want to at first but am now glad I did.

"Can you imagine the pain, to love someone deeply and watch them age, wither and die? Not grow old together, but cursed to stay youthful as they wither and fade?"

He looked as though he might cry.

Several seconds passed as he fought for composure. Finally, he continued, "It's not true that there was nothing written of her life beyond what's in the Castle book. She kept a private diary. It's hidden away in the library. I will show you later. Time to share it, I suppose."

He turned to me. "Edda was a tall woman among the Nekomata, almost your size." I am taller than Stapleya and Wisceya but shorter than Teena. Alex is taller still, of course. He was still speaking, "... why the Lady Tyrxing fits you so well. When I first saw you wearing that sword, I became unnerved. You're much like her, and not just in stature. Temperament too. With a pelt, you could be her reincarnation."

Teena spoke in a virtual whisper, "Alex...."

He turned to her with a blank expression. She continued, "I assume you have not been to Center?" He shook his head.

"Then you would not know. It is time to let our hair down." She turned to me. "Since we are in a secret-sharing mood, I may as well tell all. Jill dear, while on Center, we performed an exhaustive DNA panel on you. Without your permission or knowledge, I might add, for which I beg your forgiveness.

"We confirmed what I already suspected. You're Alex's granddaughter. His youngest son with Edda, her last child, moved to Earth and married an Irish woman. Though I lost track of them, I believe their child was your father. I knew it the moment I first laid eyes on you. I had to confirm. And yes, despite your mother's Asian influence, you do resemble Edda. You could almost be her doppelgänger. You're her heir in more ways than a beautiful sword."

Road-Trip

The following day we trotted to the Portal. We wanted to travel as early as circumstances and dinosaurs would permit. We didn't bother with weapons, supplies, or anything else. Stapleya's fragile home Portal would transport the three of us, at most. Weapons or supplies, not a chance. Our destination: Klovia — the intriguing world Alex had briefed us on the night before. The problem is, you just can't get there from here. You must go someplace else to start.

The Fur girls accompanied us to the Portal, although they had no desire to make this trip. Stapleya claimed she'd had enough space travel.

Nekomata has few Portals. I only know of two. Fitz mentioned a third one in his book, the one that connects to Ashera, or as he called it, 'Planet K.' Oops, I forgot about the one where we retrieved the ammunition; that makes four. Though, I never actually saw it. Teena had mentioned two more, but I am unaware where those are or where they port, where the terminus opens.

Earth has hundreds, perhaps thousands. But only one known Portal connects Nekomata to Earth. That Portal links to the Plaza Fitz described. Even so, Portals do not always adhere to fixed locations. Not only do they open and close, but they shift positions. Something involving complex celestial mechanics and plasma physics. Their schedules are predictable, though not by me.

Teena tried to explain it, but she did not understand it either. When not terminating in the *City by the Bay*, the plasma stream flits between other locations. One is in Oakland, where poor Shameya had the misfortune to emerge. Another lies deep in the Federal lands of eastern California. That was where Stapleya and Wisceya had emerged. I remember well the flap their furry appearance caused.

Asherans have the knowledge and technology to track and predict Portal openings and movements. They know the proper times to transit, when it is safe, and when not. We muggles depend on those conversant in the art.

We ported into *City by the Bay*, where we appeared in the plaza at 17th and Market. Yeah, like that! Just as Fitz described. This might be old hat to Teena. She has played the naked "white rabbit" to the startled city dwellers countless times. Let's just say I lack her aplomb.

Our time in the city was brief. Less than a minute, I believe. Or not much more. Teena led; I followed, telling myself that no one would notice me next to Teena. She draws the eye. I followed her lead, wearing my best poker face as Alex played caboose in our train.

We stepped into the brisk air of the city. There is an applicable Mark Twain quote. "The coldest winter I ever spent was a summer in San Francisco." Like that. Although Mr. Twain never actually said it. Acclimated to the unrelenting heat of Nekomata, I shivered.

Though I fought the urge to deploy my hands strategically, I need not have worried. No one screamed and pointed at us. No one fainted at the sight of us. Or laughed. It is no coincidence that this little plaza is ground-zero for the local urban nudist movement. Teena had explained that they intentionally encouraged the nudists and protestors.

There were a few startled glances, but the urbane city-dwellers otherwise ignored us. Nudes in this plaza are utterly unremarkable. We strolled across the plaza and stepped into the street. We walked past a trolley loaded with surprised tourists. We stepped onto the opposite sidewalk and into the next Portal as it opened to receive us. Perfect split-second timing.

Our total time in the plaza was mere seconds. It only felt like it took an hour to walk buck-naked across the open plaza and cross the street. There may have been somewhat fewer than the ten thousand onlookers I remember. I wondered which startled the tourists more, our nudity or our sudden disappearance. I now view tales of apparitions with a much different perspective.

The second transition took us to Center, but likewise, we did not dwell there. The following hop took us back to Earth again, this time to Mexico.

The heat of the Sonoran Desert was pleasant after the biting coolness of the city. After weeks on Nekomata, the Mexican heat was cool and pleasant by comparison, whereas the brief stroll in the city had been decidedly chilly.

The last leg of our trip to the Klovian Portal was inconvenient and required logistical support from the locals. The Mexican egress disgorged us in a desolate area devoid of civilization. We faced a distance of about twenty-five miles to our next Portal. Too far to hoof it naked and barefoot. Oh, we could walk it alright, we could run it in good time, but we have only a limited window to meet our Portal and no food or water. Did I mention we were in the desert? And it was hot?

Not to worry, Alex and Teena assured me. Our ride, though tardy, should be here any moment, they were confident. But, this time, split-second timing failed us. We waited. We waited some more.

Ten minutes. Twenty minutes. Thirty minutes. No place to sit, no shelter from the hot sun. Fine, I'm not sure of the time; I had no watch. But I did have our shadows on the ground and my military training. So, I think I was close in my estimation.

Finally, about thirty-five minutes after our egress, I spotted a dust cloud. Minutes later, our ride appeared. An ordinary Ride-Share, with an ordinary logo on the side and sign in the window. How mundane.

"Señor Marco?" the driver asked through the open window. Alex and Teena speak Spanish fluently. Big surprise. Is there any language these people can't speak? I followed the gist of the conversation, although my High School classes had left me far from fluent. There was some disagreement. There were several iterations before I twigged to the issue. The driver demanded more money upfront before the ride.

The whole conversation seemed incongruous; did he think we were marsupials? Where did he think we might have cached money? How he expected us to pay, had we agreed, I can't guess. Señor Gonzales acted as though oblivious to our lack of pockets. Alex, Teena, and Señor Gonzales debated the topic rather heatedly. His pay would come through the ride-share service. Forget that; he wanted more. At one point, he began to drive off as though to abandon us.

Teena had allowed Alex to lead the negotiations up to that point. When the driver threatened to abandon us, she said: "Let me handle this." Her tone took an ominous and commanding turn. Alex stepped back and suddenly became interested in the dirt under his nails. She has tools that Alex does not. Well, neither do I.

I had seen hints of her persuasive abilities before; this was the first time I saw her seriously unleash. Perhaps she emitted a burst of pheromones. Maybe she has psychic mind-control powers. I don't understand it, but I can attest to its effectiveness. Whatever she did, Señor Gonzales forgot about departing. She had his rapt attention.

She stepped up to the car and began speaking to him thru the open window. First, she apologized for not having any money to offer. Then, she asked if he would give them a ride anyway out of the goodness of his heart. He almost bought it. Her powers of persuasion had him like putty in her hands. He bought the idea of giving us the ride, but her sensual charms gave him another thought. Since we could offer no money, he suggested another way we could compensate him.

Sexual favors are a currency almost anywhere there are humans. Knowing Teena's sexual openness, I would have almost bet she might accommodate his demand.

Shows what I know!

What she might have given freely under more civilized conditions provoked a different reaction. His attempt to extort us backfired.

He knew not the danger he was in. That Alex was displaying a pointed disinterest should have been a clear warning sign.

She may look young and vulnerable. Looks are misleading. A cold and hardened warrior with genetically engineered and off-world trained muscles is underneath that flaming topknot and voluptuous figure. He had begged for an ass-kicking. He had been keeping an eye on Alex as the masculine protector in our group. He appeared unnerved at Alex's unconcern over the negotiation. He had no suspicion that said ass-kicking was to come from Teena.

In a blink, Teena reached through the open window and grabbed the unfortunate huckster. In one swift move, she yanked him bodily out the window — she performed a textbook military controlled-throw and slammed him into the desert caliche, then ground her heel into his throat.

Some textbook. Must be old school.

She didn't threaten him otherwise. She just held her heel on his throat. "debes pedirle disculpas," she said. She was convincing.

He apologized. Moments later, apology accepted, she allowed him up. "Ya se le paga para transportarnos," she said. "Then you dare to extort us when you think we are vulnerable. Then you insult ME with crassness and disrespect. Tell me why I should not take your car AND your clothes and leave YOU naked and unprotected in the desert?"

There were several more minutes of haranguing, but the outcome was preordained. Teena had impressed him.

The backstory came out. It appears the man's brother-in-law handled our particular type of transport. So our transporter should have been a man named Aguilar.

Clandestine operators within the Ride-Share community serve the specialty needs of inter-world travelers. Nude passengers are ordinary in their circle. I recalled that Julie's sister had been one such service provider. That was before they both died in that bloody Las Vegas hotel room.

Señor Aguilar had become ill and unable to fulfill his obligation. Gonzales had taken his place, although he was not getting directly paid himself. He didn't understand the rules, although perhaps he was not an innocent. Several factors drove his actions, not the least being his brother-in-law's illness.

We took a detour to verify the man's story and soon were at the bedside of an obviously sick man. His family was wide-eyed but otherwise ignored our lack of attire. You'd think they welcomed unclothed strangers into their homes every day. Well, perhaps it was not unprecedented, given his side-job.

After some discussion, Alex and Teena decided to take Señor Aguilar with us to Klovia. They felt obligated to see that he got proper medical attention. He was pale, ashen gray, and emaciated, though the cause was unclear. He appeared likely to die soon if not treated. I hoped they weren't making a mistake.

Our Portal window was fast closing. Señor Gonzales drove at insane speed on the desert washboard. Our teeth rattled; our bones vibrated with the noise. He sought the optimum speed to "float" over the washboard ridges. He never found it.

We arrived at the location of the only Portal from Earth to Klovia with mere minutes to spare. The Portal would soon close. Teena explained to Señor Aguilar that he must get naked too. He was too weak to move quickly. Teena unceremoniously shucked him of his coverings. Without hesitation, we darted through with an ashen gray Señor Aguilar in tow.

Psionic Energy

"No great discovery was ever made without a bold guess."
— **Isaac Newton**
"The most exciting phrase to hear in science, the one that heralds new discoveries, is not 'Eureka!' but 'That's funny…'"
—**Isaac Asimov**

A small greeting party awaited on the other side. The Second Lieutenant in charge met us with a couple of aides. Our guest was an unexpected complication. Teena explained his need for medical attention. She explained that she had been unwilling to abandon someone to die. She begged treatment for him. She suggested isolation. He should have as little exposure to Klovia as possible. We hoped to return him to his home with as little off-world knowledge as could be managed. One of the aides pecked on a mobile for a moment and announced a medic should soon arrive.

We started introducing ourselves. I just learned our host's name was Rice when the med team's arrival interrupted us. Moments later, our charge bundled off for diagnosis and treatment, we resumed. One of the techs passed out plain unmarked jumpsuits for our group.

Shortly, disguised as anonymous service techs, our host escorted us to a guest suite. Second Lieutenant Rice invited us to relax and freshen ourselves. "The staff will serve dinner in an hour," he said. "We will hold a briefing during dinner and afterward. Expect guests," he added.

Alex had, of course, already briefed us somewhat. My familial connection to Alex was but a small part of our past evening's conversation. We had spent almost the entire night relaxing in the warm water, talking and planning. I won't pretend to deny the DNA discussion registered near the top of my consciousness. Yet, there was much more.

We showered and refreshed ourselves just as room service brought in dinner. We had settled at the table about to begin eating when Petchy and Fitz knocked.

I had, of course, known of Petchy from Fitz's book and had met the esteemed "Dr. Shepherd" in Alex's office. At that time, I had been clueless about his secret identity. Ironic that I had to travel to another planet to meet Petchy in his own name.

Petchy was welcoming, greeted me warmly. Then Alex explained the DNA testing Teena had done and my familial revelation.

"I knew it!" he exclaimed. "When you survived that vicious attack and killed those bastards, you had my attention. I told Teena you might have Asheran blood." He held me at arm's length and squinted. "Yes, you do look like Edda. Remind me sometime to tell you the story of Edda and the snake."

The emotional family reunion was brief, to my great relief, and Petch got straight to business. Fitz had contented himself with a quick hug and a "Welcome to the family." I suspect he is as uncomfortable with the squishy stuff as I.

Let me see if I understand this. Petchy is Teena's grandson and Fitz's father. Alex is Teena's son and my grandfather. What sort of cousin does that make Fitz and me? Second? It makes my head hurt.

Petchy and Fitz had traveled to Klovia after the chance discovery of an unknown Portal. The same one we used, of course, the only known Portal connecting Klovia and Earth.

Fitz and Petchy invested weeks learning the language and assimilating into Klovian society. They confirmed that Gharlane's agents had infiltrated the Empire. The slow process of subversion and destruction is evident once you know the signs.

They also discovered someone, apparently Gharlane himself, had appeared on one of their spaceships. He killed several of the crew and attempted to sabotage the AI. By then, Petch and Fitz had ingratiated themselves with the Klovian Chief Executive, and when Gharlane's assault came to light, she gave them full access. They were able to examine the ship and its computers and neutralize the damage.

That attack on the ship may have been a strategic mistake, if we can exploit it. It appears Gharlane had expected his contagion to remain undetected, despite the blatant attack. Intended to propagate through their AI network and infect it, it would have but for Fitz. A lack of universal connectivity kept the contagion confined. It would have still propagated itself once the ship connected to another AI. The lack of a ready, always-on connection slowed the propagation.

Though delayed, the attack would have still succeeded but for Fitz. Gharlane's contagion had been a malware masterpiece — entrenched in the system, it was well hidden from scrutiny, yet somehow Fitz managed to expose it. So, naturally, I asked him how he did so. I am no computer jock, but I know enough to understand the difficulty posed by an unfamiliar system.

In typical Fitz fashion, he shrugged it off. "It's what I do," he'd said. "Unscrewing screwed-up computers and delousing them of malware is my specialty." Maybe so, but it still sounded unreasonable to me. Fitz is an expert in Earth's computers, I grant. He may be the world's most outstanding expert on data security. Klovia's AIs are not Earth's computers. Even I know that, and I'm scarcely more than conversant on the topic. I shook my head, puzzled how he had pulled off such a miracle.

I don't think he knew himself. I believe there is a mystery here we do not recognize. Computers are complex. It must be hard enough to manage the various familiar architectures. Windows vs. Mac vs. Linux is hard enough, and they are all similar. An utterly alien design? I don't buy it. He must have had help. High-powered help at that. But from where?

With no answers and no one else considering these questions, I brushed my concerns aside; Petchy was expounding on his observations.

Petchy believed our enemy commanded complete, on-demand control over Portals. This upset Petchy, and he explained the reason for his worries. "Asheran scientists have studied Portals for centuries. They have studied them, crafted theories about them, and unraveled their mysteries. Yet, we had no clue that such manipulations were possible." He professed to feeling out-classed, like a Cro-Magnon who has discovered a mobile. Perhaps able to use a few simple functions, ignorant of the underlying technology. How can we fight someone able to move across the Universe at will?

Gharlane had escaped, leaving us clueless about where he went or how to find him. We have no clue where Gharlane's home base might be. Worse, our fight has hinged on blocking the enemy Portals. We cannot block his Portals when he forms them on-demand whenever desired. Perhaps we can stymie his operatives, but Gharlane is another matter. How long until he grants his minions similar powers?

We cannot find him, so he must come to us. We need a strategy to draw our enemy. What bait would draw Gharlane into our kill zone?

We debated what we knew while dining and for some time afterward. It was late when a knock came at the suite's door. Expecting Room Service wanted to clear away the debris from our dinner, Petch answered the door. It was not room service, but Second Lieutenant Rice. He had another man with him.

"Dr. Shepherd, I believe you may have met Mr. Breen," the Lieutenant said. "Yes," Petchy answered, "How are you, Potty?" The Lieutenant blanched, and leaned into Petchy's personal space, and whispered in his ear. "Mr. Breen is not fond of the diminutive form of his name. You should call him Potipher or Mr. Breen."

Breen, of course, overheard this; he was standing right there. He laughed a great belly laugh at the Lieutenant's solicitousness. He has the belly for it.

"Nonsense," he said. "Yes, in my public persona, I discourage such familiarity, it is true. I do bristle when used in derision by those who I consider less than intimates. I encourage the foolish and ignorant to avoid me. It keeps me off their radar. Among friends and fellow warriors, I accept it in the spirit given. How are you, Petchy?"

Funny, he does not look like a warrior. My first impression was most unfavorable — I found him almost revolting. Until he laughed. Like flicking a switch, he transformed. The disgusting, vile ogre became Santa Clause. Neither Teena nor Alex appeared to notice the transformation.

Perhaps I have an overactive imagination.

The Lieutenant appeared shocked by Breen's sudden charm. I suspected the Lieutenant was not on Breen's Christmas card list. The way he arched his eyebrow when Breen used Petchy's nickname also was indicative. Petch never discouraged familiarity, except when undercover in the MiB. Is he still an undercover MiB here? Maybe.

Perhaps I read too much into a few brow-wiggles. Interpreting an opponent's body language is a skill I learned in the military. It has come in handy, although there are limits. It is a poor proxy for mind-reading.

Fitz, I have always been unable to read. Often, he has kept a poker face and gives little away. I had come to recognize when he was playing dumb. He wore a specific face for the occasion — the one he was wearing now. Unable to draw a conclusion, I shrugged and turned back to Breen.

We settled on the couches with an after-dinner coffee and dessert. Breen chowed down on a slice of chocolate cake that would have fueled me for a thirty-mile run on Nekomata. Teena gave Breen and the Lieutenant a masterful summary of our conversation. She omitted the less relevant aspects of our conversation, of course. Whatever our familial connections, they are of no concern to Klovia, or to Breen.

Petchy took the lead after Teena's summation. "The conundrum we have is two-fold. Problem one is drawing Gharlane into our combat circle. Before we resolve that, we need a weapon to kill him. He overpowered fifty trained and armed security forces on the ship. Not only did he defeat them, he dispatched them with an unimaginable ease. The video shows him doing little more than waving his hand. Drawing him into our locus does us no good if he can strike us down with a simple wave of the hand. Do we yet know the cause of their deaths?"

"Ah," said Potty around a mouthful of cake. A moment's pause while he cleared his orifice. "We know what they died of, but not how.... Or to be precise, the source of the energy that inflicted the mortal damage. They died from an intense blast of microwaves. Yet he carried no device, no projector, no weapon that could emit such a blast. It is almost as though he projected such energy by the power of his mind alone."

Fitz snorted at that. Breen tilted his head in acknowledgment. "I agree," Breen said. "Yet, there is such a thing as mental energy. Fringe phenomena lurking on the edges of science for lack of a good theory."

Petchy said, "Indeed, I have heard many convincing reports of psychokinesis and the like. Never saw a case that could stand honest scrutiny. Real or not, I am unconvinced."

"How do you explain the Psionic Egg? What causes the changes in entropy around mental activity? Was not the behavior of the Egg remarkable when Gharlane acted?"

Petchy considered Breen's question. "I don't know. I noted the curiosity, but I see no means to leverage it into a weapon. It proves nothing about telekinesis. Projecting mental energy into a death ray? Yeah, that's how it looked. Anyone who has ever watched a sleight-of-hand artist at work understands how deceiving looks can be."

Breen put his hands together, fingertips touching. He closed his eyes and rocked back and forth on the couch for a moment. Then he said, "It is true that science has no explanation for the phenomena we have noted. There is no clear mechanism by which thought alone can move anything. Further, such activity requires energy, more than glucose metabolism within the brain could support."

He reached over and touched Fitz on the arm. Fitz raised his arm in response. "We also must acknowledge that the precise mechanism by which a thought moves your arm is less clear than we might wish. But, if science must concede difficulty explaining the one, how can we say the other is impossible?"

Petchy sighed. "I don't say it is impossible. That's the thing about science, its uncertainty. Engineers are certain; scientists are not.

"The most crucial element of science is that it is uncertain. A good scientist relishes uncertainty.

"If a scientist tells you he is certain, kick him in the nuts. He is no scientist; he is an engineer at best. Most likely, he is a fraud, a charlatan, or even worse, a politician looking to put his hands in your pocket. Run him out of town, or better, put him in jail."

Petchy sighed again, closed his eyes for a second, and then continued. "After witnessing Gharlane's actions, I am bothered by the idea. I'm starting to think there might be something to it.

"Do you know of anyone who lays a credible claim of psychokinesis? I would be eager to see a demonstration of any such fringe phenomena. If possible."

"I know of no such person," Potty answered. "But I do have a thought perhaps worth exploring. Will you indulge me in a little wild speculation?"

"They say the hangman's noose focuses the mind," Petchy said in a soft, quiet voice. "I fear Gharlane has shown me my own hangman's noose. We must understand how this villain does what he does and how to stop him. For that, I am open to anything."

"Maybe this is nothing," Breen said, "but let's consider it for a brief moment. Jill dear, I understand you're rather skilled with a weapon, correct?"

Startled, I nodded mutely. I was still struggling with the language. I'd first encountered SLoTE less than twenty-four hours earlier. Alex had taught Teena and me the rudiments starting before we left Nekomata and during the trip. Since we arrived, it had been total immersion, with some support from Petch and Fitz. Teena, gifted as she is with languages, is already fluent.

The odd thing is, when Breen addressed me, he did so in perfect American English. That's what surprised me. Yet, when I later compared notes with Fitz, he was certain Breen had not spoken English. The mind sometimes plays strange tricks, I suppose.

Before I could respond, Teena jumped in. "She sure is, almost supernatural. Speed and accuracy with bow and arrow, with a firearm and a sword. She saved my life by killing a Deinonychus with only a sword."

I added, "It is an exceptional sword. Of course, Teena put her fair share of arrows into the beast as well. But yes, I killed the damn thing. I also dropped two more with a firearm." Fitz dropped his deadpan expression and looked at me with awe, releasing a soft whistle. I guess he hadn't heard that tale. Then I realized Petchy and Alex were likewise eyeing me.

She kills one little dinosaur and suddenly the men all notice the girl. Who knew?

Petchy added sotto voce, "Speaking of focusing the mind ..."

Breen had closed his eyes again as though visualizing the scene. After a moment, he again rejoined the living. "An impressive display, and one supporting my thesis. I believe that in rare instances of exceptional skill, the task is physically impossible. And yet, such impossible results are clocked all the time. Perhaps aided by non-physical forces? I believe, in some exceptional cases, the skill flows more from the mind than the body."

The room fell silent. Alex said, "It is true that exceptional feats do seem to demand a focused mental state. We call it being 'in the zone.' I can practice for hours and not hit the target. Then I am in the zone and can't miss."

I nodded in agreement. I added, "And yet when faced with a life-or-death challenge, I always find my focus. I believe adrenaline is a factor. We've all heard stories of mothers lifting giant vehicles to save a child. Perhaps more than adrenaline is involved."

"Do you think you could favor us with a small demonstration?"

"Here? Now?" I asked, almost sputtering in surprise. "I doubt our hosts would take kindly to firearms discharge indoors and at this hour."

The Lieutenant said, "There is a gym and weapons range in the basement of this building. Quite soundproofed. We train and practice any hour of the day."

Breen continued to explain his intent. "I would like to place devices containing Psionic Eggs nearby while you ply your skills. If there are non-physical forces in play, the Eggs might detect them. I am guessing we will find one such as yourself that can support my thesis."

There was more discussion and logistical details to address. First, someone must borrow a suitable weapon. Second, someone must arrange for the appropriate Psionic Egg devices. Finally, someone must book the range. We needed to ensure no one else planned to use it during our tests. We wanted no observers.

It was a bit over an hour later when we convened in the basement training room. The Lieutenant had taken responsibility for the weapons. He assembled a selection, both firearms and archery. I looked them all over and then eyed the sidearm he was wearing. Without a word, he entrusted me with his personal sidearm. Brave man. Or fool. I would not hand Ol Betsy to a stranger. Not an M1911, but close enough. It fit my hand.

Posting a target, I proceeded to introduce myself to the weapon. At first, my shots were off-center, and I went through two clips warming up, getting the feel. With the third clip, I asked for a virgin target. I then proceeded to place all seven rounds in the same dead-center hole. I think the Lieutenant would have asked me to marry him right there on the spot if we were alone. I believe I have mentioned my own particular brand of black magic.

That was merely the warm-up exercise. Now to don the cape and wave the magic wand, time for the real legerdemain. Teena knew the drill; we had practiced it for hours on Center during our convalescence. However, I doubt the others, including Fitz and Petchy, anticipated what was about to happen.

She grabbed fourteen ping-pong balls, two for each cartridge in my clip. I grabbed a spare clip. Teena stepped behind a safety barrier at the side of the range. She tossed a ball in the direction of the target. I let it bounce off the wall, then nailed it. That impressed the Lieutenant again.

Teena tossed two balls. Pew Pew. I nailed them both. Teena threw four balls. My bad, I jumped the gun. I missed my first shot but nailed all four balls with my remaining three bullets. I bagged a twofer with the middle bullet. That was just dumb luck — even I am not that good — but the fact I missed my first shot was annoying. Calm down, focus — no room for mistakes on the blowoff.

By now, the guys, not just the Lieutenant, but Petchy and Fitz too, stood open-mouthed. Potty appeared to be taking a nap. Darn it; he's missing the demonstration he asked for. Tough cookies, fat guy. Learn to stay awake or miss the fun!

Not to lose my momentum, I swapped clips and signaled Teena for the blowoff.

Seven balls flew into the kill zone. Seven shots, seven balls became useless shards of plastic. I turned, faced my audience, and bowed. As I straightened, I saw Potty was wide awake and smiling.

Physics

"These little grey cells. It is up to them."
— Hercule Poirot

We repeated the demo with various weapons. I demonstrated my skills with a bow. All the while, the Psionic Eggs spewed their random-number-laden data stream. After each session, a quick review allowed us to see exactly where in our movements the Egg would react. I soon recognized it was very much tied to my *in-the-zone* feelings.

We didn't know it then, but our sessions were also videoed at high speed for later study.

Not only was my accuracy tested, but Teena and Fitz joined in too. Watching the Psionic Eggs react as we performed captivated us. When Fitz picked up a bow, the eggs didn't just react; they went frickin' nuts. When he began throwing his missiles, the entropy ceased. Each time he drew his bow, the eggs produced a continuous string of ones. No entropy whatsoever. My efforts had caused a reaction. Fitz's provoked something else altogether.

Fitz suggested that perhaps something similar happened when he lifted weights. The gym was next door. The Lieutenant pointed out a bench and weight rack. In mere minutes we confirmed Potty's hypothesis. When lifting a considerable but non-challenging weight, the egg twiggled. As the weight increased, it began to bobble. With gargantuan weights — beyond all other human's capacity — the entropy shifts became frenetic. Far more so than anything Teena or I had evoked.

Indications were that beyond a certain level, Fitz was lifting the weight as much with his mind as his biceps—moreso, even. Perhaps that explains his impossible strength. Even so, his weightlifting produced less effect on the eggs than his archery.

Whether unique to Asheran genetics or just a factor in any elite athleticism, we have no clue. But, that we of Asheran descent appear to tap into it with greater ease does seem significant. Can others of non-Asheran genetics learn to tap the energy? Perhaps many elite athletes already do, just unnoticed.

Thus, the other question becomes whether training strengthens the non-physical effect? Can a focused regimen develop increased results? Is this the mechanism Gharlane uses? If so, can we block it? Can we do so selectively?

We returned to the suite and contemplated the implications of our little experiment. We debated the validity of our data. We questioned holes in the methodology. Finally, the Lieutenant revealed the clandestine videos. We overlaid the Egg's activity against the action.

While examining the video, I noticed something strange about my unexpected *twofer*. At 5000 frames per second, we could see the bullet turn in flight. It hit the first ball, pivoted — only a couple of degrees — just enough to clip the second ball.

"Huh!" said Fitz. "Interesting," Petchy said. Alex commented, "If this holds up to scrutiny, we have just redefined the laws of physics."

Petchy scratched his ear. "We must repeat the experiment under more rigorous conditions to consider it scientifically valid. Yet, we cannot deny that something strange is happening. Psionic energy appears real, even if we don't understand it. Significant physical skill has a significant non-physical component."

Petchy closed his eyes and drifted off to that dreamworld where scientists sometimes retreat. He began to mumble, "Hoisting a great weight requires energy. It takes 10 Joules to raise a kilogram one meter. So, lifting a 275 kg weight would equal about 2750 Joules. Human muscles produce their energy from the metabolism of Adenosine Tri-Phosphate or ATP. The brain comprises less than 2% of the body's weight yet consumes over 20% of the energy."

He paused a few moments with his eyes closed, fingers twitching, deep in thought. Then he resumed mumbling, "The brain's energy is the metabolism of glucose and oxygen. Two thousand food calories equal about 8.4 million Joules. That's about 6.7 million Joules for the muscles and about 1.7 million for the brain. Over twenty-four hours, that averages about 77 Joules per second for the body and 25 Joules per second for the mind. Close to 100 Joules per second for the total. A lift lasts maybe five seconds."

Petchy opened his eyes. "I dunno," he said. "It is a lot of energy, but there is no reason to invoke supernatural resources. Even a tremendous lift requires about a 500% burst increase over the resting metabolism. Not unreasonable."

Alex asked, "What about Gharlane's blast of microwaves. Wouldn't that be a lot more Joules than lifting 600 pounds? What about the energy required to form a Portal?"

Petchy sighed, "You got me there. Yes it would. Orders of magnitude more. Far more than any human body could metabolize from food.

"My best guess is he is controlling a greater flow of energy. Compare the bicyclist vs. the automobile driver. Like Fitz, Jill, and Teena, the bicyclist supplies the energy himself. It comes from his own body's metabolism. However, the auto driver only needs to supply enough energy to manage the controls. We are bicycling; Gharlane is driving a race car. We must learn to drive, and soon."

Teena added a nickel's worth. "Assuming he is controlling a larger source of energy, what is that energy source?"

Petchy scratched his chin in thought for a moment. "There are abundant sources of energy. Especially if one is willing to step beyond the boundaries of accepted science," he said. "For example, the Universe appears to be expanding at an accelerating rate. We don't know why, but a popular theory postulates the existence of Dark Energy. Michael Turner coined the term Dark Energy in 1998 to give a name to the hypothetical energy field.

The hypothesis of an all-encompassing energy field evolved to explain inconsistencies in our understanding. Some of these ideas go back to the work of Edwin Hubble in the 1920s and fit within Einstein's theories. If we accept these ideas, then Dark Energy constitutes around 70% of all the energy in the Universe. Is it a huge stretch to imagine non-physical phenomena might tap into Dark energy in some way?"

I had a sudden thought. I asked, "Does this non-physical force obey the laws of physics?" Everyone turned and stared at me as though I had lost my mind. Maybe I had; I'm not clear myself where I'm going with this.

Petchy said, "Good question, Jill. I don't think we know. What prompts you to ask?"

I shrugged. "The phenomenon works on Nekomata, as proven by a dead Deinonychus. Yet Teena has stated the laws of physics are different there. For example, explosives don't explode; electrons don't electronicate. So why does psionic work there?"

Six mouths fell open. What did I say?

Teena said, "The non-physical, or psionic force works on Nekomata. Psionic force may not be limited to known physics, but maybe Dark Energy is. That may mean that the larger energy source is unavailable on Planet Oz. Perhaps if we lure Gharlane to Nekomata, he will be unable to tap this larger power source. He may be limited to only the power of his mind and thus vulnerable."

Oh! I said that? Huh.

Disclosure

"Must have something to do with zero-point energy."
— Niels Bohr

Let's put a pin in the effort to develop a way to combat Gharlane and jump forward to the Disclosure Summit where the Klovian population is made aware of the Alien presence.

The chairperson assumed the dais and stepped to the fore. She paused, mobile in uplifted hand. The audience, chattering with speculation, failed to notice. She tapped the screen; a deep, resounding gong reverberated throughout the great hall. Although it required a couple of repeats, the chattering died away. A few self-appointed sergeants-at-arms aided the process. One by one, they persuaded the less compliant to focus on the proceedings.

The honored guest relaxed unconcerned on the rostrum, smiling but otherwise impassive, waiting. The chairperson began the introduction.

"Ladies and Gentlemen, you have no doubt heard hints of the momentous news we are here to disclose today. Yes, it is true. And I feel confident in stating what you are about to hear is the most profound news in the history of humanity.

"As word spreads, I expect every citizen will play the VoTE recordings from today.

"Our distinguished guest will present the extraordinary thesis. I have the honor of presenting the esteemed Dr. Shepherd." A preternatural quietude fell upon the audience as Dr. Shepherd stood and assumed the lectern.

The chairperson resumed her seat. The alert observer might find significance in her position and body language. She positioned herself as far from the third person on the dais as possible. Even after seating, her body language communicated a desire to move yet further away.

The person she strove to distance herself from took no notice. He appeared to be asleep.

Quietude gave way to impenetrable silence. The guest's stage presence demanded their attention.

The esteemed Dr. Shepherd made a minor show of laying his mobile on the lectern so the screen might be visible. He adjusted the device as though arranging notes. He took a sip of water and squared his shoulders. He then reached across, grasping the lectern on the side nearest the audience. A large man, he draped his whole body across the tiny desk. He bowed his head a moment. Then, with slow deliberation, he raised his eyes to meet full-on the audience's gaze.

"Friends," he began with a soft rumble in his voice. "I stand before you today, a man as human as any of you, yet not of your world."

A dramatic pause for his words to register.

Murmurs of disbelief trickled through the audience, ceasing as he began to speak again. "I wish to thank you for your hospitality. I have traveled light-years to tell you that you are not alone in the Universe. That by itself would be momentous news, but there is more. Not only my own people but there are other peoples than my own. You are not only not alone in the Universe, you are not even lonely."

The audience erupted in protest, unbelieving. At that, he paused, turned to the chairperson, and gave a hand signal. She stood and went to the curtain beside the stage as he continued speaking.

He raised his voice over the rising din. "Please allow me to introduce my dear friends, two lovely ladies from a planet known as Nekomata." With that, Stapleya and Wisceya stepped from behind the curtain, their spectacular pelts on full display. The audience gasped and fell silent. He charged into the gap. "You will note their beautiful, sensual pelt."

He motioned to the Fur girls; they came and stood beside him. "They are Stapleya and her daughter Wisceya."

At his words, the Nekomata women bowed. "We invite any who doubt their off-world credentials to come and meet them. I'm sorry, but they speak no SLoTE beyond a few basic words, though I can translate for them. You are welcome to speak with them and examine their exquisite fur. Trust me; there is no trickery here. Their fur is real and natural. They represent an entire civilization. But please understand, despite their gorgeous pelt, they are fully human. Please do not make the mistake of thinking otherwise. They are human to the extent of inter-fertility." He paused a brief instant, then grinned.

His staid academic manner broke, and Petchy the raconteur twinkled. He added, "Please do not mistake that for a solicitation." The audience gave a polite, nervous laugh.

The fur-clad women strutted across the stage as though modeling the latest fashion; they enjoyed the attention. They took up positions on either side of Dr. Shepherd. As they did so, two more figures emerged from behind the curtain. Dr. Shepherd introduced them. "I would also like to introduce two more associates from different worlds. Fitz of Earth, and Athena of Ashera."

Slow, poised, and seductive, Teena flowed across the stage. Captivated, the audience focused on Teena, the others forgotten. The power of her personality and influence of her pheromones captivated the hall. There was no doubting the effectiveness of her enhanced genetics. She had the audience mesmerized.

Teena mounted the podium. She stared out at the crowd. Then, with a start, she spotted a familiar, though unexpected face. Señor Aguilar! Third row, center. He'd vanished from the hospital, and after a brief search, they had dropped the matter. She must round him up after the show and get him back to Mexico. He still appeared as ashen gray as when she first laid eyes on him. She squared her shoulders and addressed the crowd.

"Citizens of Klovia, my friends call me Teena. I am the last surviving Elder of my civilization. We were once over 25 billion souls. Today we are a few scattered thousands. Many of my people hide amongst aliens on hostile worlds or live as welcome guests, as with the Nekomata." She nodded to the Fur girls. Wisceya curtsied, provoking a faint ripple of laughter from the audience.

"My world died, my people all but erased from the scroll of eternity. We thought the cause was one of our own making. We continued in this mistaken belief until Fitz joined our quest."

At her words, Fitz stepped forward and joined her on the rostrum. A soft gasp floated across the great hall as the audience noted the tremendous musculature of the man.

"Teena recruited me to help her and Dr. Shepherd pursue their mission. I accompanied her to the burned-out cinder that remains of her home world. Our mission had been to destroy an artificial intelligence, a runaway machine that continued to pose a threat. We were also tasked with recovering a genetics database and other information. We succeeded on both counts. We recovered not only the genetic data but more. We discovered incontrovertible proof that outside influences had destroyed that world."

Dr. Shepherd picked up the narrative. "Not only had inimical outside forces destroyed Ashera. Not only had an alien force brought about the destruction of a tremendous civilization." He paused for dramatic effect. "The evil bastard is still at it." A faint gasp fluttered throughout the audience. Dr. Shepherd glanced at his mobile on the lectern.

Fitz took the lead again. "Once we understood the attack vector, we knew the signs to look for. We then began to recognize their dark influence on my own world. So, we mounted a supreme effort to drive them back and block their efforts. Whether we were successful remains unclear."

Dr. Shepherd said, "While pursuing agents of our foe, we followed them to Klovia. Until that moment, we were unaware of your world. We investigated and found that indeed, humanity's enemies have a foothold here as well." He paused and spread his hands as though in frustration.

Dr. Shepherd continued speaking. "I have the unfortunate duty to be the bearer of horrendous news. Dire news that affects your entire planet, your off-world colonies, your entire civilization."

Murmurs began rumbling. He raised his hands for quiet. His demeanor elevated a notch; his voice took on a stentorian quality. "You may not know it, but your world is under attack. A near-fatal blow has already landed. A second blow averted only by swift action thanks to your Chief Executive. With her support, my associates and I blunted that attack. We held the effects to starship Z7M7-Z. More attacks are sure to follow. Swift action is the only practical response."

The audience became restless at that. A person of indeterminate gender stood in the front row, waiting for recognition. Petchy ignored the potential interruption as he plowed ahead, his voice increasing in power.

"The attack on the Z7M7-Z was violent and forceful. Fifty of your finest died at the hands of our foe. The more insidious incursion took the form of a subtle computer corruption. Thanks to my friend Fitz," he said, waving a hand in the direction of Fitz. "Thanks to Fitz, we uncovered the contagion and eliminated it. Fitz is perhaps the greatest computer scientist to have ever lived."

At this, Fitz dipped his head, shaking it with a slight grimace. He does not consider himself any sort of scientist. Dr. Shepherd continued without pausing. "Had he not done so, the contagion would have metastasized. It would spread to every computer-based intelligence in your civilization. That is the same mechanism by which Ashera died. A massive contagion spread unrestrained and destroyed the technological underpinnings of our civilization."

A delicate cough emanated from the front row.

"Beyond attacking our computer systems, they also sabotaged our scientific research. The attacks were subtle and did not arouse suspicion. The attacks masqueraded as simple scientific mistakes. They came from the realms of trusted scientists. It was a distortion of science, perverted to serve an unsavory agenda."

The standee in the front row grew impatient, shifting and making not-so-subtle throat-clearing noises.

Still ignoring the would-be interruption, Petchy thundered on. "It's striking how often we become seduced to evil following 'science.' The most educated and intelligent have often believed their behavior logical and rational. Only later do they discover their decisions have yielded morally heinous policies. Policies that were only enacted because reasonable people trusted claimed 'evidence.' Blind faith in 'science' is itself a religion. Always question authority. Always verify the data. Always!" His last words thundered from the podium.

At last, pausing in his rhetoric, he motioned to a nearby assistant. She responded by carrying a microphone toward the front row.

"You there," Petchy addressed the standee. "You have a question?"

The standee attempted to speak. The thin, high-pitched voice lacked Petchy's power. A slight delay ensued as the traveling microphone made its way to the standee.

Finally, the response came. "I don't believe you."

Dr. Shepherd seemed nonplussed. "That's good," he said. "You should not believe outrageous ideas without proof. Is there anything, in particular, you boggle at?"

"All of it!" The speaker shifted, gained confidence. The thin, high-pitched voice became shriller and higher-pitched. "I don't believe you are from another world. I don't believe he is either." The speaker pointed at Fitz.

"Fair enough," Petchy said. "I assume you would include Athena in that statement as well." The accuser nodded, his whole body shaking with his emotion. "I grant that we have made an extraordinary claim. You are quite correct to demand more than my word as proof."

Dr. Shepherd turned and placed his arms around the Nekomata women. "What about these lovely ladies. Is not their exquisite pelt illustrative to you? Do you not find them extraordinary? Would you like to come on-stage and examine them?"

"I would not. I'm not, myself, qualified to judge them. I have seen theatrical costumes as convincing."

Dr. Shepherd smiled. "Are you sure you would not at least like to come up and touch their fur? They won't mind, and I assure you that you won't either." Wisceya held out her arm toward the interrogator. Laughter percolated throughout the hall.

The inquisitor squirmed as Petchy grinned. Then, after a pause, "Your attack on science convinces me you are a charlatan. Scientific truth cannot be denied, cannot be disputed. Facts are simple, stubborn things. The power of science lies in the rejection of belief. Science tells us what you say is unreasonable. I trust science more than I do you." A flutter of applause tinkled at these words. The skinny antagonist preened before his audience.

"Friend," Petchy said, "I made no attack on science. Perhaps I expressed myself poorly. I only recently learned SLoTE. I apologize if I have erred."

"I myself claim the mantle of scientist, with advanced degrees to support it. Unfortunately, all conferred by institutions you are without question unaware of, on another planet. I place great value on science and the scientific method. It is the abuse of science to support fallacious predetermined conclusions I was attacking. Tell me, what sort of proof would you seek? I would offer you anything I might supply, answer any question."

"Can you point to any non-human characteristics? What about DNA analysis to prove your non-human claims?" The disputant crossed arms, confident of victory, smugness plain.

Dr. Shepherd asked, "Would a DNA analysis be convincing to you?" The detractor nodded.

"Then please, rather than take my word, let me introduce your own Chief Executive. I understand her word is above reproach, correct?" At his words, Kassa stepped from behind the curtain, carrying a brief. The inquisitor stood open-mouthed, surprised by the unexpected Executive appearance.

Dr. Shepherd yielded the lectern to the Chief Exec.

Holding up the brief, Kassa showed it to the audience and the VOTE cameras. "Let the public record reflect this data for all to examine. This is a comprehensive DNA panel of a sample volunteered by Dr. Shepherd. Including a forensically documented chain of custody. The full panel is available for all to study, plus a summary analysis. In short, the DNA supports Dr. Shepherd's claim of off-world origins. In my official capacity as the Emperor's Chief Executive, I vouch for the veracity of this data."

The attacker responded by preening and raising his voice again. "How can you say the DNA is off-world in origin? These people claim to be non-human. Is it human or not?"

Kassa transfixed the questioner with an icy stare. "No one has claimed they are non-human, except you. Dr. Shepherd stated that the Nekomata women are human to the point of inter-fertility. Either you fail at comprehending plain spoken SLoTE or wish to obfuscate the record." She stared him down for several seconds. The audience squirmed in sympathy.

Dr. Shepherd resumed the lectern, thanking the Chief Executive for her aid. Then he once again addressed his tormentor.

"As stated, my friends, including the Nekomata and I, are as human as you. With one possible exception, that of our enemy, all known sentient life is human. There are certainly differences across the human family. The exquisite pelt of our Nekomata friends is one example. The tremendous musculature of Fitz is another. Yet despite our variety, we are more alike than unalike."

Grasping one last straw, the inquisitor squeaked one last question. "How strong is he? Is he stronger than any human? Does his strength support non-human origins?"

Petchy sighed at the pigheadedness of his tormentor. Then he smiled. "How strong are you, my friend?"

"Huh? I don't have his physique, nor have I claimed alien powers."

"I don't have his physique either. No one has claimed alien powers. But let's address your question without responding to the rancor you seem bent on. Yes, Fitz is strong. Much stronger than I, and I'm no weakling. He works out with massive weights. I daresay his strength is beyond anything we have recorded in your official competitions. His muscles are the result of natural gifts and genetic tweaking. He has undergone rigorous training and received optimal nutrition. His strength is immense and might convince you of his off-world origins."

As he spoke, Fitz stepped to the front of the dais. He doffed his tunic and flexed his biceps, assuming various bodybuilder's poses. His muscles rippled impressively.

Dr. Shepherd continued, "Let us open the question up to a larger audience. In any large gathering such as this, there must be some power-lifters present. Would anyone care to join us for a demonstration?"

The audience began to murmur. Then, one giant of a man stood in the back. Then, more murmuring, and two more stood. Each of the three was almost of Fitz's size and well-muscled.

Dr. Shepherd rubbed his hands. "Excellent! Would you gentlemen care to join us on-stage?"

The next several minutes were cacophonous as the men made their way to the stage. They all proved to be members of a recognized powerlifting organization. Each member gave a brief biography and noted their personal record.

"Would you then say that Fitz might prove himself by out-lifting you? If Fitz were to snatch a much greater weight than any you have ever lifted? That such a lift would support the claim of otherworld origins?"

Dr. Shepherd asked the question of each member. Then he made a show of uncovering an impressive weight rack. Petchy was showman enough to avert questions of how such equipment came to be present. Instead, he invited the members to assemble barbells for a demonstration.

They each assembled a rig to match the weight they had last lifted in competition. Massive weights, lifted only by extraordinary humans. They each performed a textbook-perfect snatch. Each hoisted the weight high before dropping it to slam into the unyielding stage.

Twice, Fitz then stepped forward and repeated the snatch. The second weight was somewhat heavier than the first. Fitz appeared to struggle with it.

After the third and heaviest lift, Dr. Shepherd rushed across the stage and attempted the lift. Although much older and outmatched, he managed an awkward, clumsy half-lift. He failed at the snatch but did raise it to his shoulders before dropping it. His efforts earned a round of applause from the audience. "I told you I was no slouch," he told the audience, eliciting laughs.

Dr. Shepherd returned to the rostrum as Fitz prepared to perform the third lift. The big reveal was imminent, and he wanted to prepare for the pandemonium sure to follow. As he did so, Teena leaned in close and whispered, "Our missing patient. Don't look too quickly; let's not spook him. Third-row, center. I'm going to call security and have them grab him."

Petchy glanced where Teena had indicated and blanched. Then, he whispered to Teena, "Don't! Let him stay right there." She cocked an eyebrow at Petch. "Get ready," he added.

While this was going on, Fitz addressed the third lift. He looked it over and experimentally raised it from the floor as though judging its weight.

He hesitated. Voices in the audience jeered.

He faced the audience and shrugged. "I think I need some help with this one." The audience grumbled. "Perhaps my friends from Nekomata might lend a hand."

He motioned to the Fur girls, calling out to them in Language. Then, knowing the audience could not understand him, he said, "Let's put on our little show for the rubes. Just like we rehearsed."

Fitz turned to the audience and said, "Please welcome my friends." He started clapping as he spoke. With hesitation, uncertain of the game, the audience joined him, applauding the Fur girls. Stapleya and Wisceya joined him beside the massive weight. They took up positions at either end of the bar. Fitz positioned himself as if to lift the weight.

The ladies leaned in as though they intended to help lift the massive weight, each grasping the end. Then, just as Fitz began to raise it, they scrambled aboard. They sat astride the wheels as Fitz lifted not only the gut-busting weight but the two women as well.

The jeers turned to applause as Fitz lifted high and then lowered the weight. The ladies jumped off as he gently lowered the weight and took deep bows to raucous applause.

The three professional weightlifters conferred, discussing Fitz's performance. Suspecting a hustle, they configured a new weight much heavier than any before. It was far heavier than the weight of the prior weight plus the Fur girls. This massive barbell required all three professional weightlifters to carry it to the stage.

Fitz looked askance at the task he was to attempt. "You're kidding, right?" The audience laughed. "I know Dr. Shepherd made outrageous claims but isn't that extreme?"

The three looked at each other. They agreed perhaps they had gone too far. Chastised, they moved to remove a couple of weights. Fitz stopped them. "I will call your hand," he said.

With a great show of stretching and preparation, he addressed the monstrous weight. He hefted it a few inches and bounced it back on the floor without performing the snatch. He did this several times, each time drawing the audience to the edge of their seats. They did not know whether he would actually lift it or fail. Whether perhaps the inhuman effort might kill him.

Weightlifters die this way. Perhaps some in the audience expected the worst. Maybe a few hoped for it.

Finally, sensing he had milked the theatrics, he squared off with the great barbell. He grasped it with both hands and addressed it square. Then, with a dramatic effort, he hoisted the weight shoulder-high. He pulled himself under it, and then with a final grunt, pressed it high overhead. The audience grunted in sympathy at each stage of the lift and groaned at the final upthrust.

As he held the great bar aloft, the audience gasped in astonishment. Incredulity echoed through the hall.

Then something much more incredible happened.

Nothing! Fitz just stood there. And smiled.

Weightlifters do not hold massive barbells aloft. Not at this level. Nor smile while doing so. Instead, such weight is thrust aloft, held for the briefest of moments to qualify the snatch, and then dropped. Muscles exerting at that level soon exhaust their stored glycogen, turn to rubbery uselessness. A snatch is one thing. Holding is quite another.

Fitz stood, holding the audience in thrall as he supported the impossible weight. Then after an eternity, he lowered it. But only to his shoulders, to hoist it again. And again. Up-down, up-down, a standing Military Press as though the weight were only a few pounds. He pressed it in front, then behind his neck. Back and forth, up and down. Shocked, Ohs and Ahs escaped the audience at the casual handling of the massive weight.

Then Fitz yawned as though bored and shifted the tremendous weight. He continued the Military Press, WITH ONE HAND, covering his mock yawn with the other. Then he shifted to the other hand.

Having exhausted his theatrics, he held the barbell aloft one more time. With a laugh, he then dropped the barbell to the stage. As though to emphasize the extreme weight, this barbell crashed through the floor. Unlike the previous three, this one buried itself in the stage.

The audience sat in stunned silence for several heartbeats. Then they began to murmur in shock and surprise. They smelled a rat.

Science!

But before the blow-off, having considered how the Alien presence is to be revealed to the public, we return to the research project and reveal how the team finally taps Dark Energy and the consequences of doing so.
Energized, we tackled the research with fresh enthusiasm. Lieutenant Rice produced his mobile and manipulated it. Within hours a team of Klovia's top scientists joined us in our basement. The gym and gun range became a laboratory.

The scientists reviewed the videos of our first session and examined the Psionic Egg outputs. Then, they devised new tests designed to address aspects we hadn't considered. Finally, they crafted tests intended to yield unequivocal scientific validity.

They connected instrumentation to our bodies to determine energy and oxygen consumption. We ran for hours on treadmills as instruments measured our metabolism. We learned to tap our in the zone mode at will instead of waiting for a burst of adrenaline.

The effort continued for weeks. Finally, we confirmed the existence of non-physical psionic energy beyond doubt. The scientists agreed it was a reasonable scientific theory. They went to great lengths to exclude potential flaws in the testing.

We failed to tap energy beyond our metabolism. We suspected a vast reservoir of Dark Energy awaits discovery. Yet we accounted for every Joule of energy expended in the calories consumed.

A surprising conclusion about non-physical energy emerged. It is brutally inefficient. Fitz could hoist immense weights, his muscular effort augmented by the mental. But that mental boost came at a terrific cost.

Testing revealed the calories consumed by mental force exceeded muscles. In fact, the delta is more than a hundredfold.

Food calories to physical movement by way of non-physical force uses a lot of calories. Muscles are much more efficient.

Midway through the third week, it was clear that we were flagging. The constant testing was giving us quite the workout. Our abilities were deteriorating with use, most noticeable in tests of endurance. We were running slower, and even Fitz's strength was fading. Not a lot, but enough to measure with instruments. If not for the instrumentation, we would not have noticed. The scientists began searching for the cause.

We tried everything we could think of with no change. Two more weeks passed as we continued to slide down the slope of entropy. We were becoming slower and weaker. My aim with a weapon had not suffered, but I too lacked the fine edge in speed and strength.

There followed a whirlwind of testing on Nekomata, on Center, on Earth, and on Klovia. We made many trips between worlds, sometimes two Portal trips per day. The deterioration reversed itself after a visit to Nekomata. Consumption of GoJuice and Journey Cake staples seemed the apparent driver.

The fact that our scientists' instruments would not function on Nekomata caused endless frustration. Petchy had once stated he believed that Nekomata was not in our universe at all. Instead, he surmised it was in a strange sort of parallel dimension, linked only via the portals. In theory, one could travel from Earth to Klovia via spaceship, ignoring the problems of distance and navigation.

But travel from either of those to Nekomata would be impossible because Nekomata is not there. It is elsewhere. Perhaps even elsewhen. That, simply put, is Petchy's hypothesis of why the laws of physics go awry on Nekomata.

It is remarkable that human metabolism even functions on both worlds. Even stranger, our metabolism appears more efficient there — a lot more efficient. In light of that observation, our abilities' improvements while training there makes sense. We became stronger and faster on Nekomata because our metabolic processes became more efficient. Whether due to the nutrition, or just the environment, I dunno. That extra energy perhaps fuels increased Psionic Flow too.

That observation raised the question; could humans have originated on Nekomata? Is the Dinosaur world humanity's ancestral homeland? Could our ancestors have traveled through the Portals to all the human-inhabited worlds? Is the tale of Adam and Eve actual history, a story repeated for each human world? Is Nekomata the original Garden of Eden?

The existence of the Portals puts a new spin on the theories of human origins. The potential to cross between worlds will change everything. In the end, though, it just pushes the ultimate question back in time and moves it to another planet. There is no answer for Nekomata origins.

Is Planet Oz the ancestral home of the human race? A pretty hypothesis, but the data are incomplete. I suspect scientists will study that question for decades. Perhaps centuries. There are hints, from the seeming vast age of the Castles to the diminutive stature of the Nekomata. We know humans used to be much shorter in the past, for example. Is modern human stature a product of adaptation to an alien world?

Many questions amid a dearth of answers.

Potty Breen stayed by our side throughout our efforts. Much of the time, he appeared to be asleep, but he was usually present. I did notice several occasions when he and Fitz were in a private conference. A couple of times, I asked Fitz what he and Potty were talking about. My curiosity elicited a blank look, or at most a noncommittal response. Something was up.

Four weeks into the project, Potty appeared with a new gadget. It was an odd-looking headband with electronics and contact pads. "Let's take this for a test drive," he said. Fitz picked it up and looked it over suspiciously.

Suspicious, Petchy asked, "What's this? Some kind of brainwave device?"

Potty shrugged, "This is a widget some professional athletes have been playing around with. They call it a cranial stimulator, supposed to stimulate neurons with a tickle of electricity. The idea is to provide positive reinforcement that helps them work better—this one's modified to process feedback from the entropy generators. Positive feedback ensues when the Psionic Eggs detect non-physical energy. So in effect, we'll attempt training neurons to produce psionic energy."

Alex expressed concern. "So, you're saying this gadget zaps the brain with electricity? That's a bit scary. Has anyone examined the long-term effects of doing so?"

Potty shrugged.

Petchy said, "Yes, a scary thought. So is Gharlane. We must take risks. I volunteer to test drive it."

Teena and Fitz both raised objections. But, Potty said, "Many athletes have used the technique. It seems benign."

Fitz claimed, "Petchy, you can't muster enough psionic energy to lift a helium balloon. I think if it has any effect at all, it will have the most benefit for me. I should be the one to try it."

An argument ensued over who should be the first to try it. It became comical, outrageous. Petch claimed the right, arguing that he had the most to gain. Since Fitz already demonstrated psionic effects, Petch felt he should try it himself first.

When that argument was insufficient, he advanced the idea that he was more expendable. Should the device cause harm, he argued, better to risk himself than Fitz.

Alex jumped into the argument by suggesting if anyone was expendable, it was he.

Fine with me. I'm not one to volunteer. I learned the wisdom of volunteering in the service. I'll let the others argue over who should zap their brains. I didn't believe the fundamental postulate. Teena seemed to share my skepticism as she watched the altercation in silence.

Fitz abruptly settled the debate by grabbing the device and plopping it on his own head. Then, with a mock sneer, he dared either to try and take it.

Possession became the convincing argument; the others surrendered.

It seemed all for naught when we began testing. Nothing happened except Fitz looked like a dork with the gadget on his head. He persevered, and the scientists began tweaking the device and its software. They continued for hours, thinking up another tweak to try, one more round of careful testing. We became dejected and were close to giving up on cranial stimulation. My already well-developed skepticism grew.

Then suddenly, we had results.

Fitz tapped into the *Dark Energy*. Well maybe. We can't prove that, although it appears the logical conclusion. I am clueless about how we might prove it.

I kept talking about tapping a Dark Energy flow via psionic energy. My words morphed into a name for the phenomenon. I guess I was the one who dubbed it the Psionic Tap, though it was unintentional. But my invention or not, the term stuck.

Fitz began using less energy, less oxygen for each lift. He was lifting the same weight but expending less physical effort. Slight change at first, and then as he practiced, the gain improved. Energy was coming from somewhere other than his metabolism.

Instrumented, he began lifting larger and larger weights. He began lifting greater weights than ever, with less and less physical effort. He began lifting with one hand weights that before had required two. A week later, he was boosting impressive weights with one finger.

Two weeks followed with Fitz training on focusing his mind. He improved on every attempt to ever greater effect. Then he figured out how to lift without even touching the weight. He had to make the motions, even to grasping like his hands were around the bar. He also must close his eyes. The phenomenon would not work if his eyes could see that he was not, in fact, touching the bar. Even with these limitations, there was no longer any doubt.

Psychokinesis is real, and so is *Dark Energy*. And we can tap it.

The Game of Blood and Dust

"As flies to wanton boys, are we to the gods; they kill us for their sport." — William Shakespeare

---

Having learned to tap Dark Energy, we now resume the narrative of Disclosure. Having spotted the strange Señor Aguilar in the audience, our heroes now suspect their trap has been sprung.

The audience began to rumble in anger as Dr. Shepherd again took the stage. Clapping for attention proved futile. The chairperson stepped forward with her mobile, and once again, the gong resounded. Two, three, four times, it sounded. Fitz stepped to the rostrum. Inserting two fingers between his lips, he let loose a shrill whistle that dwarfed the simulated gong.

The audience, still grumbling, calmed, and Dr. Shepherd began speaking. "Friends, please," he began.

As though flipping a switch, the great hall fell silent. The chairperson froze, still standing, then teetered, began to collapse. Teena jumped forward and caught her, lowering her to the floor.

Dr. Shepherd squinted past the lights with apprehension. Had their trap sprung? Could they hold the quarry once caught?

The audience slumped in their chairs. In one heartbeat, the massive audience had fallen asleep. He hoped they were sleeping.

He looked at those sharing the stage. Fitz and the Asherans were the only ones moving. Their faces reflected surprise. Everyone else lay unconscious. The chairperson, even the Nekomata, all slumped, insensate. Potty appeared to be asleep as well, though that remains unremarkable. The obese Klovian could sleep through doomsday. He may well be doing so.

Fitz and Teena were staring at the audience, mouth agape. Then, a thin, pale gray man in a pale gray suit rose in third-row center and raised his hands before him.

"Well played, sir, well done," — sarcastic slow clap. "Well done, I am impressed."

"Señor Aguilar, I presume?" Petchy asked. "Or is it Gharlane?"

"Your deception worked for a while. I congratulate you on a noble effort. However, you will find it a futile one. I knew someone resisted my program. I let my guard down because I thought your race was extinct. I took down your world and scattered your people. You should have faded away, forgotten. I turn my attention away for a few brief centuries, and here you are, not extinct at all. Yet."

Petchy said, "How did you like our little demonstration? I hoped it would draw you out."

Gharlane bowed slightly in acknowledgment. "Of course, I can feel your tap into the cosmos. I congratulate you on touching the universe," Gharlane said. "You thought you could block my access. I congratulate you on your excellent effort. I could not have done it better. Although you closed this world, it did not prevent me from penetrating your blockade. The ultimate irony is your party brought me here themselves!" Gharlane laughed at the irony, a slow, almost maniacal cackle.

"You clouded my senses; I could feel your tap but not trace your location. That is impressive for one so new to the powers of the mind. I give you credit for your amazing aptitude. You do understand I cannot permit humans to walk that path. You have eaten the forbidden apple. The five of you must die this instant. The Council forbids such power to others. I must kill the four of you here and now."

Gharlane's voice tinged with anger. "One of you is hiding, masking their presence. No doubt the one responsible for the blockade. No matter, that one dies today too. Then I will hunt down the female who left this world. I will find her no matter where in the universe she hides."

Looking at Petchy, Fitz, and Teena, Gharlane then peered around the auditorium. He sensed four Taps, though one is hiding. No matter, one problem at a time, he mused. They cannot escape.

Gharlane paused a moment, then said, "I am almost sorry to take your lives. You have been worthy opponents."

"What of the Klovians?" Petchy asked. He discomfited at Gharlane's reference to a blockade and noted the discrepancy in Gharlane's count.

"These?" Gharlane waved his hands with disdain. "They're unharmed. I will, of course, topple this society. I see no need for wanton murder. They will survive in the short term. They will survive to experience a long, slow slide to humanity's natural barbaric state. Like you should have. You should have stayed down when I knocked you down."

"You attacked my people, killed my world," Petchy accused. "Why? What purpose does it serve to destroy an entire civilization?"

"Purpose? Why must there be a purpose? Isn't survival of the fittest purpose enough? The Council of Peers brooks no challengers. There can be only one cosmic sentience."

"I see," said Petchy. "You sound like a comic-book villain. Universal domination, no one may stand beside you. Is that it?"

Sardonic smile. "You mock. Yet, I can be magnanimous today. Today is the day your particular strain of the human virus dies. I was willing to tolerate a low-level infection. You have mutated, escaped your petri dish. You are a virus. You are too contagious to live. Like Prometheus, I bring the fire, though not to give, but to sterilize. Like Icarus, you flew too high. I trust you will forgive the mythology mashup. I love playing around with your religions. You flew too near the cosmic fire, and now you die."

Petchy shrugged and spread his hands in mock submission. "Today is as good a day to die as any. Death comes but once to a customer. But, before you pass sentence, would you do me the courtesy of telling me of the Council of Peers? I wish to understand the enemy I have been fighting so long. Honor your 'worthy opponent' with the knowledge before your coup de grâce."

"Why not? I will stay my hand a few moments. You have given me pleasure in the hunt. I am not the villain you imagine. I am but a workman with a task, or perhaps a soldier, following orders. I take no pleasure in the assignment. I protect the Council. No sentient being may grow to the extent that they might become aware of the Council of Peers. Once aware, they may threaten. That we cannot permit."

Gharlane stuck a casual pose, sounding almost like a lecturing college professor. "The Council of Peers is our name for ourselves. We are ancient and immortal. Our Council is made up of those peers with the most power."

Gharlane gave a sardonic laugh. "You thought with your DNA project you might reach immortality. We did something similar long before this planet's sun congealed from the cosmic dust."

He narrowed his eyes toward Petchy. "In our youth, we sought out other races to share our secrets and our power. Throughout our history, this has proven a mistake. Those races arose, some to join us, and some to conquer us. Those who joined us sought to supplant us. All failed, and we grew weary of defending ourselves.

"Before your planet cooled, we decided that no other race may be allowed to reach the stage where they may threaten the Council. Any species that discovers science must be treated with suspicion. When they become threatening, we knock them down.

"Any species may live as they wish as long as they do not seek immortality. As long as they stay on their home world and do not pursue cosmic energy."

Petchy asked, "When they do, you kill them?"

Gharlane shook his head. "My tactic is to confuse and confound those minds with potential. I dislike murder. It is much easier to sow seeds of disharmony. I stand by and watch the intelligent-yet-idiot true-believers attack and destroy their own world. It is amazing what they will do in the name of their imaginary deity. Especially if I help them along with a few signs and portents. Interject a slogan, craft a meme, and the virus spreads."

Petchy folded his arms as Gharlane talked. He nodded in agreement. Petchy said, "Perhaps it would be more correct to say you are the deity they imagine. A miracle here, a prophecy there, and behold thou art God."

"Except I play both God and Devil in one act. Good and evil both begin and end in my hands."

"It didn't quite work on Ashera, though, did it?" Petchy asked. "Perhaps our grasp of science and logic thwarted your plans?"

"Ah, your case was more challenging, I admit. Your people had progressed well beyond the *burning bush* phase. Like this world, the talking snake gambit wouldn't work. Nevertheless, Ashera was an amusing experiment. You were so determined to improve your DNA; I thought it ironic to turn your efforts to your demise.

"I should have supervised the demise more closely. I started the plan in motion then left you to attend to other demands. You should have succumbed to age and senescence. Since you failed to follow the plan, I must now destroy your entire race with my own hands. I detest that."

"Inconsiderate of us," Petchy answered in mock sympathy. "I do apologize." Petchy resisted the temptation to ask Gharlane what he meant about the blockade or why he counted four when there were only three of them. If his enemy was making a mistake, he did not wish to correct him.

Gharlane continued. "On Earth, I apply the same weapon blooming now on Klovia. An opiate as seductive as any religion. A narcotic, mesmerizing to the strongest will.

"Religion promises Utopia wholesale, in the afterlife. When a people refuse to trust in an afterlife, I cast the promises closer to hand. Sometimes it is necessary to sell Utopia retail in the physical world. Wholesale or retail makes little difference, no matter how illogical. The seductive promise of Utopia always leads to destruction and collapse. Once they partake of the narcotic, critical thinking ceases."

"You sow discontent and promise Utopia at the harvest," Petchy said.

Gharlane spread his hands apart, palms out in a classical God-like pose. "The game of blood and dust. A big, bloody reset button.

The game never ends," he said. "Civilizations die without firing a shot. The drums of war will sound. The proud, rational Klovians will dismantle their world, retreat to caves and primitive huts — science, engineering, philosophy, art — all forgotten. I need not kill a single one. Then, a few millennia hence, some archaeologists of the next epoch may rise. They will perhaps discover the decayed bones of a lost civilization and wonder. Wash, rinse, repeat. I will be there to press the reset again."

With that, he raised his hands, shifting from his God pose as though to draw the fires of heaven down on Petchy.

"And now your time ends," Gharlane said.

As Gharlane concluded, Fitz stepped forward, closed his eyes, and flexed his muscles. The massive barbell exploded from the cavity it had dug in the floor. It hurtled toward Gharlane at an incomprehensible speed, taking bits of the floor with it as it flew. A thunderous clap reverberated the room; plaster fell from the walls from the force of the sonic boom.

Although surprised, Gharlane parried the blow. The massive weight halted inches from its intended target. The unyielding steel crushed by the deceleration into a potato-shaped lump as though by an invisible hand. Then hurled anew toward Fitz, it covered half the distance before halting in midair. It hovered as two psionic minds of power grappled. It began to glow as it absorbed a minute fraction of the energies expended upon it. As the contest of wills continued, dull red turned orange, then white as it began to melt into a molten sphere. Both beings sparkled as a torrent of raw energy swirled around them.

Potipher Breen, no longer a somnolent bystander, joined in. Fitz was too busy to marvel at the unexpected assistance. Potty's human form dissipated as together they bore into Gharlane. Two minds of power, one human, one a glowing something more, linked. Together, bearing down on the villain with all the Dark Energy they could Tap. All the energy the Universe could funnel through their minds.

Gharlane enshrouded himself in a glowing energy sphere. His shield withstanding the forces, he parried the thrust. Then began expanding his sphere. Every bit of matter touched by the growing field exploded into coruscant flame. Debris and energy alike swirled as though spun by the Coriolis force of the Universe itself.

Petchy and Teena recovered from the momentary shock of Potty's revelation. They joined with Fitz and Potty, adding their minds to the Tap. Gharlane's shield ceased expanding, but neither did it retreat. Both sides held fast, each unable to gain against the other. Four against one might appear an unequal contest. Not so much.

They stood, locked in a combat of galactic proportions, for an eternity. Spacetime itself began to bend.

Then with an unimpressive '*sluurrp,*' they were gone. Petchy, Teena, Fitz, Potty, and Gharlane vanished. Dust and debris swirled as air rushed in to fill the vacuum, the empty space left by their disappearance.

Mountain Fortress

*Jill has left Klovia ahead of 'Disclosure' to return to
Nekomata to prepare their trap.*

Alien world or not, Castle Stapleya feels more like home than
Earth, at least in some ways. Don't misunderstand; I love my work
and my friends in the organization. I love adventure and
challenging missions. I also love modern conveniences. A stone-
age life is tough and unforgiving, yet the Nekomata are so
welcoming, and I feel loved and carefree. Lack of pressure to
conform to societal roles allows me to relax in ways I never can on
Earth.

I can afford only two nights under Stapleya's roof, with no time
for socializing or relaxing. We must send a call to arms to nearby
castles and recruit their aid; else, I would not have that time. No
need to run hundreds of miles cross-country; instead, I must head
into the mountainous wastelands to the west. This won't be a fun
trip.

Though it is good to be here, my cause is a dangerous one. Not
only dare I risk my own life, but our plan endangers the fur-people
too. There is no way to put a polish on this lump of excrement.

We are trading a short-term risk against a long-term certainty.
If we don't kill Gharlane here, there won't be another shot.

I need a suitable place to lure him, a battleground I can turn to a home-field advantage. Or at least one I can turn to Gharlane's disadvantage.

Stapleya had reacted with horror when we made our plans. She thought it unfair to bring another plague to their beleaguered world. She also thought it wrong to ask her to speak for her entire world. Although she heads an ancient, respected Castle, she could not represent the world. She insists she can only speak for her family, her Castle. Though distressed by the issue, she agreed that ending Gharlane with finality was the only option. If he survives, he will attack the Nekomata too. There was no time to consult the other castles. Gharlane will not wait.

The plan was set. Petchy, Teena, and Fitz will stage a public demonstration of non-physical forces. Stapleya and Wisceya will go to Klovia to help them. They planned to draw Gharlane out and lure him to Nekomata. We hoped to find an advantage here that is impossible on any other world. We hoped it would be enough.

Fitz was the first to master the Psionic Tap. It happened very late one night. Or very early one morning, take your pick. We were all exhausted, yet Fitz insisted on one more attempt. Petchy adjusted the brain-zapper to full effect. We all winced in sympathy as Fitz reacted to the tingle. Harmless, we chanted with inner voices. Only a tingle, we reminded ourselves.

Wearing the zapper, forehead twitching under the stimulation, Fitz reached for the heavy barbell. With eyes closed, mind focused, he reached out with hands and mind. He inhaled and prepared to hoist. Instead of the usual firm grip and straining muscles, something entirely unexpected happened. The Psionic Eggs might have warned us had we monitored their stream.

The instant Fitz touched the massive big-wheel, hell broke loose. Before he could even grasp the bar, it rocketed upward. Well-nigh a half-ton of steel pretended to be a crazed bottle-rocket. A barbell-shaped hole appeared in the ceiling, debris flying like shrapnel. The barbell flew upward, into and through the room above. It inflicted an impressive divot in the remote second ceiling.

Then, driving force dissipated, it heeded gravity's pull. Retracing the vertical path, it proceeded to dig a sizable crater in the gym's concrete floor. Fitz lunged backward, managing a narrow escape from the falling weight. Concrete chips and dust pelted our bodies.

Petchy stared at the still rocking, deformed weight with a wooden expression. Then, quietly, he intoned, "It is frustrating to approach the brink of complete failure, only to have success rear its ugly head." We turned our gaze from the mess to Petchy's deadpan and collapsed in laughter.

Until that moment, I had remained skeptical, even dismissive of their efforts. I suppose I still considered it supernatural. But, once Fitz proved the possibility, we redoubled our efforts. I became driven.

Several sleepless days and nights followed, with endless brain-zapping. Fitz said it reminded him of learning to juggle. Easy once you have the knack, yet difficult to learn by yourself. Except a juggler can show a student the right moves. We were teaching ourselves juggling alone and in darkness, on an airplane flying through a turbulent storm.

We had no one to teach us: our only guidance, the Psionic Egg. The output tells us when we generate Psionic energy—the Egg and the knowledge that it is possible. And, of course, we had Potty at our elbows offering his particular style of guidance. At first, I was dismissive of his help, but then I realized he was, in fact, helping. I could not explain that.

Alex was the one who developed the plan. Potty helped him a lot, too, though again, I felt unclear how that could be. Although he could not learn the Tap, Alex remains one of the finest planners and managers to have ever lived. We all provided input, but the plan is all Alex's.

Learning to generate Psionic energy is, of course, the first step. Tapping the *dark energy* flow is quite another and the more difficult step. Psionic energy allows us to tap the Cosmic Flow but is not itself the flow.

Psionic energy comes from within, from our body's metabolic resources. We don't have a good theory of how glucose transforms into non-physical force. Fitz is the largest and has the greatest metabolic reserves. Therefore, Fitz was by far our strongest generator of psionic energy.

That did not sit well; I am not content with second best at anything. So, hard-driven, or perhaps just hard-headed, I challenged Fitz for top spot.

Dark Energy is limitless. Like drawing water from the ocean, restricted only by the "pipe" we use to tap it. That "pipe" is the "diameter" of our mind, or rather the psionic energy our minds can generate. The more psionic energy, the stronger the flow we can tap. Thus, although the flow is limitless, the force we can muster is not.

We scaled the learning curb; we learned to control our psionic energy. Then, with a painful climb up and over another level of learning curb, we learned to tap the Dark Energy. We learned to engage the flow as a merged mind as though we are one.

Once we mastered the tap, we deciphered the manipulation of dark energy. From there, it was practice and practice alone.

I threw myself into the challenge. I did not quite best Fitz in raw power, but I came in a close second. Not enough glucose in my compact and efficient body, I suppose. I did beat him in tests of precision and control and sheer speed of action. Fitz is blazingly quick, but I matched him in reaction time. I beat him in precision control, though not by much.

Okay, fine, he beat me in reaction time; The difference fell within the margin of error. No need to nitpick. We're both damn quick.

We also confirmed the Psionic Tap fails on Nekomata, as suspected. Thus, the hypothesis placing Nekomata in a sort of alternate Universe appears well-founded. Our Psionic Tap and the Dark Energy of the Nekomata universe seem incompatible. We have the non-physical effects, limited to our own metabolism as the energy source. The almost unlimited energy available elsewhere is not available here.

We hope Gharlane is also unable to tap it from here. The plan is simple. We lure Gharlane to Nekomata, where we can overwhelm him with numbers. Limited to psionic energy, I am confident we can overcome him.

Our trap relies on a dangerous assumption. We are assuming he will be vulnerable on Nekomata. If we bring him here and he remains able to tap unlimited energy, we lose.

He will kill us all. But then, he will do that anyway.

The third morning we set out for the wastelands. Accompanying me were two hundred of the ablest Nekomata. Every rick-buggy available and every runner. Every skilled archer. I chose my archers with care: only the best, most skilled, and only those having no young children. I also rejected any that might be fertile. Fertile wombs are too valuable. We are not committing to a suicide mission, but I am planning like it is.

Nearby castles contributed buggies and runners, as well as archers, to the mission.

We were bristling with weapons and supplies. This may have been the most extraordinary mobilization of force in the history of the fur-people. This trip will not be easy, as there are no roads for the rick-buggies where we're headed. It is open country, but without roads, progress will be slow. We can expect to lose some of the buggies to broken wheels and such. Fortunately, the rick-buggies allow adding poles so they may be easily carried over rough ground like a litter or sedan chair. Two Fur girls in front and two in back, and it is possible to carry them over extremely rough ground with relative ease.

We distributed the supplies such that no one buggy held a critical resource alone. For example, we distributed weaponry across all buggies. Food and water too. I carried The Lady Tyrxing; I'm taking no chances with her.

Fitz's mighty Warrior bow, The Lady Seven, was well packed. Several of her sisters were in other buggies, as well as weaponry for

Teena and Petch. All the missiles we could find, too. On the relevance of sabres and archery in a war of cosmic forces, consider one point. How much more effective one of Fitz's massive arrows might become with psychokinesis? If driven, not just by the mighty bow, but by all the force the mind behind that bow could muster? Then, calculate how much greater the force should three more minds add their power to the thrust.

The same applies to other weapons too. Imagine a sword wielded not just by a strong arm but a psionic-enabled mind of power as well. Medieval weapons are not rendered irrelevant by psychokinesis. If anything, they're revitalized, made more relevant than ever.

We need a "Trinity Site," a place where we could unlimber our Ultimate Weapon. The plan was to run as far and as fast as possible into the mountainous wasteland. The area, pockmarked with caves, is undoubtedly home to nocturnal meat-eaters. We intended to reach the caves and secure a fortress amongst the caverns.

We may have to evict a local resident or two. I carried the BFR, just in case. We also carried the remaining HEIAP rounds from the defunct BMG. We lack a weapon to fire them, but I strapped them to arrows, replacing the usual arrowheads. I can hurl them with a bow, then drive and detonate them using psychokinesis. Even without the Tap, I can still drive them extremely hard. I'd bet I can kill a T-Rex. Psionic energy gives me new approaches to battling the beasts. Not that I'm anxious to engage.

We established our fortress. As expected, a few of the residents objected. We expected that and came prepared. Dinosaur hide is thick. It's suicide for an archer to engage a Deinonychus alone with only arrows. Psionic energy changes things. When a Deinonychus engages psionic-enabled archers, that's suicide too — for the Deinonychus. Imagine arrows that fly so fast that sonic booms accompany them. Imagine arrows that temper themselves into hard carbon during flight from the heat of friction with the air.

Archers ten, dinosaurs zip. Force increases with velocity squared. That's the formula of din-o-mite!

The only drawback is the arrows become single-use projectiles. When a psionic-driven arrow hits dinosaur bone, the result is catastrophic. Neither the arrow nor the dinosaur is reusable. That's fine; we have lots of arrows and fletchers busily making more. Did I mention Dinosaur meat tastes like chicken?

To be fair, the dinosaurs didn't bring their A-game. Their star player sat this one out. I was ready and waiting with my explosive arrows, but T-Rex failed to appear.

Fortress prepared and occupied; I sent the runners and rick-buggies home. We no longer have need of their services. We're dug-in, well supplied, and ready.

Dug-in and vigilant, we are ready for battle. Our counterparts on Klovia are attempting to draw the enemy into our locus. Our job is to stay honed and ready. No matter how long it takes them.

We are not going anywhere.

Emergence

Telepathy would be an asset, or at least ESP would help. Unfortunately, coordinating events across far-flung worlds and dimensions of space-time is an insurmountable challenge. The only tools at our disposal are careful planning and precise timing. Petchy, Fitz, and Teena intend to draw Gharlane out and bring him here.

Terrific plan. There are but two flaws; we don't know where Gharlane might be or what might entice him.

The core plan hinged on the belief that agents of our quarry monitored the media on worlds he targeted. Perhaps he has agents on Klovia who keep him appraised, or maybe he pops in for updates. Although as there is no evidence his agents have a method to contact him, the latter seems probable. He always contacts them, our evidence suggests. Evidence also suggests long absences when a world poses scant threat.

Since the attack on the Klovian starship, there had been no further sign of his presence. The bait for our trap is a series of demonstrations of the Tap, particularly in front of large crowds. Involving the Klovian Chief Executive herself gains us the widest possible exposure.

Our effort to draw him out kicks off with a massive 'Disclosure Summit.' We will tell the citizens of Klovia that there are aliens living among them, meaning us. The Klovians will be skeptical of our claims. Stapleya and Wisceya will appear on stage to lend credence. With the Chief executive involved, her VoTE audience and terrific media coverage follow.

If the first public appearance fails to draw our enemy, repeat until it does. Keep demonstrating, keep raising the stakes until our enemy presents himself.

Indeed, his absence has been a mystery; he should sense our attempts to tap Dark Energy. Experimenting and training, we feared, might attract him before we were ready. Yet luck favored our efforts; somehow, that did not happen. As of the time I left Klovia, there had been no interference from Gharlane. Unmolested despite our fear of discovery, we trained until we were ready.

Linking our minds together widens our Tap. The wider the Tap, the more energy we can access. With enough energy, we learned to create our own Portals. The more minds linked, the more energy and the stronger the Portal.

Our enemy generated his own custom Portal on demand when he attacked the starship, so we knew it was possible. Knowing something is possible is the first step to mastering it. Thereafter, it only requires practice and training. With enough energy, we could form a robust Portal able to transport anything we wished.

Will that end naked Portal travel?

Maybe, although I'm uncertain how I would feel if so, despite everything, I have come to appreciate the enforced deshabille of Portal travel. That aspect of interplanetary travel adds spice to an otherwise intimidating prospect. Something mundane on which to focus distracts the mind from the fear of Portal travel.

More important, control over Portals means we may transport supplies and weapons. We might be about to open the universe to free trade among all human worlds.

Special conditions extant on Nekomata are the key to our plan for trapping Gharlane. We can form a Portal from Klovia to

Nekomata and traverse it. Departing Nekomata is quite another matter. We cannot form a Portal from Nekomata to anywhere. Thus, without access to the cosmic Dark Energy from Nekomata, departure is impossible. Travel to Nekomata is a one-way proposition. Leaving Nekomata requires accessing one of the rare natural portals. The absence of Dark Energy supports the hypothesis that Nekomata is in another Universe. Or perhaps a different dimension, rendering the Dark Energy beyond reach.

Mobilizing Asheran resources to close those natural portals is Alex's responsibility. Nekomata will be our trap. We will lure Gharlane here with intent to kill him. Is this first-degree murder? Or self-defense? Either way, we must do it for the sake of humanity. Whether we kill him or not, we cannot leave this place. The entrapment protocol dictates a one-way trip. Once the trap springs, there is no possibility of transport until he's confirmed dead.

That presents a problem; how do we confirm to Alex that Gharlane is dead? And how do we communicate that to the Asherans keeping the Portals closed? The answer is, we do no such thing; Alex has a few contingency plans, but that's not my problem. I cannot know about such plans, if any. Whatever knowledge I lack, Gharlane cannot extract.

A life sentence on Nekomata is part of the deal I agreed to when I accepted this mission.

If we succeed in killing Gharlane and Alex commutes the sentence, fine. Security demands I cannot know Alex's plans. No one on Nekomata can know Alex's plans, lest Gharlane co-opts them.

If that means I spend my life on Nekomata, I'm fine with that.

As the resident military expert, my skills came in handy. Organizing our group into four teams, I planned our strategy and assigned duties to each.

Overwatch Team to spread wide, seek high ground, and keep watch for signs of our foe. A complex series of lepatata sounds and relays pass hourly status reports.

Alpha Team to forage for food. We have plenty of meat thanks to the dinosaurs, but we need more than dino-chicken.

Bravo Team to hunt Dinosaur sign. A side mission involves killing them. Exterminating them. The fur-people are reclaiming their world. If I must stay here, I will find useful work for decades to come in that job alone.

Gold Team to drill and train. Constant training and improvement. Practice, practice, practice. I joined this group daily to improve my own skills and impart my skills to others. The gentle Nekomata lack skills in this area, and I am the expert.

Each morning the teams rotate. Gold becomes Overwatch, who in turn becomes Alpha, and so on. A fresh team is always watching the sky. We stayed busy, and the days passed.

The teams assumed a series of strategic stances around our fortress. Three times per day, we drilled, falling to for battle in various formations.

Attempting to teach psionic techniques to the training group resulted in failure. I'm starting to suspect that not all minds are capable of harnessing the psionic force. Not all Asheran minds; although working at it as much as any one of us, Alex failed to master it. So far, only we four smoothies have made the leap. Why, we have no clue. Perhaps there is another unknown factor.

〰〰

Day 3 Bravo Team reported T-Rex signs a few miles away. Deinonychus and Velociraptors we knew were plentiful. So far, the T-Rex have stayed away. Fortuna, the goddess of luck, please be with us.

On Day 10, Bravo Team flushed a flock of Velociraptors. It appears they had nested in the forest, and Bravo Team happened to spot the nest. Team Bravo salvoed them as they slept, killing several outright in the nest. The rest bolted and ran.

Excoriating Bravo Team for their carelessness, I tore into them with Patton-style eloquence. Not my usual style, but I wanted them to remember this. "Godfuckingdamn cockwaffles," I said. "You were ass-shit lucky the hell-beasts ran away instead of swarming you. Stupid fucking bitches," I scolded. There was much more, but there is no need to write down every profanity.

I walked past them and engaged each one in direct eye contact. One by one, they wilted. Then I turned and addressed the team again, with a little less venom in my voice.

"You brushed elbows with Azrael, the Angel of Death himself, and were too goddamn stupid to know it. If they hadn't run, they would have killed and eaten your entire Goddamn team, weapons or no. Every one of you would be clean-picked bones in the sun. Without my psionic guidance, the only way any of you twats can kill a Velociraptor is goddam pure fucking dumb-assed luck."

"Never fuck-up like that again," I admonished them. "I decide whether or how to engage. Not you! Your judgment is horse shit! Always! I decide! No exception."

My language would not have sounded acceptable at afternoon tea, but it might save their lives. It made an impression; one they won't soon forget. More so, given they had never heard such language from me before. They had doubtless never heard the like from anyone.

Made an impression on me too. That Psyche must stay inside my head. She scares me when she gets out. By the time I got her locked away, I was shaking. I walked off and sat down away from the others and closed my eyes for a few minutes while I fought to calm myself and reel in the rage monster that had taken charge.

Having thoroughly chastised my team, I allowed them to prepare the carcasses for our afternoon meal. Dinos still taste like chicken; even so, Velociraptors are a change from Deinonychus meat.

Early in the morning on Day 23, Overwatch sounded an alarm. An odd-looking dark cloud was congealing above our position. I had just noticed it myself when the lepatata sounded. I could not be sure, but it did appear as though a nascent Portal was about to open. If so, it was high above the planetary surface, dangerously so. Anyone coming through it better have wings. Was our quarry about to appear?

Sounding battle-call, I positioned my archers. We stared at the sky. If this was the result of Fitz, Petchy, and Teena engaging Gharlane, it appeared a slow battle. How long would they engage him? If they can bring him here, what shape will they be in for battle? Perhaps my adrenaline was distorting my time sense. We waited.

The dark spot in the sky grew darker and darker. A brilliant white spot appeared. It clung there for a long time; then, with a thunderclap, they were through. They materialized in thin air, high above the surface.

I said we could form Portals using the Tap. I said nothing about accuracy of placement. We must practice our technique.

Petchy, Teena, and Fitz were in a battle with another humanoid, Gharlane, I presume. I noted a fourth figure with them, a brilliant, glowing "something." What the hell was that? And where did it come from? As they came through the Portal, the battle appeared to pause, and they were falling free.

I tried to slow their fall. Not that of the others; they could fend for themselves. I grabbed for Petchy, Teena, and Fitz and tried to hold them. I gave it my all, but I lacked the psionic strength without the Tap into Dark Energy. So, although I did slow their fall, it was insufficient. Finally, about twenty feet above solid rock, the glowing being came to my aid and the four of them soft-landed.

Well, maybe soft isn't quite the word, but they avoided major injury. Scrapes and bruises will heal. The other being had fallen free, bounced off the rocks, and fallen over the cliff into the forest below. He, or it, didn't interest me at the moment.

I presumed hitting the rocks had killed him. That was a mistake; never assume anything about your enemy. Isn't that the first lesson they teach in Warrior school?

Petchy and Teena were unconscious, Fitz though rattled and punchy, was conscious. He was quoting General Patton.

The "other" landed with a splat and collapsed in a heap. It, or he, collapsed there, drooping as though drained by the ordeal. Perhaps unconscious or injured.

I ran to Teena and checked her over. As I held her, her eyelids fluttered and she awakened. I turned to Petchy, who was also coming around.

A familiar voice shouted, "Daughter, quick, Gharlane! What has become of him, he mustn't escape." I whirled, and there stood Potty! Where the deuce did he come from? He was pointing in the direction I had last seen the other character.

I signaled to my archers, and hand on Sabre took off in pursuit of our enemy. An hour later, we abandoned the pursuit; he had eluded us. I left the archers to continue the hunt and regrouped on the mountain with my friends.

I was bitter that Gharlane had escaped. If I had focused on him instead of my friends in those first seconds, I might have stopped him. I may have even killed him. Or vice versa.

I shouted, "What happened? The plan is working, I guess; you brought him here. It must have been a hell of a fight!"

"Daughter, indeed it was," Potty answered.

"How come you are here? You were not a fighter," I asked.

He motioned for Petchy, Fitz, and Teena to come closer. "My children," he began, "There is much you wish to know. I will share what I can."

As he spoke, he dropped his 'human' disguise and once again became a — 'something.' A moment later, he returned to his 'Potty' disguise and resumed speaking. "I'm not of Klovia; in fact, I'm not human. Gharlane is my enemy as much as he is yours. Moreover, I have fought him for millennia. We have victory in hand, but we must finish the job."

I asked, "Can you find Gharlane?"

He shrugged, such a human gesture. "I'm as limited in this dimension as he. We must work together."

I had a thousand questions, but before I could begin, a lepatata sounded. Gold Team had spotted our quarry entering a cave some distance away.

I panicked that they might attempt to engage him. Thus I had my bugler sound *Stand-Down* to Alpha Team and prayed they would listen. I signaled my remaining archers, and we launched ourselves on a dead run in their direction. We set records for sprinting.

A few lepatata calls to narrow down the location, and we were soon there. We converged in front of a gigantic cavern we had not discovered before now. Dividing the archers into teams, I signaled advance into the black depths of the cavern.

We could sure use LED flashlights. I do miss technology. We had a few candles, but they provide a poor and fragile light.

We entered the cave. I admonished my forces to move slow, silent, and with care. Gharlane is not the only danger here. If we come upon a nest of sleeping Velociraptors or Deinonychus, best not to disturb them.

Leading the team into the darkest depths of the cavern, I became conscious of Potty nearby. I moved to him and whispered, "Can you give us light?" A moment later, he began to glow, soft at first, growing brighter until we no longer needed the candles. "You can do the same, daughter," he whispered in response. "Or view without light, if you wish. Use your mind."

I hadn't considered that our psionic energy could generate light. I conferred with Teena, Fitz, and Petchy for a moment. We attempted it for a few minutes without results.

"We'll work on it," I told Potty. He continued to glow as we advanced into the cavern.

The cavern was gigantic. As we advanced, we marked our trail against the risk of getting lost. Caverns pockmark the area like Swiss cheese. This may be one of the largest caverns on the planet.

About an hour into our cautious spelunking, I sensed something ahead. So did Potty. Teena and Petchy strained their ears to listen. We decided something was moving ahead of us. I signaled the team to freeze.

Teena moved ahead and took the lead. Then, slow and stealthy, one footstep at a time, we advanced. Potty's light dimmed as we moved forward, giving us just enough to pick our way.

I heard breathing; I heard a rustle of movement.

We inched forward, weapons ready. I heard a massive intake of breath as though gargantuan bellows were drawing air.

With that faint warning, a deafening roar reverberated, and leathery footsteps thundered. We dove for cracks and crevasses as a flock of Velociraptors charged from the darkness. They fled past us into the daylight as though the devil were chasing them.

Maybe not the devil, but something was. Four Deinonychuses charged forward on their heels. As they chased the Velociraptors, a Tyrannosaurus Rex chased them. Caught in tight spaces with the beasts, we were in deadly peril.

So fierce was their charge that we could do nothing but duck and cover. Several of us received scratches and other minor injuries. Teena, in the lead, received a nasty gash from a Deinonychus. The beast ran her down and stepped on her prone form as it departed, slashing her with its claw. Bloodied and injured, her fight remained undiminished.

As the T-Rex passed us, I spotted a shocking sight. On the back of Thunder Thighs rode Señor Aguilar, astride the beast as if Eragon himself! Stunned at the sight, it took me a moment to connect that Señor Aguilar is, in fact, Gharlane.

I presume he used his psionic power to control the monsters like puppets. He was escaping, not attacking us. Perhaps he's injured after his fall.

He made a mistake not engaging. Surprised and in the tight space, we were much too vulnerable. Perhaps he just was not able to fight us then. That may just prove his undoing.

Penultimate

I grabbed a couple of HEIAP tipped arrows and charged in pursuit of our prey and his pet T-Rex. Unfortunately, moments lost to surprise and gathering of weapons cost us the race. Gharlane extended an insurmountable head start. I was well in front of the others, but I could hear Fitz close behind. His longer stride let him gain on me as we both chased Gharlane. Petchy was some distance behind him, with several of my archers close on their heels.

Teena was not with us. Her injuries took precedence over the battle. Didn't matter anyway, as we failed to catch our prey. We followed the trail for miles, but we could not catch him.

Paleontologists debate how fast Earth's T-Rex could run sixty-five million years ago. Theories suggest estimates from eighteen miles per hour to forty-five miles per hour. Not that the ones here need feel bound by those estimations. Creatures that died millennia ago on a distant planet have limited relevance. Remote academics arguing over fifty partial skeletons have no theropod in this race.

The slower estimate is fast enough to escape, given the head start. Although judging from the trail left through the forest, I would go with the higher number. Perhaps Gharlane augmented the beast's speed using psionic energy. In any case, we abandoned the chase and regrouped at the cave.

"Thanks for clueing me in on Señor Aguilar," I said. A tad grumpy after the fruitless chase, I was lashing out at no one in particular.

Petchy shrugged. "In the action, we lost sight of the fact you didn't know. You figured it out, I see."

I started laughing. "That's funny," I said. "We were hunting for him and had him right in our grasp and didn't know it. So how is it that we carried him to Klovia, and he did not kill us outright?"

Potty said, "I can explain that. He was looking for me. He could sense I was near, but I could cloud his senses enough to prevent him from finding me. I kept him confused until you had disclosure arranged. Then once our trap was ready, I allowed him to sense us and drew him in."

"If I had known that was him, I would have killed him in Mexico," I said.

"No, daughter, you would have failed. He was not frail and weak, nor sickly. That was an elaborate subterfuge to get you to carry him through my psionic blockade. If you had not fallen for the trick, he would have tried some other tactic. He did not know you were my protégés, that you possessed minds of power. In your nascent state, he could not sense you. I guided you to allow him to trick you, to draw him into the trap. I watched and guided you while interacting with him."

"I thought something seemed odd about that whole escapade," Teena said.

Petchy said, "You say we are your protégés, yet we never knew you before we met on Klovia. How does that follow?"

"My children, I have known you since before your birth. I have guided your development for millennia," Potty said. He turned to Teena. "You, dear one, are my pet project. You are the culmination of more than a thousand generations of selective breeding and genetic manipulation. The series of accidents and coincidences that created your genetic pattern was my doing. It was my hand that guided the passing of your modulated genome to your descendants. I created you for one purpose, to fulfill one plan. Killing Gharlane and eradicating his kind from the Universe."

Petchy asked, "So you refer to us as your children because you formed us to be your weapon?"

Potty replied, "Yes, but more than that. You are special, you are the tip of my spear, but all humans are my children. The Cosmic Swarm is humanity's creator, not just a manipulator of the DNA of you four. The Universe creates all life. I am a tiny part of that swarm, pinched off and trapped in this space. As a part of the Cosmic Swarm, I can lay fair claim to being humanity's creator."

Teena's expression was unlike any I had ever seen her display. Then, in a low voice, she asked, "Are you God?"

Potty laughed a great belly laugh. He has less belly than he did, though. "If you mean Yahweh, Allah, or Jehovah, then no. If there is a greater God than the Universe itself, I am his humble servant the same as you. This flesh you know as Potty Breen, is but a tiny sliver of the Cosmic Swarm, or as you call it, the *Dark Energy*. A local manifestation of the First Cause."

He nudged a rock with his toe. "The Universe is alive and sentient. Every particle is a part of the Cosmic Swarm. On an elementary level, that rock is alive. It plays a role in the living entity that is the Universe, the same as the lowliest cell in your body adds to you. I suppose the Universe is God, in a sense. The me you see before you now is but a particle, like that rock, pinched off and sent on a mission. No different than if I were to skip that rock across a pond. Cast forth to follow a preordained path.

"Maybe that makes me an angel or even a messiah in the mythology you imagine. But no, that mythological construct bears but a superficial resemblance to the Cosmic Swarm. When in the Universe, I could meld with the larger Cosmic mind. In this dimension, outside the Universe, I am quite alone. I will die here, shrivel, and starve without the Cosmic Flow to sustain me. I am but a pawn sacrificed to a greater good. I can leave here no more than can you."

The silence following Potty's revelation was palpable. No one quite knew how to respond. Finally, after an uncomfortable silence, I decided to get our mission back on track. I clapped my hands for attention. "God-talk is interesting, and I'd love to know more. I want to know about reincarnation, heaven, hell, and life after death. But not right now. Potty, you may be God, god-like, an Angel or a pretender. You may be an infinitesimal slice of the Cosmic all, whatever that is. We'll sort that out when Gharlane is dead. But what I want right now is to kill Gharlane and end this farce." I was growing angry at the distractions.

Teena chimed in. She was pale and seemed in pain. She said, "There are two ways we can proceed. We can chase him or draw him to us. Either way, we'd better do it quick. The sun is getting low. We need to secure ourselves for the night. There may still be pests about."

Fitz said, "Even with psionic power, the night is dangerous. Despite chasing away predators, you cannot be certain of their absence." He looked at me. "I presume you have a refuge in these caves."

I nodded. I bristled at the idea of retreating and hiding in a cave during the night, but Fitz is right. I said, "One of them might take care of Gharlane for us."

I motioned for us to start in the direction of the caves. Unfortunately, we had to take it slow due to Teena's injuries. Petchy shook his head. "I doubt it," he said as we began walking. "He seems able to control them, and while he controls that monster, the others won't bother him."

Potty said, "He controls them for now, using his psionic powers. But he cannot relax or sleep, lest they rebel. Plus, while controlling them, he is busy, unable to find food. He is without tools, supplies, or equipment. He can survive only so long as he can maintain control. Without the Cosmic Flow, his limits are his own natural capacity."

I led the group back toward our fortress, the caves we had rid of the predators and blocked off for protection. Not as comfortable as a castle, but adequate.

At one point during the walk, I asked Potty, "You said this world is outside the Universe? You said you would starve here. Does that apply to Gharlane as well?"

"Yes and no," he said. "He may be able to survive much longer than I. He uses the Cosmic Flow as a tool. He is a corporeal being, although not human. He needs food and water much as you do. The food he might find here does not well suit him; he cannot thrive here. I crafted it that way.

"This world exists in a pinched-off dimension, away from the Cosmic Flow. Without access to the flow, I will wither and die."

"So, we win the battle then? All we have to do is keep him here. We need not kill him? We do not even need to remain alive ourselves?"

"True, daughter," Potty said. "He cannot survive in this place; although it may take years, he will die here. It is better to find him and make a clean end of it. Besides, think of the Nekomata. The fur-people would like their leader returned. Don't forget, as trapped as you are here, so are Stapleya and Wisceya trapped away from their home."

We settled in for the night but did not sleep. Instead, we spent the night talking, planning, and strategizing.

I did ask Potty about the origins of life. He explained, "The Universe is composed of two elements. Energy and Intelligence are the building blocks of all matter and every mind. All matter is a byproduct of the flow of that energy. Matter condenses where energy swirls. All matter participates in the entire Universe. Every mind in the Universe is connected to the Cosmic Intelligence. The mind coalesces from the Cosmic Mind and, when done, returns to the source from whence it came."

Fitz asked, "Is there life after death, then?"

Potty shrugged. "In a manner of speaking, yes, in that every thought pattern returns to the Cosmic Mind and remains forever a part of the Cosmic All. There is no individual awareness, only a pattern impressed upon the Universe.

"You work with computers. Think of a computer memory and data stored as a backup image. It exists but does not move. It can be restored to another computer and reconstituted, but otherwise exists as insubstantial ones and zeros in a storage medium. That is what happens to all life after death."

Fitz asked, "What of Reincarnation? Can a mind be restored to a new body and reconstituted?"

Potty did not answer for a while. He stared at the fire and simply sat quietly. Finally, he said, "Sometimes a thought is incomplete. Sometimes there is a need to extend to a full conclusion. When the Universe seeks to balance a scale, yes, a collection of thought patterns may be restored to a new body for further work. But it is not an individual personality, not a single person—only that portion that needs more processing, so to speak. So you see, it is both less and more than you imagine. Past-life regression tales, like Bridey Murphy, are hoaxes or delusions. Yet there are occasions where some piece of a past life might 'leak through,' and an ancient memory track imparts a 'Deja Vu' experience, for example. Real occurrences are rare but do happen. Perhaps a full, complete reincarnation is possible, but don't believe the tales you hear on late-night radio. When we die, we don't come back, although the Universe may remember. Trapped here, I will die. The Universe will not remember me. Death is final, especially when it occurs in Nekomata."

〰〰

Morning dawned and we were out of our cave fortress before normal curfew would lift. Guards placed, on the alert for approaching beasts, we gathered on the mountain. Though early morning, it was time to put our plan into motion.

Thin plan. We hoped we could draw Gharlane to us. We counted on his desiring to kill us as much as we wished to kill him. We hoped he believed that by killing us, he could escape the trap. By attacking, he gives us a chance to kill him first.

Teena, weak and pale, asked for help to come out into the sunshine. I worried for her. Her injuries are severe. They had dressed her wounds and applied the usual treatments. Grow Juice, and the crushed skins of root vegetables are powerful healing agents. Still, she needs to get to Central's medical facility, and that does not seem in the offing. I hugged her and kissed her, and then pulled away. I cannot be weak now; I cannot be her lover; I have a higher duty.

I am a Warrior. I must be her Warrior.

Seeing her weak and injured seems to hurt Fitz even worse than me. He had put on his rigid poker-face and hardened himself against showing weakness. Men! I understand the need to focus on the mission. But must compassion be so difficult?

Petchy seemed unaware of her injuries. We each must cope our own way.

Team Overwatch took station around the mountain top. Potty joined them, placing himself at the highest point, visible from a distance. They began regular sounding of their lepatata, calling attention to their presence. Potty hoped to draw him out. If Gharlane were within miles, he should hear them. But will he come if he hears us? What will happen if he does?

Ragnarök

"The wolf, giant Fenrir, will break his invisible chains... The skies will open, and Surt the fire-giant will come flaming across the bridge to destroy the Gods. Odin will ride out of the gates of Valhalla to do battle for a last time against the wolf. Thor will kill the serpent but die from its venom. Surt will spread fire across the Earth. At last, Fenrir will swallow the sun."
— **The Seer**

We kept up the visible presence and noise-making all day. No sign of our quarry. As dusk approached, we became aware of predators gathering in the forest below our position. We loosed a few psionic-driven arrows in their direction and knocked out a few Velociraptors, but it seemed futile. We retreated to the caves to pass another night.

The following day we noted an even larger number of beasts in the woods. Potty seemed confident their presence was the work of Gharlane. He seemed surprised that the villain could control so many beasts. Perhaps he only controlled a few at a time, flitting from beast to beast to guide the larger number. His purpose seemed unclear.

We had lots of arrows, so I lined up my archers, and with Teena, Fitz, and Petchy lending their talents, we fired salvo after salvo of psionic-driven arrows at them. For the first few volleys, we took out the beasts with ease. Then, on the last volley, our arrows turned in mid-flight and drove back at us.

That's different!

We parried all but one, which unfortunately nailed Petchy in the upper leg. A nasty thigh wound, though not life-threatening. We dressed his wound and applied the standard treatment. We are now down two warriors. Both Teena and Petchy can still exercise their psionic talents, but physical activity is problematic. Teena seems weaker. Fitz and I are the only intact psionic warriors. Unless we count Potty, he remains rather an unknown quantity.

We developed a fresh tactic. Rather than hail volleys of arrows at the target, we launched a single arrow. Driven toward a single target, with all our force behind it, we bet it would be unstoppable. Again, we penetrated the defenses at first, only to be later thwarted.

Our psionic power turns arrows into something else. For comparison, a .50 Cal bullet weighs up to 52 grams, travels at over 1900 miles per hour, and hits the target with a force of more than 20,000 Joules. That's about 20,000 times as hard as being hit by a fast tennis ball.

A heavy, metal-tipped arrow of the style Fitz shoots is more than twice the mass of the .50 Cal bullet. In fact, they can be well over 100 grams. A big heavy bow, drawn by a well-muscled man, can fire an arrow at over 350 feet per second. That's about 240 miles per hour. Note that the speed of sound is around 1100 feet per second. So the .50 Cal projectile is supersonic, whereas an arrow is not, by a wide margin. The arrow hits at approximately 70 Joules.

Now imagine that five capable Psionic Warriors can get behind that arrow and push as it leaves the bow. Fitz by himself can drive an arrow well into the supersonic realm, to the point where the arrow chars from the heat. But, if we all apply our abilities, we can drive much harder. If we can push the arrow to match a .50 Cal velocity, the impact is over 36,000 Joules. That's right, nearly twice that of the .50 Cal since the arrow is heavier. I think we can push it a lot harder than that if we put our heads together.

Working together, we should be able to kill a T-Rex with an arrow. And that's without the use of HEIAP explosive tips.

The trick is to keep Gharlane too busy to parry the driven arrow. That's where my trained archers come into play. The plan is to send them out first, to target the smaller beasts, not precisely to inflict harm but to spook them and cause Gharlane to give his attention to retaining control of his puppets.

Then a moment or two later, we drive Fitz's arrows, as many as he can hurl, at the head of Gharlane's T-Rex. Oh, and I was kidding about not using the HEIAP tips. Thirty-six thousand Joules plus explosive. I like the sound of that!

We spent the next three days laying our trap, planning our attack. The attack will occur in three waves. The first phase stations Nekomata as near the enemy line as possible, with every lepatata or noisemaker of any sort handy. Those lacking noise-makers but who can whistle loudly, even with a blade of grass between their thumbs, were invited to join.

The second phase requires placing as many archers as possible just behind the noisemakers. Their mission is not so much killing the enemy's beasts as it is to cause chaos. The theory is that the noise nearby plus flying arrows will spook the creatures and cause Gharlane to struggle to retain control.

Even if Gharlane keeps them under control and we fail at killing the beasts, it will consume his attention. Perhaps he will divert his efforts into parrying our arrows. For this reason, our noisemakers and archers are instructed to have shelter at hand, a tree they can duck behind, etc. If he flings their arrows back at them, there will undoubtedly be casualties.

Then while Gharlane is occupied, Fitz will target him and his pet T-Rex with as many HEAIP loaded, psionically driven arrows as we can drive.

We will likely only get one shot at this. We have but a few HEIAP shells, and we won't catch Gharlane unawares a second time. So, we're putting everything we have into this attack. With only one shot, we can't afford to miss. We must draw Gharlane into our sights. If we miss, we have nothing left.

Those not whistling or arching, including Petchy and myself, were deployed as spotters. I was doing double duty, as I carried both bow and The Lady Tyrxing. My role was to close in on Gharlane after the action. If I can, I intend to let my lady introduce us.

We laid out a mock battlefield inside the great cavern and planned our attack meticulously. We worked out an elaborate wig-wag code to pass commands and coordinate the action.

We placed guards outside lest Gharlane spy on us. Three days we planned and practiced. Finally, we convinced ourselves we were ready.

Teena insisted that despite her injury, she should be placed as a spotter. I helped her to a secure placement myself, equipped her with the wig-wag flags, her bow, a sword, and after a thought, gave her the BFR revolver as well. We do not have to be very close to help Fitz's arrows; we just have to see him launch.

Petchy assumed a position closer to the action. His injury was not so severe, and he is still a capable fighter even though he may not run so well.

We carefully laid out our forces, and the spotters laid to the job of locating Gharlane.

No dice; his creatures were evident but not moving. They are nocturnal, after all, so perhaps without active prodding from Gharlane, they are asleep. It's as if he lined them up to form a defensive parameter and commanded them to "stay." The hours ticked away with no sign of Gharlane himself.

I was near to calling the day's activities. Although his presence nearby was telegraphed by the creatures, Gharlane himself remained absent from our view. We suspect he was injured and resting. This could go on for days.

Just as I was about to give the signal to retire, a low whistle came to my ears. A spotter had found our quarry. Using hand signals and wig-wags, we coordinated our forces to move in the direction indicated.

We spent the next half-hour creeping stealthily through the forest as the sun dipped lower and lower. If we don't get organized and attack soon, we will be fighting this battle in the dark. Not a smart strategy when the enemy employs nocturnal predators.

Finally, I saw him. Gharlane astride his pet T-Rex, prowling his defensive line, headed toward a prominent outcropping. He appeared ghastly, as though injured, and dying himself. I almost took pity on him but dared not. However pathetic he might seem; this creature is a murdering monster of mythic proportions. He will kill us all without a whit of compassion given a chance.

I sent a series of commands back up the line and gave orders to attack as he reached the outcropping.

I readied my bow and prepared my volleys. I set my sights on several sleeping Velociraptors as targets. Two Deinonychus were in range too. Will they fall to my super-powered arrows? I will soon find out. I held my breath as Gharlane and his mount moved toward the outcropping.

Moving with glacial alacrity, the beast and its rider approached the target zone. I held my breath, awaiting the cue to begin firing. Then he stopped short of the trap. He sat there, moved as if to turn back. Then he stopped again and resumed moving toward the kill zone.

Pandemonium erupted. The noise startled the menagerie, and many creatures departed for distant whereabouts even before the arrows were airborne. I fired volley after volley until I reached for more arrows, only to discover I was dry except for one explosive-tipped arrow I had held onto. I had driven each arrow with all the force I could muster, to devastating effect on the target beasts.

Yes, I can kill a whole flock of Velociraptors, and even their larger, slower cousins just dandy. I like psionically driven archery. Quiet, clean, and effective!

The arrows had ceased, though the lepatata were still blaring. Every beast of Gharlane's defensive line had died or departed, the only one he held being the big T-Rex he was astride. I saw Fitz raise his bow for the death blow. I reached out and put all my strength behind the arrow as he unleashed.

Fitz's arrow deflected scarcely two feet from the target, exploding in mid-air as Gharlane blocked the thrust.

Fitz fired a second missile before the first had even neared the target, and I could feel the energy flow as Gharlane mustered the energy to stop it as well.

I had a sudden change of tactic. Instead of helping Fitz drive his arrows, I launched my own exploding dart, timing and driving it to arrive microseconds behind Fitz's.

He never saw me coming. He was focused on parrying Fitz's arrow, never saw my own. Dino opened his mouth fortuitously to roar. The HEIAP tip hit the T-Rex squarely in the tonsil. It would have been climatic, except for one thing. The explosive didn't. Fuck a duck, damn the luck! It was a dud!

Damned unpredictable explosives! The dinosaur was unhappy and began thrashing around, spasming and trying to dislodge the annoyance. Gharlane struggled to control the beast and stay aboard.

I grabbed The Lady Tyrxing and sprinted toward the thrashing beast. If Gharlane fell off, I intended to arrange a formal introduction between him and my Lady.

I approached, then retreated as the beast lunged my way. It bucked and whirled, and I tried to stay close enough to confront Gharlane should he fall, yet far enough to avoid being stepped on or smacked by the giant tail.

Back and forth, we lunged. Somehow Gharlane stayed on the bipedal carnivore as it lunged about. I nearly lost the battle when the tip of the giant's tail swung at me. Instinctively, I reached out with my psionic force and knocked it aside, it missed me by less than an inch. I retreated a few more feet and watched the thrashing a moment.

Abruptly I realized that Gharlane was using his own psionic power to hold onto the beast. It occurred to me that I could push him as effectively as I had the monster's tail. He was regaining control over the monster. As I watched, two more of Fitz's arrows targeted the thrashing beast, only to be deflected at the last instant.

I slammed him for all I was worth, felt him yield, then claw his way back. He slid about on the beast, down its back and away from the shoulders where he had been riding. My extra nudge broke his concentration, and now he was spending all his energy just staying aboard.

The beast continued whirling and thrashing. I ran behind it, placing Rex between myself and Fitz. Just then, the beast turned and lifted his tail — there was no longer doubt about the gender; I poked him in the taint with my sword. Sad way to use a magnificent sword, but the reaction was priceless.

The monster suddenly stood tall, tried to reach his nethers with his much too short arms, and roared in magnificent agony. I almost took pity on the poor beast in that moment.

Gharlane was fully occupied just staying aboard, and the beast faced Fitz, mouth open in full roar. That was the opening Fitz needed. His own HEIAP missile joined mine in the beast's tonsils, and his exploded. Under the emphasis, I guess mine did too. Suddenly a headless, and very dead T-Rex stopped moving entirely. It simply stood there, perfectly balanced, then began to collapse like a slowly deflating balloon.

Gharlane rode the carcass to the ground and jumped off, attempting to run. There was no way I would permit him to outrun me. As he started forward, I darted in front of him. He stopped. He turned to go another direction. I darted that way too. He pushed me psionically as if to push me aside, but he was weakened. I pushed back with all I could muster, and we stood there, face to face; he unable to budge me, and I unable to budge him. I advanced on him. Fitz was closing from behind him, holding him in place. I wondered where Teena and Petchy were; we could use some help.

Then I saw another figure nearby and felt the energy of another psionic warrior come to our aid. Potty was lending a hand, psionically speaking.

Between the three of us, Gharlane was unable to move, unable to flee. His features were hardened, but fear flickered in his eyes. We had him trapped yet could do nothing either. He was holding us off, stalemated.

I continued advancing against his pressure until I was almost within the sword's reach and yet could go no further. He could see I meant to use my sword and was fighting to keep me just out of range. I'm a better swordsman than that.

I am a Warrior!

I dropped my psionic grasp, transferring my focus to my blade. As my pressure vanished, he lunged forward toward me. The Lady Tyrxing was ready, as he fell forward, she struck with all the force and speed my arm and mind could bring to bear.

For a half-second, he simply stood there, a startled expression froze on his lifeless face. Then, his lifeless body fell one way, his head rolled the other. Our battle was ended. Gharlane was dead. Permanently so, if I believe Potty.

I glanced at Potty. He had shrunk. As he expended effort in our fight, he became smaller. I thought of a winter snowman on the first warm day. This does not bode well.

Petchy and Teena are absent. Worried, I ran back to where I left her to find Teena unconscious but alive. She was uninjured, though I surmise the exertions of the battle combined with blood loss from her earlier injury led to her collapse.

A quick search and we found Petchy, unconscious and bleeding. He had evidently been unable to dodge quickly enough when one of the beasts bolted from the pandemonium. Like Teena, he had been run down by a beast and injured by the raptorial claw. The fur-people quickly began ministering to both as we rushed back to our mountain fortress. Night was falling upon us.

Bittersweet

"It is foolish and wrong to mourn the men who died. Rather we should thank God that such men lived."
— **George S. Patton**

The threat Gharlane posed is over, and we must deal with the aftermath. Teena and Petchy lie gravely wounded; the local treatment is seemingly ineffective against the infections they incurred. I would give anything, my very life itself, for a good antibiotic.

Potty has shrunk to the size of my Nekomata archers. Clearly, the effort he expended in the fight took a toll. Without access to the Cosmic Flow, he must continue to shrivel.

If only Alex could know we had dispatched the enemy, and he can open the Portal. We need to move Petchy and Teena to Center, and Potty needs the Cosmic Flow.

We lost three of our Nekomata warriors in the fight too, victims of the battle. But, between the beasts and the wildly flying arrows, that we only had three fatalities was miraculous. Of course, there were numerous scrapes and scratches. One archer received a broken arm when she fell off a small ledge.

I remembered Patton's words and praised our people for the fact that such warriors had lived. It was poor comfort.

We buried our friends and prepared to make our way back to the Castle. Before departing our Mountain Fortress, I called the troops together for a final eulogy. I reached into my father's Irish ancestry and my own memory for the words I heard delivered at his funeral.

"Peace to each Warrior's soul that sleepeth; rest to each faithful eye that weepeth. Sleep the sleep that knows not breaking; dream of battled fields no more, days of danger nights of waking."

At that point, memories of my own parents' deaths flooded my heart and mingled with the pain of our fresh fallen. I broke, unable to continue.

Fitz stepped up, "In a large sense, we cannot dedicate, we cannot hallow this ground. The brave, living and dead, who struggled here, have consecrated it far above our poor power to add or detract.

"The soldier, above all other people, prays for peace, for he must suffer and bear the deepest wounds and scars of war."

We all stood quietly for several minutes, then without further words, began the trek homeward toward the Castle and home.

We reached Castle Stapleya before nightfall. Petchy and Teena were placed in the Queen's chambers and administered to by the Castle doctor. Not that she could do anything that hadn't already been done. The potion of leaves and Grow Juice is the most effective medicine they have. It usually is quite effective, but in this case, it seems not to be doing much if anything.

I pondered that. I had been nicked by a Deinonychus claw and had healed quickly. Not even a scar now to show for it. I could only think of one thing that was different. We were on the road, alone and without supplies, without even water to cleanse the wound when I was injured. Instead, Teena had cleansed my wound using a repulsive but effective technique.

Teena and Petchy's injuries were more severe than mine, granted, but we had plenty of water. Their wounds had been cleaned in a more conventional manner.

Could that be the difference? I asked Fitz about it. He shrugged, saying, "Maybe. The technique is ancient and usually thought effective. The water is normally sterile and slightly acidic. I doubt the drinking water we used on the mountain was as sterile. Maybe it was poison from the claw, or maybe it was something in the water. We have no way to tell here. This is a novel experience. Nekomata do not usually survive encounters with Deinonychus, even briefly, so there is no history to judge from."

Whatever the cause, we watched as, over the next few days, the infection tore through their bodies. Clearly, this was dire, and unless a portal opened soon, all was lost.

I accosted Potty. "Isn't there anything you can do?" I begged. He shook his head.

"If I had access to the cosmic flow, I could heal them. Without it, as you see, my mass is disappearing rapidly now. I shall soon be gone."

"It's not fair," I ranted. "They fought your battle, vanquished your foe. You're a supernatural being, or as near to one as the Universe allows. There must be something."

He sat with me for a while as we watched them fade away. Then Potty spoke very softly, as he said, "Give me the room, please. I cannot promise anything, but I will do what I can. Go to the other room and do not return today. What I can do, I will." As he spoke, he began to glow. I threw my arms around him in thanks, then quickly exited the room.

That was the last time I saw any of them. True to his request, no one returned to the room that evening. I slept outside the door, keeping watch. Then next morning, when I checked, they were gone. That's all I know.

Are they dead? Are they alive in some "limbo" dimension? I can't begin to speculate.

Denouement

"Children are the living messages we send to a time we will not see."
— **John F. Kennedy**

The toddler looked at her mother, her face solemn in the way that only a toddler can be. She asked, "Mommy, why does Fizzy have fur and I don't?"

"That's because they are the fur-people. This is their home. We call this place Nekomata. Your father and I are from another place called Earth. People from Earth don't have fur. So they call us Smoothies."

The child thought about the answer for a few moments. Then she posed another question. "Is Fizzy my brother? Aunt Williya says Fizzy is my brother."

"Half-brother, dear, he is your half-brother. You both have the same daddy but different mommies. Aunt Williya is Fizzy's mommy, and I am your mommy."

"Then why did daddy give Fizzy fur and not me?"

We leave the Warrior to her motherly challenges, explaining genetics to a toddler. No one expects a Warrior to become a mother. That is something those who know her best would have said improbable.

Fitz, of course, who else? What's that, you ask, dear reader? How did a confirmed lesbian become pregnant?

Excellent question, dear reader, although the how of it should seem rather obvious. Without access to proper pharmacology on Nekomata, nature is in charge. It's not as if she is unfamiliar with the dialect. Perhaps the question you meant to ask is more along the line of "how come?"

Of course, she did not suddenly decide she preferred men. Fitz's overwhelming masculinity did not magically "cure" her. Real-life isn't like that. Sexuality is not a switch that one can simply flip. She came to understand that the Warrior and the mother live on different dimensional planes. And the lesbian is on yet another plane, and the three dimensions do not necessarily intersect.

In Castle Stapleya, indeed anywhere on Nekomata, there's no shortage of distaff lovers. One never sleeps alone among the fur-people. The challenge often lies in keeping the count of bedmates in the single digits. Fitz is a strong man, but Jill is a Warrior. There is no question but that it was her idea — it could have been no other way.

Watching the Nekomata with their children may have stirred something deep in her soul. Perhaps some buried maternal instinct she never imagined, some drive awakened and demanded satisfaction. Perhaps it was merely her biological clock ticking too loudly to sleep. She contemplated the idea for months before making the decision.

The decision to have a child was Jill's alone. Fitz was hesitant to agree. Jill found that frustrating. He was granting fur-babies at every opportunity, so why not? He tried to explain the difference. The fur-babies are a sacred duty, his solemn commitment to saving their race — a baby for Jill, not the same. Sex and love are not related here. Jill refused to understand.

He insisted she must think about it a full two months before he would consent. She must understand it his way. He stipulated the condition that he not be a mere 'donor' as with the Fur-people. He demanded marriage. Not an exclusive contract, as if one could practice monogamy in Castle Stapleya.

He insisted they must become life partners. That's a different thing than lovers, or even spouses. There are many forms of love. It may not be the fairy-tale ending, yet it works for them. Perhaps it's the absence of sexual intrigue and conflict. Honesty about sex changes everything.

It was a magnificent wedding; Castle Stapleya had not had a ceremony such as theirs in several centuries. Recovery from the party required several days of Grow Juice therapy. The phrase "You may kiss the bride" takes on a whole new meaning in a Castle Stapleya wedding.

Unused skills atrophy. Neither Jill nor Fitz have use for their professional skills in Castle Stapleya. Perhaps the correct terminology is that Jill is now a retired Warrior, and Fitz is a retired Computist. Unfortunately, it appears neither of them is coming out of retirement since the Portals remain closed. There are no computers on Nekomata and no villains. There are only reptilian predators.

They stay in top physical condition with regular training, but the harsh demands of a stone-age lifestyle are the more significant factor. They mount frequent expeditions against the deadly predators. They make a powerful team against the beasts. It has been months since anyone spotted a day-walker, and even the night-stalkers are rare.

Nighttime is not yet entirely safe on Planet Oz, although it's improving. The beasts are learning to avoid humans. The roving flocks of Velociraptors are the greatest danger. The T-Rex and Deinonychus are exceedingly rare now.

The retired warrior is a terrific mommy. Her daughter is healthy and strong and growing so fast. She wishes for a camera. Unfortunately, there is no photography on Nekomata, although drawing and painting suffice. There are lovely and talented artists among the Castle's residents. Exquisite portraiture graces the Castle walls.

As we take our leave, she contemplates asking Fitz to grant a baby brother for her daughter. Train them both to be Warriors.

If you liked Chromosome Warrior, please leave a review on the Amazon Chromosome Warrior Review page.

The Story Continues...

Chromosome Warrior seems to be "The End" for Fitz, Teena, Petchy, and Jill — or is it? We've seen how resilient those Asherans can be. However, whether this is their end, or not, we can still tell the beginnings...

COMING IN SEPTEMBER 2022: A new series set in the Chromosome Adventures Universe: Undercover Alien: The Hat, The Alien, and the Quantum War

Did you ever wish to be a superhero?

Rithwick Jahi Pringle, a.k.a. Ritz, has a keen imagination, vivid dreams, and unparalleled cyber skills, but his neurodivergent brain is out to get him!

Paralyzing anxieties, symmetry-demanding OCD, and unbridled geekiness hobble his superhero missions.

He dons the superhero cape on The Dark Web. He wears a White Hat for the Agency by day but patrols the shadowy dark-web realm by night, dispensing Vigilante Justice to those beyond the Law's reach.

When a new, otherworldly Director takes charge of The Agency's cyber warriors, he is captivated, seduced, and drawn into a shadowy world beyond cybercrime, a deep underworld of dark alien villainy. https://www.amazon.com/dp/B01N984GDH

About the Author

Your humble author admits to decades of experience in data networking, telecommunications, and Internet technologies. An accomplished motivator of technical and professional staff and an experienced technical team leader, he is a technology generalist with experience covering both hardware and software disciplines in many related fields. His present day-job is in Internet Security and Crypto, where he serves as CTO and Chief Scientist for a novel internet stealth startup company.

In his spare time, he satisfies his penchant for fantasizing about the future, technology, and societal forces by writing science fiction.

Follow Nathan on:

Thank you for reading Chromosome Conspiracy. Please visit the Chromosome Conspiracy Reviews Page and leave a review. Your honest review will help future readers decide if they want to take a chance on a new-to-them author. Mysterious algorithms determine which books pop up on things such as the "you might also enjoy this" suggestions. It takes a minimum number of reviews on some sites before a book is added to those "also bought" and "you might also like" lists. Authors need your reviews.

Writings of Nathan Gregory

Science Fiction

Chromosome Quest is the opening story in the Chromosome Adventures Series, introducing the protagonist 'Fitz,' the Mentor 'Petchy,' the Goddess 'Teena,' and the stone-age world he dubbed 'Planet Oz.' Their epic fight was to shut down the runaway AI on Teena and Petchy's home planet and retrieve the genetic database at the heart of the fertility plague.

Chromosome Conspiracy brings the stone-age 'Fur girls' to Earth looking for Fitz's help with a new problem. The adventure begins as he seeks to protect the fur-bearing alien women from the machinations of Alex Marco and the 'Men in Black,' that is until Fitz's girlfriend and several others are killed, and MiB Agent Jill Smith is badly wounded at the hands of a new super-villain. Facing a common foe, Fitz joins the Men in Black to fight the evil Gharlane.

Chromosome Warrior sees the fate of all human civilization hanging in the balance as Fitz, Jill, Petchy, Teena, Alex, and the Fur girls ally with a strange other-worldly energy-being against the evil Gharlane.

Non-Fiction

Nathan Gregory's non-fiction features a pair of documentaries that tell the untold origin backstory of today's commercial Internet. The creation and funding of the ARPANET and the technologies we use today are well-told, but there is another side to the story that academia has overlooked.

From its cold-war beginnings until its commercialization beginning in 1992, the Internet forbade any form of commerce. Yet, globe-spanning commercial networks existed for more than two decades before the Internet legitimized online eCommerce.

The story of the creation of the concept of remote computing we call 'Cloud Computing' today began in the 1960s, with the first globe-spanning commercial cloud coming online in 1972. From

February 1972 until well beyond the end of 1992, these commercial networks carried the world's e-Commerce traffic while ARPANET and its cousins remained the private playground of academics and politicians.

The Tym Before... tells the story of creating these first commercial networks and the remote cloud services they powered.

Securing the Network tells the story of the subsequent commercialization of the Internet, beginning with the first commercial peering point, MAE-East, for which the initial order was placed on September 29, 1992. By mid-1993, the MAE was in place, and by 1994 it was carrying 90% of the world's commercial Internet traffic.

Kindle Vella Episodic Fiction

With the advent of Kindle Vella, I have begun some serials for publication in the episodic format.

A Walk in the Woods is a one-of-a-kind first-contact story is the first story in this format.

Tommie Powers and the Time Machine stands at four completed episodes. This story is a juvenile that is perhaps closer to a Tom Swift or Rick Brant story, and it relates the backstory of young Fitz in High School. Its fate depends on feedback from you, dear reader.

Made in the USA
Las Vegas, NV
29 October 2023

79901095R00149